W9-CBX-819

CITY OF THE DEAD

Praise for the *New York Times* bestselling
CITY SPIES

"A cinematic and well-crafted start to a new spy series for middle grades."
—*SLJ*, on *City Spies*

"Ponti writes a well-paced story laced with suspense, wit, and entertaining dialogue. Events unfold within colorful Parisian settings that include the Eiffel Tower, the Catacombs, and a deceptively shabby-looking hotel run by British Intelligence."
—*Booklist*, on *City Spies*

"Plotted with an enjoyable amount of suspense, Ponti's story features a well-drawn cast of kids from around the world forming a chosen family with sibling-like dynamics. A page-turner suited to even the most reluctant readers."
—*Publishers Weekly*, on *City Spies*

"Like any good spy thriller, this second adventure with MI6's young secret agents begins in the middle of a perilous mission. . . . The thriller is well paced, the characters animated, and the adventure engaging. A winner."
—*Kirkus Reviews*, on *Golden Gate*

"An appealing mixture of espionage, action, and personalities in a contemporary setting."
—*Booklist*, on *Forbidden City*

"A smashing success."
—*Kirkus Reviews*, on *Forbidden City*

ALSO BY JAMES PONTI

The Dead City trilogy

Dead City

Blue Moon

Dark Days

The Framed! series

Framed!

Vanished!

Trapped!

The City Spies series

City Spies

Golden Gate

Forbidden City

BOOK
4

CITY SPIES

CITY OF THE DEAD

BY JAMES PONTI

ALADDIN
New York   London   Toronto   Sydney   New Delhi

ALADDIN
An imprint of Simon & Schuster Children's Publishing Division
1230 Avenue of the Americas, New York, New York 10020
First Aladdin hardcover edition February 2023
Text copyright © 2023 by James Ponti
Illustrations copyright © 2023 by Yaoyao Ma Van As
All rights reserved, including the right of reproduction in whole or in part in any form.
ALADDIN and related logo are registered trademarks of Simon & Schuster, Inc.
For information about special discounts for bulk purchases, please contact
Simon & Schuster Special Sales at 1-866-506-1949 or business@simonandschuster.com.
The Simon & Schuster Speakers Bureau can bring authors to your live event. For more information or to book an event contact the Simon & Schuster Speakers Bureau at 1-866-248-3049 or visit our website at www.simonspeakers.com.
Jacket designed by Tiara Iandiorio
Interior designed by Tiara Iandiorio and Ginny Kemmerer
The illustrations for this book were rendered digitally.
The text of this book was set in Sabon LT Std.
Manufactured in the United States of America 1222 FFG
10 9 8 7 6 5 4 3 2 1
This book has been cataloged with the Library of Congress.
ISBN 9781665911573 (hc)
ISBN 9781665911597 (ebook)

FOR KRISTIN,
AKA MANHATTAN,
WHO MAKES THE WRITING
AND THE WRITING PROCESS
SO MUCH BETTER

PROLOGUE

Howard and Hussein

VALLEY OF THE KINGS, NEAR LUXOR, EGYPT—
NOVEMBER 4, 1922

THE TWELVE-YEAR-OLD BOY SLOWLY RODE a donkey into the desolate Egyptian landscape known as the Valley of the Kings. He had bare feet and wore a white headscarf and a tattered linen tunic called a *jellabiya*. His name was Hussein, but to the workers toiling in the desert sun, he was simply *al sakka*, or "water boy."

Twice a day, he filled two large clay jars with water from a well, loaded them into a harness strapped across the donkey's back, and took them to the excavation site where crews were searching for the elusive tomb of a

1

pharaoh named Tutankhamen. King Tut's final resting place had sat hidden and undisturbed for more than three thousand years, so long that most experts believed it was only a legend.

The heat was already stifling when Hussein reached the site at just past ten. Because the jars had rounded bottoms, he had to scoop out some sand for them to stand upright, and as he did, he felt a smooth stone just beneath the surface. He dug to reveal a step leading down into the ground.

Fittingly, the tomb of Egypt's boy king had been discovered by an Egyptian boy.

Hussein excitedly rushed to tell Howard Carter, the British archaeologist in charge of the excavation. Workers began clearing the area, and by the end of the next day, they'd uncovered a stairwell carved directly into the bedrock. At the bottom, a doorway had been plastered shut and marked with the hieroglyphic seal of the jackal Anubis above nine captives. Carter beamed, his eyes open wide with amazement as he ran his fingers across it.

It was the symbol of the royal necropolis—Egypt's ancient City of the Dead.

British Museum

ON A SLATE GRAY NOVEMBER DAY, ONE hundred years after the discovery of Tutankhamen's tomb, a group of five young people converged in a part of London known as Bloomsbury. Like Howard Carter, they were looking to recover treasures of Egyptian antiquity. Except they weren't going to dig a tunnel in the desert. They were going to sneak through one in an abandoned section of the London Underground. And the artifacts they sought weren't concealed in some long-forgotten tomb. They were on

3

display at one of the busiest museums in the world.

This was no excavation. It was a heist.

"Testing comms, one, two, three," Kat said into the microphone hidden in the red remembrance poppy pinned to her lapel. "Can everybody hear me?"

"Loud and clear," said Paris.

"Perfectly," answered Rio.

"All good on my end," Brooklyn replied.

There was a pause as they waited for a final voice to check in.

"Sydney, are you not responding because you can't hear me?" Kat asked. "Or is it because you're still pouting?"

After a moment, Sydney replied, "I'm sorry. I was under the impression nobody cared what I had to say."

"So, pouting," Paris commented.

"I'm not pouting," Sydney said defensively. "I'm just . . . *disappointed*. All I asked was that we slide the break-in a couple hours so we could see the fireworks at Battersea Park. You know how much I love Bonfire Night. It's going to be huge and everyone's going to be there."

"Which is exactly why *we're* going to be *here*," Kat said. "The police will be spread thin, and there are no celebrations scheduled for Bloomsbury. That means they'll be elsewhere, which dramatically improves the probability of us not getting caught."

Kat was the alpha on this mission, which meant she had to come up with the plan to break into the British Museum. She'd studied dozens of famous robberies and noticed that many took place on holidays or during special events, when police and security altered their normal patterns and were understaffed. She picked this date because of its connection to one of the most infamous figures in British history.

On November 5, 1605, a soldier-turned-radical named Guy Fawkes was captured before he could execute his plan to use thirty-six barrels of gunpowder to blow up Parliament. Ever since, Britons had marked the occasion with raucous public displays that included bonfires, burning effigies, and fireworks.

For Sydney, a born rebel who loved "making things go boom," it was as if Bonfire Night had been created specifically with her in mind. And here she was in London, so close to some of the biggest celebrations in the country, yet she was going to miss out.

"Just tell me this," Kat said. "Are you good to go with the mission? Or is this going to be a problem?"

"Of course I'm good," Sydney replied. "I never let anything affect our work."

"Excellent," Kat said. "And if it makes you feel better, I'll try to find something for you to blow up."

"I really appreciate it," Sydney replied with a smile. "That means a lot."

Rio cleared his throat and said, "Now that we've got everybody's feelings sorted, can we please get started?"

"Yeah," Brooklyn added, "you know we can't do anything until you give us the word."

As the alpha, it was Kat's responsibility to say the good luck phrase that kicked off every operation.

"Okay, then," she said, surveying the museum entrance from her vantage point in the Great Court. "This operation is hot. We are a go."

And just like that, the City Spies were in action. The five of them were an experimental team of agents, aged twelve to fifteen, who worked for MI6, British Secret Intelligence. They were called in for assignments in which adults would stand out but kids could blend in.

In this instance, the job was to steal two items on display in a special exhibition called *Wonderful Things: One Hundred Years of Tutmania*. They didn't know why they were stealing them; after all, spies weren't supposed to ask too many questions. All they'd been told was that it was in the best interests of the British government for them to do so.

Kat had never been the alpha for a mission this big, and she'd prepared for it like she did most things, as though it were a series of complex math equations. She split the heist into two parts so they could, in her words, "isolate the variables." The theft wouldn't happen until after the museum closed. But now, while it was still open, they had to set things up for later.

"Everyone good with what they're supposed to do?" she asked.

"Yes," Rio groaned. "We've gone over it and over it and over it."

"Good," Kat replied. "Repetition leads to fluency, and fluency leads to confidence. It's a cornerstone of executing complicated mathematical processes."

"Except this isn't math," Rio said. "It's a break-in."

"You're so funny," Kat told him. "*Everything's* math. Now blend in and disappear. Do your best to stay invisible."

"Don't worry," Sydney replied. "We'll be ghosts."

"Yeah," Rio added. "Math ghosts."

With so many kids at the museum, they had no

trouble blending in as they went to work on their specific assignments. Kat had even managed to get uniforms that matched those of schools visiting on field trips. This let them enter with large student groups that bypassed the normal security line.

"We're at the west stairs, and there are no surprises," Sydney informed the others.

She and Rio were double-checking the route they needed to take later that night. The team had plotted it using a virtual tour of the museum they found online. This let them carefully study every room and look for vulnerabilities. Now, they had to make sure that nothing had changed or been added in the time since the tour was filmed.

"There's a CCTV camera on the ceiling," Rio said. "And the entrance to the Egyptian gallery is protected by a roll-down gate that's operated by a keypad next to the doorway."

"We'll be able to control those once Brooklyn hacks their computer system," said Kat.

"Grab a photo of the keypad," Brooklyn said. "Make sure it shows the name of the manufacturer so I can download an operator's manual."

"Got it," Sydney answered.

She motioned for Rio to stand near the pad so it

would look like she was taking a picture of him and not the device.

"Smile," she said, and he flashed a goofy grin.

Next, they walked through the Egyptian sculpture gallery, where they noted and took pictures of three different security features. There were motion detectors along the wall, closed-circuit television cameras on the ceiling, and sensors eighteen inches above the floor that were part of a laser trip-wire system.

They made special note of these locations because, unlike in the movies, there wouldn't be brightly colored beams of light they could dance around. The lasers would be nearly invisible, and tripping any one of them would mean disaster for the mission.

As they mapped the location of two sensors near a giant statue of Rameses II, Rio noticed a security guard standing nearby. His nametag read OFFICER HAWK, although his droopy mustache and lumpy physique seemed more walrus than bird of prey.

"Target acquired," Rio said in a low voice to Sydney.

"Why him?" she asked.

"Two things," Rio answered. "He's friendly *and* he's awkward."

Sydney gave him a curious look.

"Security guards are supposed to be standoffish to intimidate you," Rio said. "But notice how he smiles and makes eye contact with people. He wants to connect and be liked."

"And awkward?"

"His tie's crooked, and his shirt's tucked in unevenly," Rio explained. "Not only that, but his ID badge is clipped to his belt instead of his shirt pocket, which makes it easier to lift."

"It's scary how well you read people," Sydney said.

"I've got skills," Rio said. "Nice of someone to notice for a change."

For years, Rio's ability to read people had been essential to his survival. He'd lived on the streets of Rio de Janeiro and made money by performing magic for tourists on a sidewalk near Copacabana Beach. To do that, he had to know how to read an audience and be able to perform amazing sleight of hand maneuvers. He was doing both to steal a security card they'd need later.

The lift was a two-person job that they'd done many times. Sydney's role was to be the diversion.

"Excuse me," she said, approaching the guard. "Do you think you could take a picture of me with this statue in the background?"

According to regulations, the guard wasn't supposed to do anything except keep an eye on the gallery. However, like Rio said, he was friendly and had trouble saying no. "Of course," he replied with a smile. "Let's make it quick."

She handed him her phone and struck a pose. He snapped the shot and gave it back to her, but when she looked at the picture, she frowned.

"Ugh," she said. "I'm sorry. Could you do it again? My eyes are closed, and it's backlit, so you can't see my face."

She directed him to move over a few feet, and as she became more difficult, the guard became more distracted. This was when Rio brushed past him and deftly slipped the badge off his belt. Next came the tricky part. Rio had to copy the badge and put it back before the guard noticed it was missing. If it was reported lost, the protocol was for that card to be deactivated, which would render it useless.

Rio slid it into his pocket and pressed it against his phone, which had a built-in scanner and cloning app. After a few seconds, he heard a single beep that told him it was done. Then he moved back to them, where Sydney was unsatisfied with another picture and the guard's patience was running thin.

Rio nosed into their conversation. "The problem is the light from that window," he said, pointing at the photo on Sydney's phone. "You need to be on the opposite side of the room."

The guard wanted no part of this. "I'm not moving to . . ."

"Why don't I take it?" Rio offered.

"Good idea," said the guard.

As he handed Sydney's phone back to her, Rio clipped the ID badge back to the guard's belt.

"Here you go," replied the guard.

"Thank you for your help," said Sydney.

They walked away, and once they were out of earshot, Rio whispered, "Friendly and awkward, my two favorite traits." They crossed the room to take the picture with better lighting so as not to draw suspicion from the guard, and then they went directly to another gallery and found a door marked STAFF ONLY. They waited until no one was around before Rio held up his phone next to the ID sensor. A light on the sensor turned from red to green, and they heard the lock click open.

"We're all set with the security doors," Rio said proudly.

"Nice job," answered Kat.

Kat was still in the Great Court, which sat in the middle of the museum's four vast wings. Originally, this two-acre area had been outdoors, but since 2000 it had been enclosed with a giant glass roof above, making it the largest covered public square in Europe. She'd picked this as the ideal location to study the security staff. Kat had an innate ability to see patterns where others saw only chaos, and she was analyzing the guards' movements, trying to figure out the exact route they took while making their rounds.

She noticed they tended to move floor by floor from bottom to top and in a counterclockwise direction on each level. She couldn't be certain that they'd do the same at night, but she thought it was likely that they would.

"Brooklyn, Paris, how are things for you?" she asked.

"Tricky," answered Paris.

"Yeah," Brooklyn added. "It's crowded over here."

The pair was in a hallway between two galleries featuring artifacts of Ancient Greece and Rome. There, beneath a stairwell, a computer storage room held servers for the west wing of the museum. Brooklyn wanted to use them so that she could "patch into the subnet and take over the entire system." This would give her remote control of the CCTV cameras, motion detectors, and other security features when they came back that evening. But to get into the room, Paris needed to pick the lock on the door, and he was having trouble because there were too many people nearby. Brooklyn was acting as lookout and signaled him with a nod that the coast was finally clear.

"If you need some help with a diversion or picking the lock, Sydney and I can always come to the rescue," Rio teased.

"We've got skills," Sydney added, giving Rio a wink.

"Just hold your horses," Brooklyn said. "We don't need the cavalry quite yet." She muted her mic for a second and turned to whisper to Paris. "We don't, do we?"

"No," Paris answered confidently as he jiggled the lockpick and opened the door. "We're all set."

They swapped positions, and now Paris became the lookout. Once he was sure it was safe, he gave Brooklyn a nod, and she slipped into the room.

Moments later she said, "Um, we may need some help after all."

"Why's that?" asked Kat.

"Because the servers are gone," Brooklyn answered.

"What?" everyone else asked in unison.

Inside the room, all Brooklyn found was some stray cable and a row of metal brackets and supports.

"They've been moved," she said. "All that's left are the racks to hold them."

"What does that mean?" asked Rio.

"For one thing, it means that I can't hack their network from here," Brooklyn said.

In the Great Court, Kat's mind was racing. Up until this point, everything had gone exactly as planned, but in order to pull off the heist, they needed to access the security system. One weakness with giant equations was that if a single number was wrong, all the other calculations were ruined.

"Is there another server room in the east wing?" asked Sydney.

"Yes," said Brooklyn. "But it's probably empty too. The only reason they'd take them out of here is because they've consolidated everything into a central location. Unfortunately, we have no idea where that is."

"Is there anywhere else you can hack into the system?" Sydney asked.

"There's always the main security office," Brooklyn joked. "Although, I doubt we can get in there without getting caught."

"What if you use a computer outside the building?" asked Rio.

"If I could do that, I already would've," said Brooklyn. "Their network is *air gapped*. That means it's completely disconnected from the internet. It's local access only."

"So, what do we do?" asked Paris. "Postpone the mission? Cancel it?"

"No way," Sydney interjected. "This mission came straight from Tru," she said, referencing the high-ranking MI6 official who had ultimate authority over the team. "We can't let her down. We've got to do it."

"Kat, you're the alpha," Paris said. "What do you think?"

Kat had planned things down to the smallest detail, but now they were slipping off track. It was her biggest mission as an alpha, and she felt like she was failing. Almost imperceptibly, she began to bounce on the balls of her feet and twitch her fingers at the second knuckle, telltale signs of growing anxiety.

"I don't know what to think," she admitted.

"I say we go straight to plan B," Sydney said confidently.

"Do we have a plan B?" asked Brooklyn.

"Maybe . . . kind of," Sydney answered, formulating one on the spot.

"*Maybe, kind of?*" said Rio. "Why do I not feel confident about this?"

"W-w-what are you thinking?" Kat asked with a slight, nervous stammer.

"I'm still piecing it together," said Sydney. "You'll just have to trust me on this one."

There was a pause on the comms channel.

"Kat?" Paris asked. "It's your call."

"O-okay," she said reluctantly. "Tell us what to do."

"I need Brooklyn to meet me at the Rosetta Stone, and I need everybody else to keep a safe distance. Looks like I'm going to get to celebrate Guy Fawkes after all."

"Tell me you're not going to set off an explosive in the middle of the British Museum," Kat exclaimed.

"Of course not," Sydney said. "I'm not asking you to keep your distance because I'm worried about you getting injured. I just want to make sure you're clear of things in case this goes wrong and someone needs to get us out of jail."

"Now *I'm* the one who's not feeling confident," Brooklyn protested. "I thought we were being ghosts?"

"We are," Sydney said. "Except we're going to be like the ones in the attic who howl and rattle loud chains."

The Rosetta Stone was the most famous artifact in

the museum. Nearly four feet tall and weighing just under seventeen hundred pounds, the granite slab was inscribed with three different languages and was the key to how Egyptologists deciphered the code to understanding hieroglyphics. It stood in the center of room four, the Egyptian sculpture gallery. When Brooklyn reached it, Sydney was already waiting for her.

"You ready?" Sydney asked.

"For what?" Brooklyn answered. "You've been kind of vague."

"Yeah. I'm pretty sure if I'd said my plan out loud, it would've been rejected on the spot."

Brooklyn gave her a concerned look.

"Don't worry," Sydney said. "Just trust me and follow my lead."

They looked out across the gallery and could see the others watching from a distance.

"Here goes nothing," Sydney whispered to herself. Then she started chanting, "Remember, remember, the fifth of November, gunpowder, treason, and plot!"

It was a well-known rhyme taught to schoolchildren across the United Kingdom to commemorate the capture of Guy Fawkes.

"Remember, remember, the fifth of November, gun-powder, treason, and plot!"

Sydney turned to Brooklyn and prodded her to chant along with her.

"Remember, remember, the fifth of November, gun-powder, treason, and plot!"

They kept chanting and getting louder. It didn't take long for a small group of visitors to begin looking on curiously. Moments later, a security guard rushed onto the scene.

From her vantage point, Kat looked on, worried and once again bouncing and twitching ever so slightly. There was no mathematical equation for what was happening. All she saw was chaos.

Guy Fawkes

THE SECURITY GUARD RUSHING TO STOP Sydney and Brooklyn wasn't the friendly and awkward one Sydney had encountered earlier. Officer Peter Ryan was more no-nonsense and by-the-book. He had broad shoulders, a buzz cut, and an endless supply of self-confidence. If his bosses allowed it, he would've worn his mirrored sunglasses inside the museum.

"Pete, do you need help?" came a voice over his walkie-talkie.

"Hardly," he scoffed as he strode toward the commotion. "Just some silly schoolgirls making noise. I've got this."

"Remember, remember, the fifth of November, gunpowder, treason, and plot!" Sydney and Brooklyn had found a steady rhythm in their chant, and some of the growing crowd around them playfully joined in. At least until Officer Ryan arrived.

"All right now!" he commanded. "Everybody, quiet down!"

The crowd hushed, as did Brooklyn, who didn't know what the plan called for next. Sydney, however, remained undaunted.

"Remember, remember, the fifth of November, gunpowder, treason, and plot!"

The officer stared her down as he said, "You've had your fun. Now you need to be quiet."

"Quiet?" she said defiantly. "Don't you see that's the problem? We've been quiet for too long. That's how you've gotten away with your crimes."

The guard scoffed again. "And what crimes have we committed, love?" he said with a tone that was meant to sound paternal but was totally patronizing. "Have we broken the laws of fashion? Let me guess, we didn't use the right designer for our uniforms?"

Sydney rolled her eyes. "I was thinking more about your violations of the 1970 UNESCO Convention on the Means of Prohibiting and Preventing the Illicit Import, Export, and Transfer of Ownership of Cultural Property." She waited a beat before adding, "Love."

Officer Ryan sagged as he realized these schoolgirls might be a little more of a challenge than he first thought, and it was all Brooklyn could do to keep from bursting out laughing.

"Can I get some assistance to room four?" he said into his walkie. "We've got a disturbance at Rosetta."

While preparing for the break-in, Sydney had learned about a controversy surrounding artifacts, such as the Rosetta Stone, acquired by museums during European colonization. The dispute centered around who should be the rightful owners of a country's cultural heritage. It riled her sense of justice, and she decided to share that opinion with the dozen or so people who were watching the scene unfold.

"The Rosetta Stone was stolen from Egypt during an invasion by Napoleon's army," Sydney informed them. "Then, after the British defeated the French at Waterloo, it was brought here to London as part of the spoils of war. This is a priceless cultural treasure, not a combat trophy. It belongs to the Egyptian people."

"Think about it," Brooklyn said, joining in. "How would you feel if the Magna Carta or the crown jewels were stolen from us and put on display at a museum in Cairo?" She turned to Officer Ryan. "You wouldn't like that one bit, would you?"

He didn't have an answer for this, and he keyed the mic on his walkie again and asked, "Is that help on the way?"

Across the gallery, Kat, Paris, and Rio watched from in front of a giant bust of King Amenhotep III. No longer anxious, Kat flashed a grin when three guards rushed past them toward Sydney and Brooklyn.

"She's bloody brilliant," she observed. "Never in a million years would I have come up with this."

"With what?" Rio asked, confused. "What makes you think this is brilliant? Now there are even more guards to deal with."

"Exactly," Kat answered. "And soon those guards will take them straight to the main security office. You know, the one where Brooklyn said she could hack into the system."

"That *is* brilliant," Paris said, piecing it together.

Having heard the conversation on the comms channel, Sydney looked at them and nodded slightly. Kat nodded back, her emotions a mix of admiration and envy. It was great to have Sydney on her side, but she couldn't help but wonder how great it would feel to have Sydney's self-confidence.

"What have we here?" asked the lead guard arriving on the scene. Her nametag identified her as V. GARFIELD, DIRECTOR OF SECURITY. She was slender and tall with shoulder-length black hair and a fair complexion. Importantly, she had two teenagers at home and was not about to underestimate Sydney and Brooklyn.

"First, they were chanting about Guy Fawkes," said Officer Ryan. "Then this one brought up Napoleon and some convention."

"The 1970 UNESCO Convention on the Means of Prohibiting and Preventing the Illicit Import, Export, and Transfer of Ownership of Cultural Property," Sydney said, "Director of Security Garfield."

She added the last part for the benefit of Kat and the others, who instantly whipped out their phones and started searching for information about the woman.

Garfield smiled at Sydney. "So you're not just mischief-makers. You've done your homework," she said, impressed by her knowledge.

"Yes, ma'am," Sydney said.

"Well, they've taught you well at the . . ." Garfield checked the crest on the school uniform Sydney was wearing. "City of London School for Girls."

"And they've taught us to be passionate about our beliefs," Sydney said.

"Good." Garfield turned to one of the guards who'd come with her. "Contact the group visitors' desk, and get the name of the head chaperone from the school. Find where she is in the museum, and bring her directly to the central command center."

Sydney went into instant panic mode. "Wait, please don't." In coming up with her plan B on the fly, she hadn't considered this. She was wearing a fake school uniform, and if the chaperone from that school came on the scene, the situation could quickly spin out of control. "If you do that, we'll get in serious trouble."

"I'm afraid there's often a price to being passionate about your beliefs," said the woman.

"We're passionate about a lot of things," Sydney said, "including our education. If we get in trouble, we may get expelled. And that could derail my dream to one day attend . . ."

"Cambridge," Kat blurted into her hidden mic. She was looking at her phone. "According to Garfield's LinkedIn page, she went to Trinity College Cambridge and studied History of Art."

"Cambridge," said Sydney.

Garfield smiled at the mention of her alma mater. "So, it's Cambridge for you and not Oxford?"

"Like my mum," said Sydney. "She was at Trinity College."

"Nicely played," Kat whispered.

"I want to study History of Art there," Sydney continued. "I want to work at an institution like this. I love the British Museum with all my heart. That's why I'm so troubled by that fact that it exhibits treasures that do not belong here."

Garfield weighed the situation for a moment. "We seem to be at a crossroads," she said. "You don't want to get in trouble with your school, and I don't want a disturbance in my museum. How should we resolve this?"

"Perhaps we could stop making the disturbance," Sydney offered. "And then we could go somewhere with you where we would express our concerns so that they could be shared with the proper channels."

"I'm not sure I get your meaning," said Garfield.

"If we can file a formal complaint, we'll feel like at least we've shown that young people have opinions on this issue and want to share them."

Garfield looked at the group of people watching and noticed several were shooting videos on their phones. The last thing she need was for one to go viral and turn into negative publicity for the museum with a title like "Museum Guards Bully Courageous Schoolgirls."

"That sounds reasonable." She turned to the guard. "Forget the chaperone. I think we can handle this among ourselves."

Minutes later, they were walking in a behind-the-scenes area as Garfield led them to the central command center, a suite of offices located on the basement level underneath the Great Court. This was the headquarters of the museum's security force, and unlike the ancient relics on display in the galleries above, everything here looked modern and state of the art.

"You're not wrong, you know," Garfield said as they entered her office. "Although I think you have a stronger argument with regard to the Parthenon Marbles on display in room eighteen."

Sydney realized they'd caught a break because the woman was sympathetic to her argument.

"You agree with us?" she asked.

"I didn't say that," Garfield responded. "Just because you're not wrong doesn't mean that you're right. The world's not as clear-cut as you think. The stewardship of cultural treasures is a complicated situation with valid points to be made on both sides. But I agree that it's a worthy topic for discussion."

"Thank you," said Sydney.

"Still, I don't want you to raise a ruckus in my museum ever again," she said. "Just because you're well-intentioned doesn't mean others with lesser motives won't follow suit. These artifacts are irreplaceable, and it's my responsibility to protect them. Understand?"

"Yes, ma'am," they both answered.

She sat them down and tossed a legal pad on the table in front of them.

"I've got to answer emails for the next ten minutes," she said. "That should give you plenty of time to eloquently express your feelings. I'll deliver them to the appropriate person, so write well and be persuasive. Don't make me look foolish for giving you a chance."

"Got it," Sydney answered.

"Thank you," Brooklyn said.

They huddled around the notepad, and Sydney began writing. It wasn't hard, because she honestly felt passionate about the issue. Brooklyn pretended to confer with her but was actually scoping the office for a computer terminal she could access. This was complicated by the fact that Garfield was sitting at her desk just a few feet away.

"Excuse me—do you have a computer I can use?" Brooklyn asked the security director.

"For what?"

"I want to look up some specifics about the convention." Brooklyn turned to Sydney and asked, "What was it again?"

"The 1970 UNESCO Convention," Sydney answered.

"That's it," Brooklyn said. "I want to make sure we have the exact language from the agreement, and my phone doesn't have any service down here."

"You don't need the precise language," Garfield said. "They'll know what you mean."

"But you wanted us to make a compelling argument," Sydney replied, "so you don't look foolish for giving us a chance."

The woman sighed and said, "Okay, you can use that

one." She motioned to a terminal on a nearby desk.

Brooklyn eagerly hopped onto the computer and did a search for the information. While she was doing that, she also slyly plugged in a tiny USB drive. She'd placed a program on it before the trip that bypassed the museum's security structure so she could create a VPN, or virtual private network. This would allow her to fully access the system from her personal device when they returned after closing.

Five minutes later, Garfield escorted the pair back up to the Great Court.

"Thank you for not turning us in," Brooklyn said.

"Don't make me regret it," Garfield replied. "I don't want to see you causing trouble again."

"Don't worry," Sydney said with a sly smile. "You won't see us at all."

Bonfire Night

LATER THAT NIGHT

THE BEAM FROM PARIS'S FLASHLIGHT sliced through the darkness as the team walked single file through an unused section of the London Underground. They were headed toward the long-abandoned British Museum Tube station, which had been closed since 1933. In the years since, it had served several roles, including military office, command center, and subway storage area. Most importantly to the City Spies, it was a bomb shelter during World War II, when a special tunnel was built connecting it to the museum's basement so artifacts could be brought in and shielded during the Battle of Britain.

Now they planned to use it to sneak back into the museum.

"How much farther?" Sydney asked.

"It's hard to say," Paris answered. "There aren't a lot of visual references down here in the dark, but I think we're getting close."

"We'll know we're nearby when we hear the shrieking of Amun-Ra," Rio said.

"The supreme god of Egyptian mythology?" Kat asked with a raised eyebrow.

"They say his ghost haunts the abandoned Tube station," Rio answered.

"Where'd you come across that tidbit?" Sydney asked.

"While I was researching the mission, I found a great blog about paranormal activity in the London Underground," Rio explained. "There have been multiple sightings of him, and his screams have been heard as far away as Holborn. He was even blamed for the disappearance of two women in the 1930s. Apparently, he escapes through a passageway that connects to a sarcophagus inside the museum."

"You realize how ridiculous that is, don't you?" Kat replied. "First of all, ghosts aren't real. Second, even if they were, Amun-Ra wasn't real, hence the term 'mythological character.' And finally, even if he was real, why would a ghost need a tunnel? Couldn't he just walk through any walls?"

"I didn't say I believed it," Rio mumbled defensively. "I just pointed out that it was a legend."

The mumble caught Sydney's attention, and she pointed her flashlight at him.

"Are you eating?" she asked, incredulous.

Rio paused for a moment before answering with his mouth full. "Maybe."

"Where'd you get food?" she asked.

"At the café in the Great Court," he said with a swallow. "I put it in my backpack in case I got hungry."

"*In case?*" Sydney said. "As if there was ever a time you weren't hungry."

"So, I like food. Big deal. It's just an egg salad sandwich. There's no harm in that."

"Tell that to the burglars who were arrested after the Antwerp diamond heist," Kat responded.

"Consider for a moment that maybe some of us didn't

prep for this mission by memorizing the details of *every* major robbery in history," Rio said. "What happened in Antwerp?"

"It was the biggest jewel theft of all time," Kat said. "The bad guys got away with more than one hundred million in gold, silver, and diamonds. But they were caught because of a half-eaten sandwich that one of them left behind."

Paris laughed. "Then we don't have to worry."

"Why's that?" asked Kat.

"Because Rio's never left anything half-eaten in his life."

The others laughed, and Rio put the last bite in his mouth and held up his empty hands. "All clear," he announced.

Just then, they were startled by a massive whoosh of air and the clatter of a train speeding through an adjacent tunnel. They quickly turned off their flashlights and stood motionless to make sure no one could see them through the windows of the train.

Once it was past, Brooklyn let out a sigh of relief and said, "Just for the record, I'm all good if we stop using creepy tunnels and passageways. I saw enough subway rats in New York to last a lifetime."

"It's not just the rats," joked Sydney. "Don't forget the smell, which might be best described as . . . I don't know . . ."

"Disgusting?" suggested Paris.

"Revolting?" Brooklyn said.

"Let's go with disgustingly revolting," Sydney offered.

"Good call," Paris said with a chuckle.

"I mean, it's one thing to deal with all that on a critical mission," Brooklyn contended. "But this mission doesn't make sense to me. Why are we even down here?"

"It's simple," Kat explained. "It's the best way to access the museum without alerting the security staff."

"I don't mean 'why' as in 'how best to break in,'" Brooklyn answered. "I mean 'why' as in 'why do it in the first place.' I get the Antwerp diamond heist. They were criminals who were motivated by money. But why is the British government stealing two artifacts from a museum owned by the British government? You spent a lot of time planning this. Didn't you think about that?"

"Not really," Kat said. "From a planning point of view, the reason doesn't matter. It's like an absolute value in an equation. There's no good or bad, positive or negative. It just is."

"I've thought about it a lot," Brooklyn said. "I mean,

we're supposed to be the good guys, right? How is *this* good?"

"I have a theory," Sydney interjected. "I think it has something to do with the Mukhabarat."

"Egyptian secret intelligence?" said Paris.

"I didn't just make up that stuff earlier," Sydney explained. "The Egyptian government desperately wants the museum to return the artifacts, but the prime minister has refused, claiming that Britain is their rightful owner. My guess is that MI6 needs some help from the Mukhabarat with regard to Middle Eastern intelligence, so they made a deal. We'll give you back a couple of your priceless treasures, and in return you do us a favor. All hush-hush under the table, of course."

"That's not a bad hypothesis," suggested Kat. "But it may not matter if we don't reach this station soon." She checked her watch. "There's a small window of about twenty minutes during which we know the guards will be elsewhere. That's the only time it will be safe to enter the basement. That means we need to be in the tunnel and ready to go in less than half an hour."

"Good news, then," Paris said, "because I think we're almost there." He moved his flashlight beam in a little circle, and a glint of light shimmered ahead of them.

"See that reflection? It looks like it's from an old platform sign."

"Great. Let's pick up the pace." Kat was relieved. They'd already strayed from her plan earlier, and she was determined that they stay on schedule for the break-in.

A few minutes later, they climbed up onto the platform of the abandoned station. Even without the specter of Amun-Ra, the creepy factor was high. There were decades of dirt and grime on the tiled walls, and they could hear little creatures scurrying in the dark.

"Here are some pictures of the platform during World War II," Kat said, holding up her phone so that she could match the layout of the station with the images.

"You've got service down here?" Brooklyn asked. "How? Because I don't have any bars at all."

"I assumed there wouldn't be any," Kat said. "So I saved all the pictures to my phone while we were aboveground."

Paris and Sydney shared a look. They were impressed.

"Just for the record," Paris said, "you're killing it as the alpha."

"Definitely," Sydney said.

"That couldn't be further from the truth," Kat said. "We've only made it to this point because of your quick thinking at the Rosetta Stone. So far, my plan has failed."

"Your plan worked perfectly," Sydney said. "The only problem was that they moved the server. My quick thinking, by the way, was just an example of utilizing chaos theory, which I learned from you."

"I appreciate what you're trying to do," Kat said, "but rather than worry about my feelings, we really need to access the tunnel." She swiped through a couple images until she reached one of a sculpture being moved into the bomb shelter. It showed the location of the passageway to the museum. "The doorway should be over there," she added, pointing to the far end of the station.

They found it quickly, but just like the entry to King Tut's tomb, it had been plastered shut. Although this one didn't have royal seals with hieroglyphics, just an uneven paint job left by the army.

"It's hammer time," Paris said as he unzipped his backpack and pulled out a couple of rock hammers and a chisel. "We'll start in the middle, where the plaster should be the weakest."

"Or . . . ," Sydney said.

"Or what?" asked Paris.

"Well, Kat said we were in a rush," Sydney replied. "And she also said that I could blow something up."

"I didn't specifically mean tonight," Kat said. "Do you even have any explosives with you?"

"What do you think?" Sydney said with a grin. "I always bring a couple bangers along just in case." From her backpack she pulled out two small silver cylinders and held them up for the others to see. "These were how I planned on celebrating Bonfire Night."

Kat did some quick calculations and liked the idea that this would be quicker than hammering. "All right, then," she said. "Show us what you've got."

"Brilliant," Sydney replied, excited. "Just move back and get behind something." She thought for a moment. "Oh, and make sure to cover your ears."

The Break-In

SECURITY OFFICER BARBARA CURTIS was doing her nightly rounds of the museum's ground floor and had just entered what was known as the lion hunt room when she heard a pair of muffled bangs and a crash coming from one level below.

She paused for a moment to listen for more, then keyed her walkie-talkie and asked, "Did anyone else hear that?"

"Hear what?" came the reply from the night shift supervisor in the command center.

"Two bangs and a crash down in the basement," Curtis answered.

"I didn't hear a thing," replied a guard doing rounds in Medieval Europe.

"Neither did I," said another in the reading room.

"Well, I didn't imagine it," Curtis said.

"There's nothing on the monitors," said the supervisor, scanning a wall of video screens in front of him. "It was probably just someone setting off fireworks for Guy Fawkes."

"Downstairs?" she asked, skeptical.

"Noises have a funny way of bouncing around," he said. "Maybe it sounded like it was downstairs, but it was probably really out on the street."

"Maybe," she replied. "But I'm going to go check it out."

Curtis had worked the night shift long enough to know that the two-hundred-year-old building had plenty of unexplained creaks and noises, but this felt different. She took the stairs down to the sepulchral basement, a maze of rooms whose name came from a word meaning "related to a tomb or funeral." Each chamber was filled with an eerie mix of sculpture fragments, stone slabs, friezes, and other items related to burials and the dead.

The central hallway had vaulted ceilings and was lined with archaeological treasures dating back thousands of years. Disembodied statue parts and marble torsos sat next to partial sculptures of animals and mythological creatures. Each was marked with a tag listing a description of the artifact, its time and place of origin, and its museum number, a five- to eight-character alphanumeric code used to identify it in the collection's database. There were also large wooden crates and various packing materials used to ship objects when they went on loan to other museums around the world.

The guard carefully moved from room to room, looking and listening for anything out of the ordinary. Everything was as it should be until she reached a workshop marked EGYPT AND SUDAN DEPARTMENT—CONSERVATION. This was where scientists and restorers studied and repaired ancient artifacts from along the Nile valley. The work required precision, and the room was always neat and tidy.

Until now.

"What happened here?" Curtis asked herself as she saw that a large wooden shelving unit had toppled over. Luckily, there didn't seem to be any damage to the artifacts or equipment, but books and papers were scattered everywhere, and there were hand tools and a broken wall clock on the floor.

The scene was baffling, and she wondered if perhaps a small earthquake or tremor had somehow triggered the fall. She didn't suspect an intruder because this was far from any entry point to the museum. Or at least that's what she thought.

Unbeknownst to her, and practically anyone else on the staff, the workshop bordered the World War II tunnel that connected to the old Tube station. The shelves and clock had fallen because of reverberations from Sydney's explosives, which she'd packed with an extra wallop in honor of Bonfire Night.

Once they were in the tunnel, the team entered the room by removing a large ventilation grate in the wall. They'd put that back into place and were trying to stand the shelves upright when Rio heard the guard coming their way. Now, they were trapped and hiding as Curtis came closer to inspect the scene.

Brooklyn was balled up underneath a desk and had a clear view of feet and legs as the guard knelt down to check the base of the unit.

"Why'd you fall over?" Curtis wondered aloud. "Were these books too heavy?"

Eighteen inches away, Brooklyn held her breath and tried to remain perfectly motionless, although she flinched when she heard another voice. This one belonged to the security supervisor, who was speaking over the walkie.

"We have a smoke alarm going off in the southeast corner of the upper floor. Do you copy?"

"Copy that," one guard replied.

"On my way," said another.

"What about you, Barb?" asked the supervisor. "What's your twenty?"

"I'm down in Egyptian conservation, and I think I found the cause of that—" she started to answer, but then he cut her off.

"Okay, now we've got an alarm going off on the ground floor too," he said. "I need you there."

"Roger that," Curtis said. "I'm on my way."

The possibility of a fire was one of the gravest threats to any museum's collection. One alarm might be a malfunction, but two signaled a potential emergency. Barbara Curtis raced out of the room to help her coworkers locate the cause.

Once she was gone and the door closed behind her, things were quiet for a moment, until Paris sat up from his hiding place inside a marble tomb from the thirteenth century BCE. He'd hidden in there and covered himself with a canvas drop cloth.

"The coast is clear," he informed the others.

Sydney stepped out of a closet, Brooklyn came from under the desk, and Kat stood up from behind a large wooden shipping crate.

"Well, that was close," Sydney said sheepishly.

Kat shot her the stink eye and said, "Much too close. I can't believe how loud that was. How much explosive was in there?"

Sydney shrugged. "It's hard to say exactly, but the noise wasn't just because of the explosive. There was a lot of echo in that tunnel."

"Does anyone else hear a constant buzzing?" Brooklyn asked as she made repeated biting motions, trying to pop her ears. "I keep hearing buzzing."

"I warned you to cover your ears," Sydney said in her defense. "Although, I'll admit those bangers might have been just a bit stronger than we needed for the job."

"Just a bit?" Kat asked, incredulous.

"But, on the plus side, my smoke bombs seemed to do the trick right on schedule."

Paris nodded. "You can't argue with that."

Sydney had made four smoke bombs that looked like air fresheners. Each had a built-in timer, and the team had hidden them in bathrooms earlier in the day.

"Wait a second," said Paris. "Where's Rio?"

"I didn't see where he hid," said Sydney.

"Neither did I," added Kat.

"Rio," Paris called, "you can come out now."

"Maybe he can't hear you," suggested Brooklyn, who was speaking louder than usual and still wiggling her jaw, trying to clear her ears. "Maybe he can't hear anything."

They looked around the room, but there was no sign of him. Then their eyes fell on a wooden sarcophagus.

"You don't think he . . . ," Kat said.

They rushed over to it, and Paris lifted the lid to reveal a terrified Rio, who scrambled up and out of it.

"Are you okay?" Brooklyn asked.

"I was holding the top so that it stayed slightly open," he said, shaking and nearly hyperventilating, "but it got too heavy, and when it shut, I couldn't budge it. You can't imagine how dark it is in there."

Paris looked at the attached label and read it aloud. "'Coffin of Horaawesheb containing the mummy of a female. Thebes. Twenty-second dynasty. Nine hundred BCE.'"

"Mummy?" Rio said anxiously. "You're saying I was in a coffin that's held a mummy for the last three thousand years?"

"Well, at least she's not in there now," Paris said. "She's probably in some preservation lab or something. But yes. That seems to be the case."

"And to think, you were worried about the ghost of Amun-Ra," Sydney joked.

"That's not funny," Rio said, trying to brush off any mummy dust. "Not funny at all."

"Funny or not, we are now on the clock," Kat said, taking charge. "The smoke alarms will only keep them busy for so long, which means we don't have much time. You're up first, Brooklyn."

"I'm on it," Brooklyn said as she pulled a laptop out of her backpack and set it up on the desk. She was a virtuoso on a computer keyboard, and she quickly accessed the VPN she'd set up earlier and breached the museum's security system. "And we've got CCTV."

The others huddled behind her and looked over her shoulder as the camera feed came onto her screen.

"Here's how this system works," she said. "The top two monitors are controlled by the operator in command central. At the moment those are locked on the southeast corner, where the smoke alarms went off."

"You can see the guards right there," Paris said, pointing at one.

"Meanwhile, the bottom row continually rotates through all the cameras in the museum," she explained. "But, and here's the great part, the cameras are ranked by value to make sure they see the most important ones more often. All you have to do is assign a camera a value of *zero*, and it disappears from the feed."

She typed a zero under one of the camera feeds, and the image vanished from the screen only to be replaced by video from another.

"Just like I told you, Rio," Kat said with a grin. "Everything's math."

"I'll get rid of the cameras for your route, and you'll be invisible," Brooklyn said.

"That's great," Kat said. She turned to the others. "Now get moving."

"Aye, aye, Alpha," Paris said with a wink and a smile.

Paris, Sydney, and Rio slipped out into the hallway of the basement, while Kat and Brooklyn set up in the workshop. Kat monitored the CCTV feed to keep an eye on the guards, and Brooklyn used a second laptop to access the VPN so she could take control of the additional security measures. By the time the others reached the stairs, she was ready to go.

"We are at the gate to the Egyptian gallery," Paris said. "What do we do with the keypad?"

Brooklyn quickly pulled the specs up on her computer and made a few adjustments.

"I just changed the passcode," she said. "All you've got to do is activate it with the badge clone on Rio's phone, and then enter the numbers one-one-two-zero."

"You used your birthday as the passcode?" said Paris.

"Thought it might be good to remind you guys," Brooklyn said. "After all, it's just a few weeks away."

Rio held his phone up to the keypad, and when it turned on, he entered the numbers. An interface appeared on the screen with up and down arrows.

"Just lift the gate high enough so that we can slide under," Sydney said.

"Yes, I know," Rio replied as he pressed the up arrow. "This is not my first mission."

The metal gate clattered to life, and the sound of its gears echoed through the cavernous exhibit hall. Sydney and Paris winced, nervously checking to make sure it hadn't alerted any guards. Once it'd risen about two feet off the ground, Rio stopped it.

"Gate's open," Sydney said. "Now you need to take care of the lasers and motion detectors."

"Already doing that," Brooklyn replied.

On the screen, she'd opened a diagram of the entire ground floor. There were overlays for the different security measures. First, she turned off all the trip-wire lasers. Next, she deactivated the motion detectors, but as she clicked the last one, the entire screen went blue.

"Wait, what just happened?" Brooklyn asked. "Did the system crash? Or is this a reboot?"

"My screen looks fine," said Kat, who still had the security feed on her laptop.

"Yeah, but mine just blue-screened," Brooklyn said.

"Is it the computer or the system?" Kat asked.

"Definitely the system," Brooklyn replied. "All my other windows are good."

"Is this normal?"

"No," Brooklyn said. "It isn't."

"Hey, remember us?" came the call from Sydney. "What's going on?"

"I'm not exactly sure," said Brooklyn. "I was turning off the last motion detector, and then the system crashed. Maybe it's a normal maintenance reboot. Maybe it's . . . something else."

"Did it happen before or after you clicked the last one?" asked Paris.

"At the same time," Brooklyn responded.

"So, you don't know if it's off or on?"

"No."

There was a pause. "Any idea how long it will take if it's a reset?"

"None."

"We can't wait here too long," said Sydney. "As soon as they finish with the smoke bombs, at least one of those guards will be headed back this way."

"Do you *think* you clicked it off first?" Rio asked.

"Maybe," Brooklyn answered. "And maybe the motion detectors shut off automatically when the system went down."

"We can't risk it," Kat said, disappointed. Once again, her meticulous planning had been derailed and her mental equations rendered useless. "Come back, and we'll exit through the Tube station. We need to call this off. The plan didn't work."

"Come on, Kat. You're more than your plan," Paris said. "We can figure this out."

"How?" asked Kat.

"Think about all those robberies you studied," Paris

said. "Certainly one of them involved beating a motion detector without the aid of a world-class computer hacker. What about that diamond heist you told us about earlier? The one with the sandwich."

"Antwerp?"

"Did they have motion detectors in Antwerp?"

"Actually, they did," Kat said.

"And how'd they beat them?" asked Paris.

"Hairspray," Kat answered. "They sprayed it on the sensors, and that did the trick."

"Well, that's not going to help us," said Rio. "We don't have any hairspray."

"I have hairspray," Sydney said.

"You do?" Rio said, incredulous. "Explosives are one thing, but who brings hairspray to a museum heist?"

"Asks the boy who packed an egg salad sandwich," Sydney replied. "Technically it's a mist elixir, and I didn't *bring it to the heist*. I just always keep a small bottle of it in my backpack."

"Because?"

"Because I have amazing hair," Sydney replied. "And every now and then, it needs a little spritz."

"That's great," said Brooklyn. "But you'd still have to get close to the motion detector to spray it. And there's no way to approach it without moving and setting it off."

"That's not exactly true," Paris said. "They're thermal motion detectors. They only trigger if there's movement *and* body heat. That way a stray mouse or some giant mutant cockroach won't set it off."

"And do you know a way for a person not to generate body heat?" asked Rio.

Paris just smiled and said, "In fact, I do."

He hurried back down the stairs, and the others were left wondering what he was up to. Two minutes later he returned and was carrying two items he'd noticed in the basement hallway—a mover's dolly and a thermal blanket.

"What's all this?" asked Rio.

"A dolly normally used to move marble statues, and thermal wrap that protects artifacts from temperature damage when they're being shipped."

"And we're going to use them how?" asked Sydney.

"I learned about this in my SERE training," he said, referring to a survival skills course he'd taken with the Royal Air Force. "The thermal blanket is designed to keep you warm in cold climates by trapping your body heat. We're going to wrap this around Rio, put him on the dolly, and slide him toward the sensor so that he can get close enough to squirt it with your hairspray."

"Mist elixir."

"Sorry. Mist elixir."

"Why me?" asked Rio.

"Because making a person disappear is the ultimate magic trick, and you are an amazing magician."

"I can't see what it is you're talking about, but we've completely strayed from the plan," Kat protested. "Let me think through the math."

"There isn't time for that," Rio said.

"You can stop us, Kat," Paris said. "That's your right. But I know in my heart that this is going to work."

"What's that Motherism?" Sydney said, trying to remember one of the rhyming couplets they'd learned as part of their training. *"You're at your best . . ."*

". . . when you trust the rest," Kat said, finishing it.

"It comes down to trust," Sydney said. "It comes down to *team*."

Kat thought for a moment, and her fingers began to twitch again. "All right, make Rio disappear," she said. "But do it quickly. We don't have much time."

Rio laid across the dolly on his stomach while Paris and Sydney tucked the thermal blanket around him. The motion detector was about fifteen meters away, and they had to give him a big shove to get him close.

"We can't see, so tell us what's happening," Kat said.

"Okay," Sydney said. "He's sliding out there toward the spot, and he's coming to a stop just short of it."

"You need to go about another two meters to your right," Paris called out to Rio, who started moving the dolly just by using his fingers on the floor.

"He's getting closer, and there are no alarms yet," Sydney told the others. "This may actually be working."

"You're almost there, mate," Paris said, encouraging. "Keep going until you reach the wall."

"He's there," Sydney said. "Now he has to stand up."

"Careful," Paris instructed.

Rio rolled off the dolly gently and slowly stood up, holding the thermal blanket in front of him like a shield.

"You're so close," Paris told him. "Just a hair more."

"Lucky for me, I have hairspray," Rio joked as he shuffled his feet and slid into the perfect position. Next, he carefully lowered the blanket with one hand and kept the rest of his body perfectly still. This was where his sleight of hand came into play. He was so nimble and quick that he moved in a flash and sprayed the mist on the sensor before it could go off.

Once he was done, he kept as still as the statues around him.

"Did you get it?" Paris asked.

"We'll see," Rio whispered into his comm. "Get ready to run, in case this didn't work." He let out a breath and then waved his hand in front of the sensor.

Nothing happened, and he flashed a proud grin.

"Got it!" he said.

There was a moment of muted celebration. "That's amazing," Kat said. "But we still have to hurry. On the monitor, it looks like the guards are almost done."

Paris, Sydney, and Rio quickly moved through the room and went directly to the special exhibit on Tutmania. Their targets were a jeweled necklace and a gold chest plate.

Just as they reached the display, a woman's voice filled the gallery and instructed them to "Stop right there!"

Sydney froze and recognized the voice from earlier in the day. It belonged to Valerie Garfield, the museum's director of security.

London Bridge

"STOP. RIGHT. THERE!" VALERIE GARFIELD repeated.

The security director walked briskly across the gallery, her heels clicking against the tile floor. Sydney, Paris, and Rio all stopped in their tracks and slowly turned to face her. Each was contemplating making a run for it but changed their mind when they saw who was walking with her.

"What's going on?" Kat asked urgently over the comms channel. "Whose voice was that?"

"It's hard to explain," Sydney said, "but you'd better come up here."

"What?" asked Kat.

"She's right," said Paris. "Both of you. Just leave your gear in the workshop, and come straight to the Tut exhibit. This isn't what we thought it was."

"I've seen enough," Garfield said to her companions. "I wouldn't have believed it any other way." There were three people with her, and they weren't part of museum security.

They were MI6.

"Mother? Tru? What are you doing here?" Rio asked.

Mother was the agent in charge of the City Spies, but he was much more than that. He was also their father, having adopted all five earlier in the year. They were quite literally a family of spies, and at the moment he looked every bit the proud papa. Striding alongside him was Gertrude Shepherd, better known as Tru, a tall woman with a slight limp and a legendary career as a spy. She was Mother's boss and a high-ranking official in the Intelligence Service.

"Bravo!" she said. "Bravo!"

"That was really great work," Mother added. "So impressive."

Although Mother and Tru were beaming, Valerie Garfield's expression was less positive. After all, a team of burglars too young to drive had just infiltrated the museum she was in charge of protecting. She stopped directly in front of Sydney and shook her head before offering a begrudging smile.

"I literally escorted you into the command center," she said, furious with herself. "I'm guessing you're not a student at the City of London School for Girls."

"No," Sydney said sheepishly. She wasn't one to gloat, especially considering the fact that she'd taken an instant liking to Garfield. "I'm not."

"Then who are you?" the security director asked.

"I'm afraid that's classified," said the fourth member of the group, an aristocratic man in his sixties who had thinning hair and wore a finely tailored suit. It was dark in the museum, so it was only now, as he stepped into a slash of moonlight, that they got a good look at him.

"Wait a second," said Paris. "Are you—?"

"Yes, I am," the man said with a smile. "Sir David Denton Douglas, although you can call me C."

This bit of information put a smile on Paris's face.

C was the designation given to the chief of the Secret

Intelligence Service. He was Britain's top spymaster.

"Tru has told me about your exploits," C continued, "but I assumed the stories were more embellishment than actual accomplishment."

"As if," Tru said. "Have I ever exaggerated anything to you?"

C gave her a pointed look, and she cracked a wry smile.

"Point taken," she said. "But not about this team. Every word was true."

He nodded. "I can see that."

Kat and Brooklyn arrived on the scene and didn't know what to make of it.

"What's going on?" Kat asked.

"Tonight, you were functioning as what's known as a red team," Mother said. "You were testing the museum's security systems."

"And we failed," Garfield said. "Miserably."

"MI6 received credible intel that the museum is a target for an upcoming attack," Tru said. "The information specifically mentioned the Tut exhibit."

"The Intelligence Service reached out to me, and I assured them that all was secure," Garfield said. She looked at the five of them. "Obviously, I was mistaken."

"Luckily, it was the good guys this time," Tru said. "We'll write up a report and detail the vulnerabilities we discovered." She caught herself and smiled at the team. "Rather that *they* discovered."

"I'd greatly appreciate that," Garfield said.

"Now, if you don't mind, we need to speak with the team," C said.

"Of course," Garfield replied. "Just as I need to speak with mine."

As she started to walk away, Sydney called out to her, "There's no fire."

"I beg your pardon?" Garfield replied.

"At the moment, your staff is trying to figure out if a fire has set off several smoke detectors," Sydney said. "They were just smoke bombs. Completely harmless."

"Thank you," Garfield said.

"And there's something wonky with your computer system," Brooklyn said. "It went offline about ten minutes ago. I'm not sure if it was a crash, a reboot, or something else, but you should check it."

"Okay." Garfield nodded wearily. "Anything else?"

After an awkward pause, Rio said, "On the positive

side, the egg salad sandwich I bought at the café was delicious. It had just a hint of paprika. Very nice."

This made the security director chuckle. "I'll pass it along."

Once she was out of the gallery, Tru turned to the team. "Rough night for them. I imagine that's not going to be a fun conversation."

"But their failure is our success," said C. "It was quite an impressive display. Please tell me who was in charge of this operation."

All eyes turned to Kat.

"I was the alpha," she said. "But my plan didn't work."

"It looked like a total success from my vantage point," C proclaimed.

"The team was successful, not the plan," Kat replied. "There were operational mistakes and contingencies that I failed to factor in."

"The team and the plan are one and the same," C said. "There are going to be bumps along the way, but the end result is what determines success or failure."

"Exactly," Sydney said. "Your plan was great."

"I've got a question," Paris said. "I thought red teams always knew it wasn't an actual infiltration.

Why didn't you tell us the real purpose of the mission?"

"Because we weren't just testing the museum," Tru explained. "We were also testing you."

"Your team has had tremendous success," C said. "But I wanted to see it firsthand."

"And he wanted to make sure that what he observed was all you," Mother said. "That's why I didn't help you with any of the planning. What he saw tonight is what I see every day."

"And it was brilliant," said C. "Absolutely brilliant."

They talked a while longer, going over the key points of the mission, and were still smiling thirty minutes later as they took the Tube back to their safe house in Notting Hill. Tru, who preferred public transportation to chauffeur-driven cars, was with them and grinning biggest of all.

"You're now rising stars in the Service," she said. "Tonight's performance will open the door for bigger and better things to come." She chuckled. "And here I thought the show at Battersea Park was impressive."

"You saw the fireworks?" Sydney asked, her voice laced with envy.

"It wouldn't be Bonfire Night without them," Tru

said. "We have a great vantage point from the roof at Vauxhall Cross, and they were magnificent."

"We didn't get to go," Sydney said, "because Kat hates Bonfire Night."

"It's not that I hate it," Kat corrected. "It just didn't fit into the schedule."

"I'm not buying it," said Sydney. "Deep down I think it's hate."

Kat fought it for a moment and then laughed. "Okay, you're right," she said. "I absolutely despise it."

Tru gave her a curious look. "Why?"

"Where do I begin?" Kat responded. "It's loud. It's crowded. There are fireworks and explosions everywhere. It's absolute chaos."

Sydney was incredulous. "*Those* are the best parts!"

They rode for a few more minutes, laughing and talking, until the train inexplicably stopped in the middle of a tunnel, far from any station.

"That's odd," Tru said.

"What's going on?" asked Mother.

Just then, a slowed-down and eerily distorted version of "London Bridge Is Falling Down" started playing over the loudspeakers in the train. It sounded like it was coming from a warped jack-in-the-box, and when the tune reached its end, all the power went off, and they were plunged into darkness.

There was a concerned murmur among the passengers in the train car, and then Kat said, "And I repeat. Absolute chaos."

The Gawky Fuse

THEY'D BEEN STUCK IN THE UNDERGROUND for a few minutes, and the interior of the train car was still dark, with the exception of some flickering security lights and the flashlight apps from passenger phones. Despite some moaning and groaning, no one seemed to be panicking. Yet.

"We've got torches in our backpacks," Paris whispered to Mother, using the British term for flashlights. "Should we bring them out?"

"Hold off for now," Mother said. "It might seem odd

for you to have them, and we don't want to attract any unnecessary attention. Hopefully, this is just a blip, and we'll be back and running in a jiffy."

"Got it," Paris said.

Tru's phone dinged, indicating the arrival of a message.

"You're getting a text down here?" Brooklyn said. "How do you have service?"

Tru smiled and answered, "Let's just say my phone doesn't come from a retail store."

In fact, Tru's phone had been built especially for her by the covert comms team at HMGCC, Her Majesty's Government Communication Centre. Its many special features included military grade encryption software, connectivity to a secret "ghost network" that included antennas within the London Underground, and a real-time direct feed of breaking news alerts from the information desk at the Secret Intelligence Service.

One such alert had just arrived, and she related it to the others.

"It's not just us," she said. "Apparently, the entire London Underground's at a standstill."

"Is it a blackout?" asked Mother.

"I think it's just the Tube."

Another ding.

"Well, well, what's this?" Tru asked as she looked at the screen. "With regards to the shutdown, a cryptic message has been sent to multiple news and government outlets."

"What does it say?" Rio asked.

"'The London Underground cannot be used, because it's blown a gawky fuse,'" Tru answered. "And it's signed, 'Mr. Bevin Hoffet.'"

"Bevin Hoffet's not exactly Shakespeare, is he?" Sydney said.

"No, I'd rate that around a mid-level Motherism at best," Paris joked.

"Mid-level?" Mother said with mock indignation. "My couplets are poetic, and this is—"

"Not a poem," Kat interrupted. "It's just a prank. All of it. The rhyme. The Underground shutting down. It's a Bonfire Night prank."

"What makes you say that?" asked Brooklyn.

"'Gawky fuse,'" Kat replied. "It's an anagram for 'Guy Fawkes.' Just like 'Mr. Bevin Hoffet' is an anagram for 'November fifth.' As in, 'Remember, remember the fifth of November.'"

The others paused for a moment in stunned amazement until Brooklyn asked, "How do you do that?"

"Do what?" Kat asked.

"Hear a sentence and instantly find anagrams hidden in it?"

"It's incredible," Mother added.

"Breathtaking," Tru added.

"You know that thing about patterns I talk about?" Kat said. "I can't just turn it off and on. It's always there. Some things fit and some things don't. 'Gawky fuse' doesn't fit. It's awkward. Normally someone would say a fuse was faulty or dodgy, so the instant I heard it, I wondered why someone would use the term 'gawky fuse,' and that led straight to Guy Fawkes. Once I had that, 'November fifth' was kind of obvious."

"To you, pet," Tru said. "Only to you."

The shutdown lasted exactly eleven minutes and five seconds, another nod to November fifth. Once that time had passed, "London Bridge" started playing over the loudspeakers again, and the trains came back to life.

At first glance, the only damage caused by the stoppage seemed to be the inconvenience of passenger delays and public embarrassment for Transport for London, the government agency that oversaw the Underground. A few hours after Kat solved it, someone at the BBC figured out the Guy Fawkes references, and by the time the morning news was on, the media was framing the story as an elaborate Bonfire Night prank. Depending on who was being interviewed, it was either a serious crime, an indication of a poorly run government, or a humorous lark worthy of commemorating the fifth of November.

For the City Spies, the stoppage was just what Mother had called it, little more than a blip on a night dominated by their infiltration of the British Museum and their praise from the nation's top spy. But that perception began to change three days later, when the team was back in school at Kinloch Abbey.

Brooklyn and Kat were in an English class where the assignment was to write a descriptive essay about something they found beautiful. Kat was describing her love of polynomials, and Brooklyn was trying to come up with the perfect adjective to evoke the mouth-watering aroma of her favorite New York pizza parlor, when there was a knock on the door and in walked Dr. Graham, the school's headmaster.

"I'm sorry to interrupt, Ms. White, but I need Christina and Supriya to come with me," he said, using their cover names.

"Of course," responded the teacher.

Brooklyn and Kat shared a glance; neither had any idea what this was about. Their curiosity only intensified when Dr. Graham instructed them to "bring your things."

"What's going on?" Brooklyn asked once they were in the hall.

"You have a visitor," Graham answered. He turned and spoke in a confidential whisper. "I believe you call her Tru."

"'Curiouser and curiouser,'" Kat said, quoting one of her favorite books. "Why would she come here?"

Graham smiled and answered, "I know better than to ask such things."

Before pursuing a career in education, the headmaster served as an army intelligence officer with the Royal Scots and had been heavily recruited to join MI6. Tru was the handler who had tried to enlist him, and their professional relationship was why Kinloch had been chosen as the school for the team. Tru knew that he could be trusted to keep secrets, but up until this point, she'd never visited the campus in person for fear of someone wondering what a high-ranking member of MI6 was doing at a prep school in Scotland. Yet there she was sitting with

Mother when they arrived at Graham's office.

"Thank you, Christopher," Tru said. "Now, if you don't mind, we need some privacy."

"Of course," Graham replied.

"No one can hear us when we're in here, can they?" Mother asked.

"No," the headmaster assured them. "It's secure."

Brooklyn and Kat shared a look, unsure what to do, and Brooklyn said, "You might want to close the heating vent behind the desk."

Graham gave them a surprised look.

"It's directly above the reading room in the library," Kat explained. "And sometimes you might be able to pick up a word or two of what's said in here."

"At least that's what other people have told us," Brooklyn chimed in. "Of course, we would never eavesdrop."

"Of course," Graham said. "Thanks for bringing it to my attention."

He left the room, and Mother reached down and closed the vent tight before they moved to a sitting area on the other side of the office.

"Why are you here?" Brooklyn asked, showing concern for the first time. "Is everyone okay?"

"Everybody's fine," Mother answered. "Tru came up from London with a pressing need that I'm afraid can't wait until you get home from school."

"Quite pressing." Tru spoke directly to Brooklyn. "At the museum, you said that the computer system acted . . . I believe the term you used was 'wonky.'"

"That's right," Brooklyn answered. "It just blue-screened out of nowhere."

"And 'blue-screened' means what, exactly?"

"Some people call it the blue screen of death," Brooklyn said. "It's an error screen that usually means a total system failure and shutdown. But this was different. I think it may have been some kind of update or reboot, because when we returned to get our laptops, everything was back to normal and looked fine."

"It may have looked fine, but it wasn't," said Tru. "Which is why I need you to be totally honest with me about something."

"Of course."

"Did you do anything to the security system?" she asked.

"Are they blaming me for the shutdown?" Brooklyn asked defensively. "Because that was not my fault. I didn't—"

"No one's blaming you for anything," Tru said in a calming tone. "I just need to know if you did something like perhaps install a program other than the VPN."

"No," Kat answered. "The plan was to slip in and out and leave no trace of us being there."

"Actually," Brooklyn said with a guilty shrug. "I may have diverged from that a bit."

"In what way?" Mother asked.

"I installed a RAT," Brooklyn admitted. "A Random Access Trojan."

"Why'd you do that?" Kat replied. "You weren't supposed to leave any trace."

"And I didn't," Brooklyn said. "It's invisible. No one can find it but me. It's an old hacker trick. You leave a backdoor just in case you need to get into the system someday."

She looked at Tru, worried that she was about to get into trouble, but instead was greeted with a big smile.

"Well, it turns out that *someday* is today," Tru said. She turned to Mother. "Have Dr. Graham get the others so we can head straight for the FARM."

"You're not mad?" Brooklyn said.

"Quite the opposite," Tru said. "But now we have to get to work."

"On what?" Kat asked. "What's going on?"

"It turns out that the subway stoppage was more than just a prank," Tru said.

"What does that have to do with the security system at the British Museum?" Brooklyn asked.

Tru looked directly at her and said, "Everything."

The FARM

THE FOUNDATION FOR ATMOSPHERIC
Research and Monitoring, or FARM, was a weather station based in a centuries-old manor house in the north
of Scotland. For generations, the sprawling three-story
house and surrounding estate belonged to a series of
barons and baronesses of Aisling. In 1953, when the
final one died with no heirs, the property was turned
into a meteorological research center, perfectly situated
to study changing weather patterns from its perch over-
looking the North Sea.

To anyone passing by, the FARM was little more than a once-grand estate that now did the none-too-exciting work of analyzing yesterday's weather and predicting the paths of potential storms. Few people paid it any attention, which is exactly how the Secret Intelligence Service wanted it.

That's because it was actually an MI6 cover operation. While the foundation did produce authentic weather reports, the primary purpose of those was to hide the real work being done there. During the Cold War, the estate housed a team of spies that used its northerly location to eavesdrop on communications in the Soviet Union. More recently, it became a cryptography center because the type of supercomputer used to predict the path of a hurricane was exactly the same as the type used to break complex codes. And, for the last six years, the FARM had been home to the City Spies. This is where they lived and trained under the protective eyes of Mother and an agent named Alexandra Montgomery, more commonly called Monty, who was the cryptographer in charge of the facility. And this is where Tru met with them all to explain why she had rushed up from London.

"Four government targets have been hacked by someone, or some people, calling themselves Horus, spelled *H-O-R-U-S*," Tru told the team, which was gathered around the conference table in the priest hole, the FARM's secret underground situation room. "Parliament, the National Health Service, the London Underground, and the British Museum."

"Wow," Rio said. "Those are big targets."

"Huge," Paris said.

"What does the hacking entail?" Monty asked.

"Their systems were breached, and the hackers installed some kind of ransomware," Tru explained. "Now that information is being held hostage. Either the government pays millions of pounds for the cipher key, or Horus starts deleting files and disrupting life throughout Britain. The shutdown on the Tube the other night wasn't a prank. It was a demonstration to show how capable and serious they are."

"Any idea who Horus is?" Rio asked.

"We know that they're connected with Umbra," she said, referencing the global crime syndicate that the City Spies had come up against before. "But it's likely that they're independent and just using Umbra for technical support and muscle."

"When is the ransom due?" asked Mother.

"That's being negotiated as we speak," Tru answered.

"But I can't imagine they'll be very patient. That's why C wanted me to pluck you all out of school."

"C sent you?" Paris asked, incredulous. "To put *us* on the case?"

"Yes and no," she said. "He sent me, but you're not officially on the case. Our hands are a bit tied on this. We have no proof yet that this is the work of anyone outside of the UK, which means that it falls under the jurisdiction of MI5 and the National Cyber Security Centre, not MI6. C, of course, is in charge of both MI5 and MI6, so he's keeping us looped in. He's given all the official assignments to the appropriate groups, and they're working in conjunction with Scotland Yard and liaising with the prime minister's office, the Government Communications Headquarters, and . . . well, you get the idea. There are many people working on this, and that's not always efficient."

"Then what does he want us to do?" Sydney asked.

"We need to identify Horus and figure out how to neutralize the attack."

"But we have to do our bit without anyone on either side knowing we're involved," Mother said.

"Exactly," Tru said. "You'll sneak along the edges and poke around without being seen."

"There are a lot of teams inside MI6 he could use," Paris said. "Why us?"

"Several reasons," said Tru. "First of all, you really impressed him the other night. I don't know that I've ever seen him quite so delighted. Second, you have detailed knowledge of the museum's security, both physical and cyber. That could come in very handy since they're one of the targets. And finally, there's WannaCry."

"Who wants to cry?" Kat asked, confused.

"No, dear, *WannaCry*," Tru said.

"It was a cryptoworm," Brooklyn said. "The North Koreans launched it as a worldwide botnet attack, and it infected hundreds of thousands of computers in more than one hundred fifty countries. It threatened to crash the entire internet."

"And what does that have to do with us?" Sydney asked.

"The world's biggest tech companies and top intelligence agencies, not to mention thousands of the most skilled and well-funded cybersecurity officers on the planet, were all trying to stop the attack before it destroyed the digital universe as we know it," Tru said. "And the person who actually saved the day was a young man, just a few years older than you, working by himself in the basement of his parents' house. He lived out in the middle of the Devon countryside and stopped the attack by creating something known as a 'sinkhole' with a domain name he purchased for ten pounds."

"He became an instant legend in the hacking community," Brooklyn said.

"And, while he's had somewhat of a checkered legal history, on that day he was heroic. Which is why C said, 'Never underestimate the potential of a young, precocious Brit working on a computer in their parents' basement.'" Tru motioned to their surroundings and smiled. Then she handed a folder to Mother. "Here's a dossier, rather thin I'm afraid, that includes what we know about the hack and what the specific threat is to each of the targets."

"Here's something I don't get," Sydney said. "Kat's always talking about patterns, but the pattern of these targets doesn't make sense."

"In what way?" Monty asked.

"The Tube is how millions of people move around the city. Parliament runs the government. The NHS looks after everybody's health and medical care," Sydney said. "They're mammoth operations, but the British Museum isn't. I mean, I love it, and the collections are priceless, but this whole thing feels like Horus is robbing three banks *and* a candy store. It doesn't fit."

"Unless the candy store is how you get into the bank," Kat said.

"What do you mean?" Rio asked.

"The Baker Street robbery was one of the heists I studied while I was prepping for the mission," she said. "In 1971, a gang broke into a Lloyds Bank and got away with millions. Rather than attack the bank directly, they went in through a leather goods shop two doors away and tunneled under the ground to reach the vault. Maybe the museum's like the leather goods shop—an access point."

"Just like we used the abandoned Tube station to break into the museum," Paris offered.

"Exactly," said Kat.

"Except, unlike the Tube station, none of these targets are nearby," Rio said. "They're spread all over London."

"You're thinking of a physical break-in," Brooklyn said. "This was a cyberattack, and all the targets are part of the British government, which means on some level they're all connected to the same computer network."

"That makes a lot of sense," Mother said. "If we can

identify that the museum was where the breach started, that would let us focus on a smaller group of potential candidates."

"Why don't I go look for it?" Brooklyn said. "I'll fire up Beny and see what I can find."

Beny was the nickname for the Cray XC40 super-computer that filled an entire wall of the priest hole. Brooklyn moved over to a terminal and started typing, while the others passed around pages from the dossier.

"I need to get back to London before my absence becomes conspicuous," Tru said. "Keep me in the loop of anything you uncover, and just . . . do good work and make us proud."

"Don't we always?" Mother said.

Tru smiled. "You absolutely do."

"I have one question before you leave," Monty said. "How do you know Umbra's involved?"

"What do you mean?" Tru asked.

"Earlier, you said that you know Umbra is involved," Monty said. "But you don't know Horus's identity, so how can you be certain?"

"The original intel came from a source deep inside the organization," Tru answered. "That's how we knew the museum was a target in the first place."

"But that information was inaccurate," Kat said. "You thought objects in the Tut exhibit were the target. Why didn't your source tell you it was a cyberattack?"

"And why only mention the museum, when there were other much larger targets?" Sydney asked.

"It's hard to understand what it's like to spend years as a deep cover agent inside an organization as dangerous as Umbra," Tru said. "There are no phone calls or direct communications. This source is one of the most valuable assets MI6 has. They can't give us everything, because if we knew too much at once, Umbra would realize that there was a leak. All the agent can do is send us coded messages and hope we figure it out."

"We're good with codes," Kat said confidently. "Can we see the message?"

Tru considered this. "All the message did was warn us that the museum was a target. That's been confirmed."

"Then why is it a problem for us to see it?" asked Paris.

"Because it also includes highly sensitive information," Tru said.

"You mean about the identity of the source?" said Monty.

"Potentially," Tru said. "But there's something else. Something I'm not inclined to share."

"This is a serious threat, and you want us to help solve the problem," Mother said. "You came to us, and you can trust us."

She thought about it for a moment and nodded. "That's fair."

She reached into her briefcase and pulled out a manila folder marked TOP SECRET. She opened it to reveal a single sheet of paper, which had been stamped EYES ONLY in several places. Written in the middle of the paper was:

Wonderful Things

515194001270

389523771458

Cleopatra

"That's the entire message?" Rio asked.

Tru nodded. "That's it."

"How was it sent to you?" asked Monty.

"That, I cannot tell you," Tru said.

"Okay, *Wonderful Things* is the name of the Tut exhibit," Kat said. "And Cleopatra?"

"The mummy of Cleopatra, not the queen, but another Cleopatra, is in the same gallery at the museum," Tru explained. "When we thought it was going to be a robbery, we assumed that it was a target along with the Tut exhibit."

"But you didn't tell us that," Kat said. "That wasn't part of our objective during the break-in."

"Because we didn't really want you to steal anything," Tru explained. "We wanted you to demonstrate that the collection was vulnerable. Once you reached the inside of the room, that was proven. The mummy is extremely large and heavy, so we switched the target to the necklace and the chest plate."

"What are the numbers?" Paris asked.

"Latitude and longitude," Tru answered. "The first is for the British Museum. That, along with the mention of the *Wonderful Things* exhibit and Cleopatra, gave us full confidence that it was the target."

"And the second number?" Mother asked. "If the first is the target, then the second might be whoever planned the attack."

"*That's* what has us worried," Tru said. "It is the latitude and longitude for the CIA."

Anything Goes

AFTER TRU LEFT, THE TEAM QUICKLY raided the kitchen to grab leftovers for lunch and then returned to the priest hole to start working. Mother brought down some cold pizza for Brooklyn, who'd stayed in the room and was in full hacker mode, sitting in a gaming chair and wearing headphones as she focused on the screen.

"Thanks!" she replied louder than she intended as he handed her the pizza.

Mother motioned for her to take off the headphones for a moment.

"We're going to try a round of Anything Goes, if you want to join in," he said, "but feel free to keep working on this."

"I'll join in while I'm eating," Brooklyn said. "That way I won't get any pizza grease on the keyboard."

"I'm sure Monty will appreciate that."

Anything Goes was a brainstorming technique the team often used at the start of an operation. It got its name from a Motherism: *There are some solutions that everyone knows, but for many, the answer's anything goes.*

The concept was that, during one of these sessions, no theory or suggestion was too silly, unconventional, or far-fetched to be considered by the group. This encouraged broader thinking and creative problem-solving. Everyone gathered around the conference table with their lunches in front of them, while Mother stood at a dry-erase board so he could write out the different ideas.

"Who wants to go first?" he asked.

"I do," Brooklyn said. "As the lone American at the table, let me say that I totally believe that the CIA could be involved. We should seriously consider them."

"I was thinking about that," Sydney said. "I know that countries spy on their allies, so I'm certain the CIA spies on Britain. But why would they attack these targets? What good does it do the United States if people get stuck on the Tube or hospitals can't run?"

"They might not have done it on purpose," Brooklyn said.

"How could anything this sophisticated be an accident?" Paris said.

"Just look what happened to the Americans with WannaCry," Brooklyn said.

"I thought you said that came from North Korea," Rio said.

"It did," Brooklyn answered. "But it was built using a worm developed in the US by the National Security Administration. That code was leaked, which is how the North Koreans got it."

"So, you're saying the CIA may have created some cybertech that Horus got its hands on and used to launch the attack?" Mother asked.

"Either that or the Americans did it themselves for some reason we don't know," Brooklyn said.

Mother wrote "CIA? On purpose? Accidental?" on the board.

"I think we should consider mythology," Paris said.

Rio, who was using chopsticks to eat chicken lo mein from a take-out box, laughed and said, "You always think we should consider mythology."

Sydney shot a humorous look at Rio. "No judgments during Anything Goes."

"I wasn't judging," Rio said, "just pointing out facts."

Paris was a mythology buff and had even started a Folklore and Myths Club at Kinloch. "I grabbed these from my room," he said, pointing at a stack of books on the table next to his pizza. "So I could study up on Horus."

"What'd you find so far?" asked Monty.

"He was one of the most important deities in Egyptian mythology," Paris said. "He was the god of the sky, including the sun and the moon, and was usually depicted as a man with the head of a falcon. He was kind of like an Egyptian version of Apollo."

"How can this help us?" Rio asked.

"If we can figure out why they picked this as a name, we might get an idea of how they see themselves," Paris said. "It may even give a clue as to who they are."

"That's good," said Mother as he wrote "Horus myth" on the board.

"And then there are the four sons of Horus," Paris continued. "They are the four gods who represent the canopic jars that accompanied mummies for the afterlife."

"What are canopic jars?" asked Brooklyn.

"During mummification, the organs are extracted from the body and placed in special jars," Paris said. "One jar each for the liver, lungs, stomach, and intestine."

"What about the brain and the heart?" asked Kat.

"The ancient Egyptians thought the heart contained the soul, so they left that in the body," Paris answered. "And they thought the brain was just for making mucus, so they liquefied it."

Sydney made a gagging noise and held up her take-out carton. "Anybody want my moo shu pork? Suddenly I'm no longer hungry."

"Here's what I'm thinking," Paris said. "What if they chose Horus because the four targets correspond to the four sons? Kind of like these institutions are the essential organs that make it possible for the UK to run. There might be some connection that the myth can help us figure out."

"That's an interesting theory—we'll add that to the list," Mother said as he wrote "Four sons of Horus" on the board.

"Put Guy Fawkes up there too," Rio said. "This all started on Bonfire Night. And when they attacked the Underground, they sent the message with the Guy Fawkes references."

"Excellent point," Kat said. "Especially when you consider that it's common for hackers to use Guy Fawkes masks to hide their identities."

"Absolutely," Brooklyn said, liking this train of thought. "The Guy Fawkes mask is a huge symbol of anarchy in the hacker world."

Mother wrote "Guy Fawkes/hackers" on the board. Then he turned to face the group. "Now I've got one that I'm not even going to write out," he said as he put the cap back on his marker. "I just want to talk it through."

He sat at the head of the table, and the others leaned forward in anticipation.

"Does anyone else think Tru acted strangely with regard to the message from the source inside Umbra?" he said. "Like she was hiding something?"

"Tru's always hiding something," Rio said. "That's the definition of her job."

"Besides, even though she resisted at first, she still showed us the message," Paris said.

"But why'd we have to push her?" asked Kat.

"My guess is that she's worried about the CIA connection," Brooklyn said. "I'm sure it's got everyone in panic mode at MI6. If even a hint of it went public, it would be huge news."

"I just think she's naturally secretive," Sydney said. "It comes with her position at MI6."

"That's true," Monty said. "But everything about this is sensitive, and that was the only part she was reluctant to share. My gut tells me this is something else, and I think it's that she's worried about her source."

Mother looked at her and smiled. "So do I. What makes you think so?"

"Because a deep cover asset inside Umbra has to be one of the biggest secrets at MI6," Monty reasoned. "She mentioned that it's someone who's been undercover for years. I wouldn't be surprised if Tru and C are the only two people in the Service who know the agent's identity."

"And, if you're right," Mother said with a nod, "that would make me number three."

"She told you who it was?" Sydney said, amazed.

"No," he answered. "I figured it out. Or at least I think I did. I can't be completely certain."

"Who is it?" asked Rio.

Mother took a deep breath and answered, "Clementine."

"Clementine, as in Clemmie, your wife?" Rio asked.

"As in the woman who left you to die in a burning warehouse in Paris?" added Sydney.

"Yes, Clementine, my wife," Mother said. "And we all know what happened in Paris, so you don't need to bring it up every time her name is mentioned."

"I think I do," Sydney said. "I want to keep it fresh, so we don't forget what kind of person we're talking about."

"I know exactly what kind of person she is," Mother said, his finger gently moving across the burn scars on his forearm. "I just don't know why she's trying to send me a message."

Kryptos

IN ADDITION TO BEING HUSBAND AND wife, Mother and Clementine were once a highly effective spy team. They were MI6 stars until a mission in Paris went horribly wrong. The plan was to lure and capture Umbra's leader, but Clementine flipped the script and joined the organization instead, betraying Mother and the UK in the process. In the aftermath, Mother was trapped in a burning warehouse, where he would've died if he hadn't been rescued by a boy who secretly lived in the building. That boy was Paris, and the rescue was the beginning of the City Spies.

By the time Mother made it back to England, Clementine had disappeared along with their children, Annie and Robert. It had been more than five years since he'd seen them, but now he was convinced his wife was trying to make contact.

"Why do you think the message is from Clementine?" Monty asked.

"Because it mentions Cleopatra."

"I thought that was a reference to the mummy in the British Museum," Brooklyn said.

"That's what MI6 thinks," Mother said. "But look at it."

Wonderful Things

515194001270

389523771458

Cleopatra

"*Wonderful Things* is the name of the exhibit, and 51.5194 degrees north by 0.1270 degrees west is the latitude and longitude for the British Museum," Mother said. "If she was referencing the mummy, she would have put Cleopatra at the top with them. But she didn't. She put it at the bottom."

"Like a signature," Monty said, getting it.

"Exactly," Mother said.

"Then how come MI6 didn't figure that out?" asked Rio.

"Because they don't know about Clemmie's nickname," Mother said. "Cleopatra was an inside joke in our family. One day, Robert came home from preschool and started calling his mother Cleopatra. We thought he'd somehow confused it with Clementine, because both are long and start with the same three letters. But when she asked him why he was calling her that, he grinned and answered, 'Because you're my mummy.'"

Everyone laughed, and Mother smiled at the memory.

"Even at that age, Robert had a great sense of humor," Mother said. "After that, I'd call her Cleopatra as a joke, especially whenever she exhibited any diva-like behavior. But over time it turned into something more serious."

"How do you mean?" Brooklyn asked.

"On Victoria Embankment, not too far from MI6 headquarters, there's an Egyptian obelisk, about twenty meters tall, that's covered with hieroglyphics," Mother said. "It's called Cleopatra's Needle, and the little area around it became our secret meeting spot. There's also a loose brick in a nearby wall that we used as a dead drop."

"A dead drop?" Paris asked, confused.

"That's a secret location where two operatives hide messages for each other," Mother said with a sarcastic tone.

"I know what a dead drop is," Paris said with an eyeroll. "I just can't figure out why you'd need one. You lived and worked together. It seems like you'd have plenty of opportunities to pass messages without hiding them in a park along the Thames."

"We lived and worked together *most of the time*," Mother explained. "But there were occasions when we'd have to split up before a mission, while we were building our legends." He gave Paris a humorous look. "A *legend* is a cover story a spy uses to hide their identity."

"Yeah, I know what a legend is," Paris replied.

"For example, in the six weeks leading up to our mission to Paris . . ."

"The one where she left you to die in a burning warehouse?" Sydney interjected.

"That one," Mother said. "I was developing a legend as a black marketeer who specialized in stolen art masterworks. We told the kids I was going on an extended trip for work, and I moved into a loft down by the canal in Camden. Clemmie and I couldn't have direct contact, but every day I'd go for a jog along the

Thames and check to see if she'd left me a message."

"So, Cleopatra isn't just a nickname," Brooklyn said. "It's a nickname that ties directly to hidden messages?"

"Yes," Mother said. "But the question is, where did she hide this one?"

"Maybe it's at the dead drop site," Sydney suggested. "In that loose brick in the wall."

"No," Mother said. "I already checked, and there's nothing there."

"How could you have checked?" Rio asked. "Cleopatra's Needle is in London, and we just found out about it thirty minutes ago."

"*We* just found out about it," Mother said. "But the message was sent a while back. That's why Tru had you infiltrate the museum."

Monty closed her eyes as she figured it out. "And you checked it last week when you all were down in London for the break-in."

"I've checked it every time I've been in London for over five years," Mother admitted, his voice fighting not to show too much emotion. "I guess I'm always hoping there'll be some note that explains what happened."

There was quiet around the table until Sydney started to speak. "I just want to say—"

"I know," Mother said. "She left me to die in a fire."

"No, that's not what I was going to say. At least not this time. I just want to say that I'm really sorry that happened to you."

"We all are," Brooklyn added. "I don't understand how someone can be like the woman you describe and then do what she did, but we're sorry you had to go through that."

"Thank you," Mother said. "I'm sorry it happened too. But, in a not so indirect way, it led me to all of you, and I'm not one bit sorry about that."

No one spoke for a moment as they let this sink in. The good and the bad were all tied together.

"Can you tell us about her?" Kat said, breaking the silence. "I think we've always been reluctant to ask, but it might help us better understand her and any clues."

"Sure," Mother said. "Her father was a career diplomat, and she grew up in capitals around the world. She was recruited to join MI6 while she was still a student at Oxford, just like Monty. She's smart, charming, and amazingly talented with languages."

"Where'd you meet?" Brooklyn asked.

"At IONEC," he said. "That's the Intelligence

Officer's New Entry Course, a six-month training program at Fort Monckton in Portsmouth."

"You said she grew up in capitals around the world; was Washington one of them?" Paris asked. "If so, that might have something to do with her mention of the CIA."

"No," Mother said. "But she did spend a couple weeks there as part of an exchange program between the CIA and MI6."

"Did she do CREEP?" Monty asked, surprised.

"Yes," Mother said. "How'd you know?"

"I did it too," she said. "Probably about five or six years later."

"What's CREEP?" Brooklyn asked. "Sounds . . . creepy."

"That's just what we called it," Monty said. "Officially it was the Crypto-Research Educational Exchange Program. Every year, the head of Codes and Ciphers at MI6 took the top five cryptography students from IONEC on a two-week trip to CIA headquarters. She always insisted that we go in October."

"Because?" Sydney asked.

"Because October is the rainiest month in London

and one of the driest in Washington," Monty answered. "The CIA headquarters are right outside the city. We'd spend all day in a darkened room learning about code-breaking techniques with the Americans, but we got to eat lunch every afternoon on picnic tables in the courtyard as we enjoyed the sunshine. It was pretty great all around."

"So, Clementine was that good at code-breaking?" Brooklyn asked. "She was one of the top students in the training program?"

"The top in our class," Mother said. "She was torn as to which direction to go in the Service. She would've been happy spending her career with codes and ciphers, but I think she chose field ops because that's where I was going to be. Still, she was really good at it."

Kat picked up the message and studied it for a moment before something clicked and her eyes opened wide in amazement. "That's an understatement."

"What do you mean?" asked Paris.

"I think she may be incredible at it," Kat said, getting excited. "Let me check something."

She took the message over to a computer terminal and did a quick search while everyone watched with eager anticipation.

"She's got that Kat face," Rio whispered.

"I know," Paris said as he signaled him to hush. "Don't break her concentration."

After a couple searches, Kat turned to the others and said, "Genius!"

"What's genius?" Sydney asked.

"Think about it," Kat said. "What's the perfect code?"

"One that can't be broken," Rio answered.

"Close," Kat said. "But even if a code can't be solved, the other side knows that it's there, so it affects the way they act. In World War II, before the Allies broke Enigma, they still knew it existed, and they reacted accordingly. The perfect code is one that has two meanings, so that once it's solved one way, the other side is unaware of the additional message."

"You're losing us, Kat," Brooklyn said.

"She gives us *Wonderful Things* and the coordinates for the British Museum," Kat said. "And she even throws in Cleopatra, all of which leads MI6 to conclude the museum is a target, which it is. I mean, it's brilliant because it's quality intel and a coded message, so MI6 thinks their work is done."

She walked back to the table and showed them the note.

"But Cleopatra has a double meaning," Kat continued.

"It means something different to Mother, but only to Mother, so that means there's a hidden message just for him."

"Hidden where?" asked Sydney.

"In this message," Kat answered, holding up the paper.

"All that's left are the coordinates for the CIA," Sydney said.

"Also a double meaning," Kat said. "MI6 sees it and worries that the Americans are involved in the cyber-attack. But they're not just the coordinates for CIA headquarters. That's what I was checking. Those coordinates are on CIA property, but they're a specific location in the CIA's central courtyard. The courtyard that Monty was just talking about. That's what made me think of it."

"Unbelievable!" Monty exclaimed, seeing what Kat was getting at. "It's *Kryptos*!"

"That's right!" Kat replied.

Monty shook her head in amazement. "That *is* brilliant."

"Okay, um, you realize that means nothing to the rest of us," Paris said.

"*Kryptos* is a sculpture located in the courtyard of the

CIA," Monty said. "How did I miss this? I looked at it every day during lunch. It's legendary among cryptographers around the world. It features four panels, and each one has a separate coded message created by the artist."

"It was put up more than thirty years ago, and code breakers everywhere have tried to decipher it ever since," Kat interjected. "And after decades of attempts, so far only three of the four panels have been solved. Every crypto on the planet wants to be the one who cracks the last one."

"So, you think she's referencing the sculpture as part of a communication with us?" Mother said.

"I know that she is," Kat said, "because just like Cleopatra and the CIA coordinates have two meanings, so does *Wonderful Things*."

"The third panel," Monty said, putting it together. "You're right, Kat. She's brilliant, but you're right there with her. Wow."

"What's the third panel?" Brooklyn asked.

"The coded message in the third panel is an excerpt from Howard Carter's diary," Kat answered.

"The archaeologist who discovered King Tut's tomb?" Paris asked.

"Yes, I have it pulled up here," Kat said as she went

back over to the computer. "The entry describes the moment when Carter broke open a hole big enough so he could look into the chamber and see what was inside." She began reading from the monitor. "'I inserted the candle and peered in. The hot air escaping from the chamber caused the flame to flicker, but presently details of the room within emerged from the mist.'"

She looked up at the others. "The entry ends at the point when someone asked, 'Can you see anything?'" It doesn't include Carter's answer, but what he said is famous. 'Yes, wonderful things.' It's where the exhibition got its name. And it's how Clementine is ensuring that we know she means *Kryptos*."

"So where do we go from here?" asked Mother. "Say you're right, and I'm convinced that you are: How is she talking to us through a sculpture at CIA headquarters?"

"I bet she wants to use the internet forum as a dead drop," Monty said. "There is a very active online community of amateur and professional cryptographers trying to decipher that final panel. Kat and I are both members."

"Seriously?" Rio said.

"It's fascinating," Kat said. "The code-breaking community is incredibly friendly and supportive. There are so many great minds out there debating everything from running keys and encryption schemes to transposition methods and cryptograms."

"There's a thread about corollaries between *Kryptos* and Enigma that's riveting," Monty added.

Sydney laughed and said, "I think you guys have different definitions of 'fascinating' and 'riveting' than the rest of us."

"That may be so, but I think you're definitely onto something," Mother said. "So, what we need to do is post a topic on this site that looks like it's about one of those *riveting* subjects but is actually a message to Clementine."

"Exactly," Kat said. "And if she responds, we'll know we're right."

Kat and Monty worked out a carefully phrased post for the *Kryptos* message board. Its post title read "Cleopatra's Needle," and the message proposed a possible connection between the *Kryptos* code and the hieroglyphics on the side of the obelisk. It was believable enough not to seem out of place, but so obscure that it was unlikely to get much attention from anyone else.

Forty-seven minutes later, the computer dinged, signaling a response.

The others watched as Kat clicked on the message.

"What does it say?" Brooklyn asked.

Kat read aloud from the screen. "'How is *Kryptos* analyzed thus?'"

"*Thus?*" Paris said. "Is Clementine the type of person who uses 'thus' in a sentence?"

"The grammar's correct but awkward," Monty said. "She's letting us know that she's speaking in code."

"What kind of code?" asked Brooklyn.

"It's one of the most basic of all," Monty said. "An acrostic."

"You take the first letter of every word to spell out the message," Kat said. "*H-I-K-A-T.*" She looked up from the screen. "She's saying, 'Hi, Kat.'"

"She knows it's you?" Sydney asked, alarmed. "How? Did you sign your post? Is it part of your user ID?"

"No," Kat said, perplexed. "She just knows."

"It's a logical guess," Mother said. "It was either going to be Kat or Monty who deciphered the message."

"That's only logical if she knows who Kat and Monty are," Sydney said. "Since we're all part of a top-secret operation, I'd say it's troubling."

"She's an amazing spy, far better than me," Mother said. "And if she's a double agent still working for MI6, Tru might've filled her in."

"This just keeps getting worse," Sydney said.

"You need to respond with another acrostic," Monty said to Kat. "So that she knows the message has been confirmed. But, in case somebody else sees it, the response has to also be a legitimate answer to her question about how the code is analyzed."

Kat nodded and read her answer aloud as she typed it. "'Cleverly, like every other puzzle and tricky riddle's analyzed.'"

Paris tried to decipher as she read it. "C-L-E—oh my goodness! You just spelled out Cleopatra in an acrostic like it was nothing. How'd you come up with that so fast?"

Kat gave a shrug. "I don't know how to answer that. I just did it."

There was another ding.

"What's her response?" Mother asked.

"A 'wow' emoji and a 'laughing with tears' emoji," Kat answered.

"That's because she's impressed with how quickly you did that too," Mother said.

"Now we know that it's Clementine," Monty said. "She reached out to us, so we should wait to see what she wants to say."

After a moment, there was another ding, and Kat read it out to the others. "'This is a very interesting idea. I think you should take a look at what we already know about the fourth panel and go there.'"

Another ding, as another message came in.

"'I have to leave now, but we should discuss again in twenty-four hours.'"

A final ding signaled the last message.

"'Keep at this,'" Kat said.

"Another acrostic," Monty said. "She's spelling out 'Kat.' That's the end of her message."

"So, she wants to talk again in twenty-four hours," Paris said. "What was this about the fourth panel?"

"It's been so long since anyone's solved one of the panels that the artist who created the sculpture has given three hints," Monty said. "He's told us what three of the words are."

She walked over to the dry-erase board and wrote "Northeast. Berlin. Clock."

"She doesn't want to talk again in twenty-four hours," Mother reasoned. "She wants to meet in Berlin." He leaned in and pointed at the message on the computer screen. "When she said 'go there,' she wasn't being meta-phorical. She literally meant *go there*."

"That's not a good idea," Sydney said. "We can't go. This could all be a trap."

"You're right," Mother told her. "We can't."

"That's a relief," Sydney said.

"But *I* can."

"Wait, no," Sydney objected. "I understand that you want to—"

"Sydney, I appreciate your concern," Mother said. "But this is not a debate. We were given an assignment straight from C, and this is where it leads. Despite what you may think, I am well aware of what Clementine is capable of doing." He pulled back his sleeves to show the burn scars on both arms. "But I am going to go to Berlin to see where this path leads." He turned to Kat. "Confirm the meet."

"I will," Kat said, "but you can't go alone."

"I'm more than capable of handling myself," Mother pointed out.

"It's not that," Kat said. "It's the clock. There's been a huge debate ever since the clues came out about which clock it is. There are three different candidates in Berlin. You can't be in three places at one time, which means you're going to have to bring two of us along."

Berlin

PARIS LOOKED OUT THE WINDOW AT THE German countryside as the ICE train, or Intercity Express, raced from Hamburg to Berlin at speeds over two hundred kilometers an hour. He was sitting at a table with Rio and Mother, and though they'd gotten up before dawn to catch a flight from Edinburgh, they were wide-awake in anticipation of the day ahead. If they'd interpreted the message correctly, they were about to meet up with Clementine.

"Situational awareness is the key to everything,"

Mother explained as he drew a diagram on a tablet lying on the table between them. "You have to pay attention to the entire field of play in order to map out possible attacks and escape routes."

If anyone paid attention to them, it would've seemed as though he was diagramming tactics for the football pitch. That's because their jackets, sweatpants, and travel bags all featured the red-and-white logo of the Aberdeen FC Youth Academy. These props were left over from a cover story that was developed but never used for a canceled mission and gave the impression that the trio were a coach and two players on their way to a youth tournament in soccer-mad Germany. In truth, Mother was sketching out countersurveillance strategies for the meeting.

"She's totally put us at her mercy," Mother said. "She's given us no time to prep and three possible locations, so the key for us is that we be careful and flexible. We'll each stake out one of the clocks from a secure location, and if you see her, you call me, and I'll rush to the scene."

"What if she approaches one of us?" Paris asked.

"You still call me right away," Mother said. "But I think she's looking for me, not you."

Mother's phone vibrated, signaling a text, and the others shared a knowing look.

"Wonder who that is?" Rio said. "Again."

Mother looked at the screen and nodded. "Sydney."

Although she was opposed to the mission, Sydney was disappointed that she wasn't part of it. With Brooklyn trying to hack the hackers and Kat as the expert on all things to do with the British Museum, it made sense for the two of them to stay at the FARM and continue working on Operation Find Horus. That left Sydney, Paris, and Rio as candidates for the two spots on the Berlin trip, and she had been certain she'd be one of them.

"Let me guess," Paris said. "This one says, 'Hey, guys, you forgot to bring me.'"

"She's reverted to poetry." Mother read the text aloud. "'*The spy is wise with wide-open eyes.*'"

"Is that a Motherism?" Rio asked.

"Not one that I've heard," Mother said. "And since I make them up, I should've heard them all."

"She's writing her own," Paris said. "That's how desperate she is."

"She's just worried about us," Mother said, defending her. "She wants us to look out for ourselves and be careful."

"It's not about us being careful," Rio replied. "It's about her being here, which is what she wants."

"She totally thinks you're punishing her for what she said about Clementine," Paris said.

"It's not that," Mother said. "I explained that we didn't have time to create a legend from scratch and that the Aberdeen FC cover was ready to go. Uniforms, passports, travel bags, everything."

"And what did she say when you told her that?" Paris asked.

"That I was punishing her for what she said about Clementine," Mother answered. "And I probably am. Not punishing, exactly. But she was so opposed to this, I worry that if she were on lookout and saw Clemmie, she might not say a thing about it, and we'd lose this chance."

"So, if it wasn't for that, she'd be here instead of me," Rio said, wounded.

"No," Mother replied, trying to boost his confidence. "This is the right team for this mission. It's tricky, but we're ready."

They exited the train at the modern, glass-enclosed Berlin Hauptbahnhof, the city's main railway station. There, as they walked along the platform toward the exit, Mother turned to Rio and said, "Why don't you say it?"

Rio flashed an arched eyebrow and asked, "Does that mean I'm the alpha?"

"I'm the alpha," Mother said with a laugh. "It just means you get to say it."

Rio shrugged as if there'd been no harm in trying. "Fine with me," he said. "This operation is hot. We are a go."

All three shared a smile.

There were three very distinctive clocks in Berlin, and each was a potential candidate for being the clock referenced in the *Kryptos* code.

First, they visited the *Mengenlehreuhr*, whose name was German for "Set Theory Clock." Among those trying to break the code, this was considered most likely to be the one referenced by *Kryptos*, because it was commonly referred to as the Berlin Clock. It made the *Guinness World Records* because it was the first public clock to display time using only colored lights, no numbers or hands. Rather than a clockface, it featured twenty-four lights aligned in four rows with the lights blinking on and off to signal hours, minutes, and seconds. It was installed on the sidewalk outside of a popular Berlin shopping mall called the Europa-Center.

"Paris, this one's going to be you," Mother said as they stood across the street from the mall. "If you sit at this café, you have a clear view of the clock and everyone going to and from it. Keep a close eye on that hotel entrance; it's a logical place for the approach."

"Got it," Paris said confidently.

"Now, let's go inside and look at clock number two," Mother said.

The second notable clock was also at the Europa-Center. The Clock of Flowing Time was three stories tall and stood in the middle of the atrium inside the mall. It was unique in that it displayed time by the placement of a bright lime-green liquid that flowed through glass spheres arranged in columns. It was as much a sculpture as it was a timepiece.

"Okay, Rio, here's a quick test," Mother said. "Where do you think is the safest place for you to wait?"

Rio surveyed the scene and pointed to a balcony on the third level. "Up there," he said. "It gives the best vantage point of the atrium and is protected in back so that no one can come at me from behind."

Mother smiled. "Very good," he said. "Now what are your escape routes if anything goes bad?"

"Whichever direction has the most shoppers," Rio answered. "I want to disappear into a crowd."

"That's absolutely right." Mother turned to them. "Okay, so you're going to be close to each other, Rio on the third floor here and Paris across the street at the café. If there is even the slightest hint of trouble, I want you two to meet up and get out of here. Where's the rendezvous?"

"Just inside the entrance to the zoo," Paris said.

"That's only a couple blocks away," Mother said. "Also, I want you each to check in on the comms channel every two minutes."

"Isn't that a little overly cautious?" Paris asked.

"There's no such thing when it comes to Clemmie." Mother checked his watch. "It's fifty minutes until we reach the twenty-four-hour mark from yesterday. Stay together for thirty, and then get into position. I'm heading to Alexanderplatz."

"Be careful," Rio said.

"Right back at you both," Mother said.

The third of Berlin's unique clocks was the massive World Clock in Alexanderplatz, one of the city's busiest public squares. The clock weighed over sixteen tons, was built turret style in the middle of the square, and rotated throughout the day. Its twenty-four sides represented the main time zones of the world and featured the names of one hundred forty-eight major cities, displaying the current time in each.

Mother had decided that he'd stake out this clock for two reasons. First of all, because the other two were so close to each other, it meant Paris and Rio would be on hand to help one another if needed. Moreover, after reading up on the clocks, Mother was convinced that this was the one Clementine would likely choose. The nonstop flow of people in and out of the square meant that it would be easy for her to show up and disappear when needed.

He had just enough time to go to the observation deck at the top of the Berlin TV Tower, one of the city's most famous landmarks and the second-tallest building in Europe. This gave him a perfect aerial view of Alexanderplatz. He studied all the ways into and out of the square and decided that the best location for him to wait was a spot near a carousel that was popular with tourists. It was ideal because it was close to the clock but gave him plenty of hiding places.

"Testing comms, are you two in position?" Mother asked as he took his spot near the carousel.

"I hear you loud and clear," Paris responded. "I'm at the café."

"Are you eating?" Rio asked, suddenly jealous.

"Well, I've got to blend in, don't I?" Paris said.

"I think I lost out on assignments," Rio said.

"Don't worry. We'll feed you soon." Mother checked his watch. "In sixty seconds, we're at the twenty-four-hour mark from when Clemmie sent the message. Keep an eye out for her, and let me know if you see anything suspicious."

"Copy that," said Rio.

"And how often are you all checking in with me?" Mother asked.

"Every five minutes," Paris said.

Mother cleared his throat.

"Okay, every two," Paris responded. "But I still think that's overkill."

"Luckily, I'm the alpha, the handler, and the parent," Mother said. "That means there are three reasons I get to overrule you."

"Speaking of overkill," Rio said. "How many texts have you gotten from Sydney since you left us?"

"Only three," Mother said, eliciting a laugh from the others. "She's either losing interest or getting tired."

For the next thirty minutes, they waited patiently, looking for any sign of Clementine, but all they saw was the normal flow of people. It was a cold day, which was unlucky for Paris and Mother, because they were both outside. Not only were they cold, but because most people wore bulky coats, it was harder to identify anyone. Mother had the added irritation of hearing the same carousel music playing over and over again.

"How long do we hold out until we call it?" Paris asked.

"We've come all this way; we'll give it at least an hour," Mother answered.

"Copy that," Paris said.

Mother's phone vibrated. Sydney again.

Any sign of her? read the text message.

None, Mother typed back.

I need to talk to you, wrote Sydney.

I'm really not trying to punish you, Mother wrote. But I need to keep my focus on the clock.

Moments later Mother's phone rang. He checked the ID, and it was Sydney.

"I just need you to listen for a second," Sydney blurted when he answered.

Mother sighed, frustrated by Sydney and the fact that the mission was washing out. "What is it?" he said curtly.

"It turns out you should've taken me after all," Sydney said.

Mother had had enough. "I know you're disappointed, but—"

"Because there's a fourth clock," she said, "and I think it's the one she's at."

"What clock?"

"Egypt has been the key to this whole thing," Sydney said. "First at the British Museum and then with Cleopatra and the quote on *Kryptos*."

"Get to the point," he replied. "We're facing a time crunch here."

"There's a museum in Berlin that is entirely dedicated to Egyptian art and antiquities," Sydney said. "It's called the Neues Museum, and its collection includes the oldest known sundial in the world. That's a type of clock, right? Kind of an important one at that."

"It could be," Mother said, thinking it over. "Or it could just be grasping at straws."

"That's what I thought," Sydney said. "So I looked at a virtual tour of the museum, and do you know what's right next to it? A bust of Cleopatra."

Mother was sprinting toward a taxi before he answered. "Text me all the info about the museum and where it is. Also which exhibit room has the sundial."

"Copy that," Sydney responded.

Mother caught his breath for a second and said, "Thank you, Sydney. This is great work."

"Glad I could help."

Mother used the comms channel to alert Rio and Paris, both of whom decided the best thing to do was to meet him there. The taxi took him across the bridge to an island in the middle of the Spree river that was home to the Neues, which housed one of the world's most significant collections of ancient Egyptian artifacts, including the iconic Nefertiti bust.

Mother had no time to study or scout the building, and when he raced toward its columned entrance, he realized he was breaking many of the rules he taught the others. He was rushing into a possible trap with no real plan. But after years of searching, he was closer than ever to catching up with Clementine.

He was willing to take the risk.

"I'm at the museum," he said as he reached the entrance. "I hope I'm not too late."

"We're on our way," Paris responded as he and Rio got into a taxi outside the Europa-Center.

Mother tried to slow his heart rate as he walked through the marble foyer. He needed to blend in and calm down. Surprisingly, it was Sydney's attempt at a Motherism that did the trick. *The spy is wise with wide-open eyes.* He took a deep breath, bought an admission ticket, and took a map with a layout of the museum's exhibits.

Three minutes later he was looking across a large room toward the sundial. Just as Sydney had said, a bust of Cleopatra stood next to it. Unfortunately, there was no sign of Clementine.

"I'm at the exhibit," Mother said over the comms channel.

"Is she there?" Paris asked.

"No," Mother said, disappointed. "I think I'm too late. All I see are a pair of men, a man and woman with two small children, and a boy with a backpack."

"Any chance the woman with the children is her?" asked Rio.

"No," Mother said. "It's not her. It's a washout."

And then it clicked.

"Oh my goodness," Mother said, his voice full of emotion. "Oh my goodness!"

He sounded like he might cry.

"What is it?" Paris asked urgently. "What's wrong?"

"The boy," Mother answered. "It's Robert."

A Change in Plans

MOTHER HAD IMAGINED THIS REUNION countless times, scripting out endless variations of what he might say. But now, as he walked across the mosaic floor, he was so overcome with emotion that he was speechless.

In the nearly six years since they'd last seen each other, Robert had grown a foot and a half taller, and his once-pudgy face had started to thin out. Still, there was no mistaking who he was. The same couldn't be said for Mother. After the fire in Paris, he'd gone through nearly a dozen surgeries, and MI6 had used the opportunity to alter his appearance. This did a great job of hiding his identity among spies, but he worried that his own son wouldn't recognize him.

"Robert?" he asked tentatively.

The boy looked up at him with a quizzical expression, as if he were trying to place the face. "Dad?"

"I know you don't recognize me," Mother said, instantly self-conscious. "There was a fire and surgeries and—"

Robert cut him off. "I know who you are," he said. "I just can't believe you're really here."

Robert wrapped his arms around him, and Mother swept him up in a giant hug, at one point lifting the boy's feet off the ground.

"I have scoured the earth for you," Mother said, his voice cracking. "I've looked everywhere."

"I'm here now," Robert replied.

They stood locked in the embrace until Mother forced himself to let go. He was a father, but he was also a spy. He had no idea what forces were at work, but he needed to protect his son.

"Where's your mother?" he asked as he scanned the room.

"I don't know," Robert said. "We said our goodbyes last night."

"Goodbyes?" Mother asked, perplexed. "What do you mean?"

"All of this was arranged so that you and I could be together," Robert said. "So that I can go home with you."

"She's letting you go?" Mother said, trying to process the information.

"She said it was my choice, and I told her I wanted to live with you."

Tears streamed down Mother's face, and he wiped them away with the palms of his hand, trying to control himself so as not to draw attention.

"She said this would catch you off guard and that you might be emotional," Robert continued. "So, I'm supposed to remind you that we have to get out of here right away and make sure no one follows us. She said you need to get me out of Germany as fast as possible."

"Even in this, she's trying to tell me what to do." He thought for a moment before continuing. "Although, of course, she's right. We need to leave immediately. What do you have with you?"

"Just this backpack," Robert answered. "I travel light."

"Good," Mother said, taking charge of his emotions and the situation. "Let's get going." He activated the mic on his comms. "Paris, Rio, where are you?"

"In the taxi, about to pull up to the museum," Paris answered.

"Is it large enough for four passengers?" Mother asked.

"I guess," Rio answered. "If someone sits in front."

"Tell the driver to wait," Mother responded. "We're heading for the exit and need to get out of here right away."

"We?" Rio asked, confused. "Is Robert joining us?"

"You bet he is."

Moments later, Mother and Robert exited the museum and hurried toward the street, although careful not to go too fast so that they wouldn't attract any attention. It was cold, and Mother flipped up the collar of his coat as he scanned the surroundings for any hint that someone might be watching or following. He was certain Clemmie was there somewhere, observing to make sure that everything had gone okay. He also knew that she'd be hidden in a way that he'd never see her.

Before getting into the cab, he turned back and momentarily placed both hands over his heart. This was his way of thanking her for letting Robert come home.

"Alexanderplatz," Mother instructed the driver as he hopped into the passenger seat. "Quickly, please."

The boys were crammed in back and took care of introductions.

"Nice to meet you, I'm Rio."

"And I'm Paris. We're . . . um . . ." He wasn't exactly sure what he should say.

"They're your brothers, and they call me Mother, even though I'm their adoptive father," Mother said from the front seat. "A lot's happened since we saw each other last. I'll explain it when we get a chance."

"Nice to meet you both," Robert said, confused but going with it.

Mother picked Alexanderplatz for the same reason he thought Clemmie might have chosen it for a rendez-vous. It was easy to get lost in the crowds of people, and that's exactly what he wanted to do. Robert put on Rio's Aberdeen FC Youth Academy jacket, to help blend in with the others, and Mother called Monty to have her book new travel arrangements.

"I need four tickets out of Berlin Brandenburg. Use the three names from the Aberdeen cover story, and add . . ." He stopped for a moment as he checked the name in the phony passport that Robert was carrying. "Benjamin David Dobrow."

"Who's that?" Monty asked.

"It's Robert," Mother answered.

"Wow," Monty said. "I can't wait to hear this story."

"Neither can I," Mother responded. "It'll take us about an hour to get to the airport and then an hour for security. Put us on the first plane you can get us on after that."

"Where to? Edinburgh?"

Mother paused before answering. As excited as he was that Robert was back, he still had to worry about Clementine. Perhaps this was all an elaborate trap. If Clemmie was working for Umbra, she might be tracking Robert in hopes of finding where Mother and the team were based. It would be dangerous to go straight to the FARM. "Make it London," he said. "It's the city he knows as home."

"That's good, because we need to go there too," Monty replied.

"Why?" asked Mother.

"New developments in the case," Monty said.

Mother was so focused on Robert and trying to make sense of things that he didn't know what she was talking about. "What case?"

"The cyberattack," Monty answered, trying not to laugh at his befuddlement. "You know, the case we were assigned by the head of intelligence. It kind of affects the whole country."

"Of course," Mother replied. "My mind's a million places."

"Understandable," Monty said. "But we've made some good progress here today, and there are some leads we want to follow in person."

"Perfect," Mother said. "We'll need a safe house big enough for eight."

"I know just the place," Monty said. "I'll text you the address along with travel arrangements as soon as I get everything locked down."

"You're a lifesaver, Monty."

"Be safe and congratulations. You must be so happy to have him with you."

"You have no idea," Mother said.

From Alexanderplatz, they hopped on a train to the airport, and two hours later they were flying to Munich, where they caught another flight to London. Within thirty minutes of taking off, the three boys were out cold, exhausted by a busy day that was not yet done. Mother, though, was wide-awake as he gently squeezed Robert's hand as if checking to make sure this was really happening, that he hadn't just imagined it all.

The Sacred Sisters of St. Joshua

THE PLANE DIDN'T TOUCH DOWN AT
Heathrow until after midnight, and it was nearly two
in the morning by the time Mother and the boys finally
arrived at the address Monty texted them. It was a narrow brick-faced building squeezed between a pair of
Victorian town houses in a quiet section of Hyde Park.
Next to the door was a small plaque with the image of
an eye inside a triangle and the Latin phrase "*semper
occultus.*"

"Looks nice," Mother said as they walked up the front steps.

"All I care is that it has a bed," Rio said as he knocked on the door. "I'm exhausted."

"Me too," Robert added.

"What time did this day start anyway?" Paris asked. "For that matter, was it even today, or did we wake up—"

He never finished the question because they were all startled when the door opened and, instead of Monty, they were greeted by a woman in her sixties with white hair, horn-rimmed glasses, and chubby cheeks. Despite the late hour, she seemed cheerful.

She was also dressed in a nun's habit.

"I'm so sorry, sister," Rio said. "I didn't mean to knock that loudly. I mean, I didn't mean to knock on your door. I mean—"

"We apologize," Mother said, taking over the conversation. "I'm afraid we're at the wrong address."

"Nonsense," said the nun. "You must be Monty's friends."

Rio and Paris shared a confused look, as did Mother and Robert.

"I'm Sister Christine," said the woman. "Please come in. The others are in the kitchen."

They stepped into a narrow hallway devoid of all decoration except for a large wooden cross hanging on the wall.

Paris looked around, still trying to figure things out. He started to ask, "Is this a—"

"A convent," said Sister Christine. "Yes, it is. We're members of a small but very dedicated order, the Sacred Sisters of St. Joshua."

Mother thought about this for a moment and then let out a laugh.

"St. Joshua," he said. "That's perfect."

"Why?" Robert asked him, confused.

"He's the patron saint of spies," explained Mother.

"Aren't you the clever one?" Sister Christine said with a cherubic smile.

As they walked up the stairs to the second floor, Mother wondered if there actually was a Sacred Order of St. Joshua or if the nuns were part of a cover operation, just like theirs with the Foundation for Atmospheric Research and Monitoring. Part of him hoped that they were a clandestine spy ring run by the pope.

"Welcome," Monty said as they entered the kitchen.

"You waited up for us," Paris said, pleasantly surprised.

"We just got here about an hour ago," Sydney answered.

"Besides," Monty said, "we all wanted to greet our special guest." She turned to Robert and gave him a warm smile. "It's a pleasure to meet you. My name's Monty."

"It's nice to meet you," Robert said tentatively, trying to make sense of his rapidly changing life. He looked over at the others and tried to read their expressions.

Brooklyn was the first to make a move. She strode over to him and offered a hand. "I'm Brooklyn."

"Hi, Brooklyn," he said, shaking it.

"What should we call you?" she asked. "Robert? Benjamin? Something else?"

"I'm not sure," Robert said. "I haven't actually gone by Robert in a long time, and Benjamin's just a name on the passport my mother handed me . . . I don't know . . . was it yesterday? The day before that? I've kind of lost track of time."

"These are all things we can figure out tomorrow," Mother said. "We all need to get some sleep."

"Brilliant idea!" Rio exclaimed.

Just then, they heard the sound of a handbell ringing

from the basement level. Sister Christine listened to the notes, and when they were done, she pulled a handbell from the pocket of her habit and responded with another series of notes.

Mother and the boys looked confused, but Kat was beside herself with excitement.

"Isn't it amazing?" Kat asked.

"What?" Rio responded.

"They speak in code," Kat said. "With the bells."

"Just when we're on separate floors," said Sister Christine. "We're not much for devices as it were, and it saves us from walking up and down the stairs too much. Sister Neve wanted to see if you needed anything, and I told her you were fine."

"See what I mean," Kat said. "I'm totally on board with us getting our own set of bells to use on the FARM."

"Maybe if you have some time tomorrow, I'll teach you our code," said the nun.

"Yes, please," Kat said. "Sign me up for that."

"But for now, you need to all go to sleep," Mother said.

"Let me show you to your rooms," Sister Christine said. "I'll warn you, they're not what you'd call deluxe. We each took a vow of austerity to live a simple, unadorned life."

"Do the rooms have beds?" Rio asked.

"Of course," said the nun.

"Then they sound perfect," Rio answered.

Sister Christine led the kids up to the third floor, while Monty and Mother stayed in the kitchen. Robert was at the back of the line, and he shared a look with Mother, who said, "I'll be up in a few to check on you, son."

"Good," Robert said.

Monty beamed, and once the others were out of ear-shot, she said, "How lovely is that?"

"I still can't believe it," Mother said.

"Clemmie just let him go?" she asked.

He nodded. "It appears so."

"What a surprise."

"Speaking of surprises," Mother said, "a convent?"

"There used to be twenty-four sisters here, but now there are only six, and they all sleep on the ground floor," she explained. "That leaves two levels of empty bedrooms that they're more than happy to rent out at a reasonable rate. Besides, they're shut off from much of the outside world, so it gives us all the privacy we need."

"It's absolutely perfect," Mother said. "I'm tempted to believe the sisters are just a front for MI6, like the FARM."

"I have my suspicions," Monty said. "But they guard their secrets religiously."

They both laughed at her accidental pun.

"How'd you even hear about it?"

"They have convents in capitals around the world," Monty said. "I used them for a few missions early in my career. Don't forget, I was a spy long before you stepped into my life. I know things about the clandestine world of espionage."

"I know you do," Mother said. "And I'm afraid I'm going to need to borrow that expertise before you can go to sleep."

"What is it?" Monty asked.

He motioned to Robert's backpack, which was sitting on the kitchen table.

"I'm his father and would never forgive myself for digging through his things to make sure there weren't any bugs or trackers, but . . ."

"You're also a spy and know that it needs to be done?" Monty replied.

Mother nodded.

"I'll take care of it," Monty said. "You get some sleep, and I'll get to work."

Regent's Park

PARIS WAS SLEEPING DEEPLY WHEN HE was woken by the sound of someone breathing in his room. He opened his eyes and was startled to see another pair staring right back at him, just inches away. Before he could react, a slobbery tongue licked him on the face, which served as an introduction to the convent's overly friendly black Labrador.

"Blech," he said as he wiped off the drool and sat up on the edge of the bed. "Are you my alarm clock?" He gave the dog a good scratch behind the ears and read her name off her collar. "Hannah, huh? Nice to meet you."

Even with the slobbery wake-up call, he was still groggy as he walked down the stairs, guided by the sweet aroma of freshly baked bread coming from the kitchen.

"Are we the first ones up?" he asked Sydney, who was sitting at the table, finishing off a bowl of cereal.

"Guess again." Sydney laughed. "You're second to last. Robert's the only one who's still asleep."

"Where's everyone else?"

"Mother went to talk to Tru, and the others are trying to identify Horus and stop the cyberattack."

"How?"

"Working off the theory that the hackers used the British Museum as the 'candy store' to access the other targets, Brooklyn was able to identify three potential leads as to who might be behind it all," she explained. "One's an Egyptologist, one's a computer company, and one is a bit of a mystery."

"How do you mean?"

"Brooklyn found a username, but we don't know who it belongs to."

"Who's doing what?" Paris asked.

"Brooklyn and Monty are heading over to the computer company, while Kat and Rio are working on the Egyptologist."

"Great, that leaves the mystery to you and me," he said. "What's the plan?"

"Actually, that leaves the mystery to me," Sydney answered. "The plan for you is to stay here and keep an eye on Robert." She stopped to emphasize the next point. "And make sure you keep a close one."

"How do you mean?"

"Think about it. After years of hiding him, Clemmie just lets him go?" she asked skeptically. "I don't buy it. I don't trust her, and I don't trust him. He could be spying from inside the team. My worry is that Mother's so happy to have him back that he won't see it."

"I don't think that's the case," Paris said. "I think he's good."

"I hope you're right," Sydney said. "Because if you're not, it could be disastrous."

Unknown to them, Robert got up right after Paris and had started down the stairs to join them but had paused when he heard his name and was now listening in. The look on his face was equal parts angry and brokenhearted.

"I can't believe you woke me up so early," Rio complained to Kat as they exited the Russell Square Tube station onto Bernard Street.

"I know you need your beauty sleep, but the chief of intelligence did assign us a rather important mission," Kat said, unsympathetic. "Besides, you claim to be the best at picking locks."

"I don't *claim* to be the best," Rio replied. "It has been proven over and over again that I am the best."

"Which is why I didn't let you sleep in," Kat replied. "We need to break into the flat of an Egyptologist who's a potential suspect. Besides, as a bonus for you, I found a top-rated bakery around the corner from the target."

"Ooh, you should've led with the bakery," Rio said, suddenly engaged. "Are we going there before or after?"

"After," Kat answered. "Don't want you to get sticky fingers."

"Good point," Rio said. "Besides, I don't want to be in a rush while I eat. In order to give the food an accurate evaluation for my database, I need to make sure I have enough time to savor and digest it properly. Now, tell me more."

"About the Egyptologist?" asked Kat.

"No, about the bakery," he said, as if it were obvious. Then he laughed and said, "Just kidding. Why are we breaking into the flat?"

"Brooklyn used Beny to search all the activity on the British Museum's servers in the days leading up to that cyberattack," she said. "She identified three examples of users logging on in a suspicious manner."

"And this flat belongs to one of those users?"

"Dr. Imogen Gaisman," Kat replied. "She's a big shot Egyptologist and a frequent consultant for the museum. She was one of the two curators who developed the *Wonderful Things* exhibit and brought it to London. The day before the attack, she logged into the system at three in the morning."

"That's it?" Rio said, unimpressed. "She might've had trouble sleeping and decided to catch up on her emails."

"Maybe," Kat said. "But Brooklyn got into her bank account and discovered that she'd made three large deposits totaling fifty thousand pounds in the preceding week."

"That's a lot of money," Rio admitted.

"And, on the day of the attack, she took a sudden trip to Cairo."

"What makes you say it was sudden?" Rio asked.

"Because she booked it that morning and flew out without a return flight scheduled."

By this point they'd stopped walking and were across the street from Gaisman's apartment building.

"That may all be a bit curious," Rio said, still skeptical. "But I don't see what any of it has to do with a cyberattack on major British institutions. It seems like breaking into her flat is an unnecessary risk. Maybe we should come up with a different strategy at the bakery."

Kat considered this for a moment and nodded. "That's what I was concerned about."

"What do you mean?" asked Rio.

"Her apartment building's nice, relatively new, and you're worried that you won't be able to break in."

"Hardly," Rio protested.

"Don't feel bad. I totally understand. I probably should've asked Paris. He's got more experience."

"Are you joking? Look how long it took him to pick the lock the other day at the museum. He'd never be able to get in here."

"And you think you can?"

"Try to stop me," he said confidently as he checked traffic and hurried across the street toward the apartment building.

Kat followed closely behind and tried not to laugh as one thought ran through her mind. *Some people are so easy to manipulate.*

LOVELACE & HOPPER CYBER SOLUTIONS

In a part of East London known as Tech City, Monty and Brooklyn entered a modern office building that had an industrial feel, with concrete walls, exposed beams, and large open spaces that made it look as if it had once been home to a factory or textile mill. They took the elevator to the fourth-floor offices of Lovelace & Hopper Cyber Solutions.

This was the company that had installed the new servers. While scouring the files, Brooklyn noticed they'd made frequent maintenance visits and had full access to the museum's computer systems. This would've given them ample opportunity to secretly launch the cyberattack. In order to figure out if they did, Brooklyn needed to find a way into the network at their headquarters.

"You ready?" Monty whispered as they walked from the elevator to the office suite.

"Angry mother, grumpy daughter," Brooklyn answered. "Should be fun."

They opened the door, and Brooklyn was surprised at the size. Or rather, lack of. Based on what she'd read about the company, she expected it to be bigger. There were only a handful of offices and a reception desk but no receptionist.

"Hello, anyone there?" Monty called out. "Hello?"

A twentysomething woman with cropped magenta hair poked her head out of the nearest office. She was wearing black jeans, Converse high-tops, and a baseball jersey.

"Who are you, and what are you doing here?" asked the woman.

"We're a mother and daughter looking for help with our computer," Monty replied. "This is Lovelace and Hopper Cyber Solutions, isn't it?"

"Yes, but . . ."

"Wait a second, I just got it," Brooklyn said, gleeful. "The company's named after Ada and Grace."

The woman was pleasantly surprised. "You know Ada and Grace?"

"Ada Lovelace, pioneer of computing and the world's first programmer," Brooklyn said. "Grace Hopper, a programming genius and naval rear admiral known as Grandma COBOL. They're legendary." Brooklyn turned and saw that a few more people had looked out from their offices. They all had one thing in common. "Is this an all-female tech company?"

"Maybe," said the woman. "Who are you again?"

"My laptop won't turn on," Monty said, getting back on script as she pulled a silver laptop from her bag and placed it on the counter. "My daughter broke it."

"I didn't break it," Brooklyn said. "I was just trying to free up some space, and I accidentally deleted some system files."

"Which sounds exactly like breaking to me," Monty said.

"Mom, why don't you ever—"

"I'm sorry, but I can't help you," the woman interrupted. "We don't do tech support here."

"Isn't your slogan 'There's no problem too big for us to solve?'" Monty asked.

"Yes, but there are plenty that are too small," the woman replied. "There are just a few of us working on some big projects, and we don't have time to fix laptops."

Brooklyn felt the opportunity slipping away, so she just blurted out, "My brothers will say it's because I'm a girl."

"What?"

"When they find out the laptop's broken, they'll say

it's because I'm a girl and don't understand computers." She gave the woman a desperate look.

This connected with the woman, who gave a begrudging smile. "Why don't I take a look and see what's going on?"

"Thank you so much," Brooklyn replied.

KNIGHTSBRIDGE

Although Brooklyn had been able to identify Imogen Gaisman and the computer company, she hadn't been as successful with the third potential suspect. This person had been much better at covering their tracks, and the best she could do was find a log-in by someone with the username KV66. It wasn't like any of the employee IDs assigned to staff members at the museum, and she couldn't find an actual name associated with it anywhere.

Sydney had an idea about who might be able to help them, although she wasn't sure that person would be happy to see her as she knocked on the front door of an elegant house in Knightsbridge. Moments later, it opened, and Sydney smiled at Valerie Garfield, the British Museum's director of security.

"Interesting that you knocked," Garfield said when she

saw who it was. "I thought your preferred method of entry was blowing a hole into a wall and walking through that."

"No, ma'am," Sydney answered as she tried to read the woman's mood. "Only when that's the assignment."

"And this is what? A social visit?" Garfield leaned out from the door to look for the others. "Or are you diverting my attention while your friends sneak in through the back door?"

"I'm all alone," Sydney said. "But my friends and I do need your help."

"You need my help?" Garfield laughed. "Do you have any idea what my life has been like since you came into it? The break-in was bad enough, but now I'm dealing with MI5 and the Cyber Security Centre. I suppose you know all about what's going on because of your secret girls and boys club."

"The cyberattack," Sydney said. "That's why I'm here. We have a lead that we're trying to follow as to who may be behind it all."

"You have a lead?" she said, incredulous. "Do you know how ridiculous that sounds? No offense, but you're children. This situation is now out of my hands, and I have been instructed not to discuss anything with anyone else. So, I'm sorry, but I can't help you."

She started to close the door, but Sydney used her foot to keep it from shutting.

"Can you at least tell me if you've ever heard of anyone named KV66?"

Garfield's expression changed completely. "Is he part of this?" She shook her head. "I should've thought of that."

"Who is he?" Sydney asked.

Garfield took a deep breath and sighed before opening the door all the way, signaling for Sydney to come in.

"Let's talk about him over a cuppa," Garfield said. "Just promise me that you're not going to steal anything or hack into my computers while you're here."

"I'm not the one who hacks," Sydney said with a grin.

"No," Garfield replied. "You're the one who makes her way into places she's not wanted."

Sydney grinned again and said, "Pretty much."

"I won't ask how you got my address."

"It's probably better that you don't."

REGENT'S PARK

Mother's message to Tru said only that it was urgent for them to meet face-to-face, so they rendezvoused near the boating lake in Regent's Park. It was a picturesque setting as autumn leaves of orange and brown carpeted the ground while vibrant yellow blooms clung to otherwise barren tree branches. Tru was sitting on a bench reading an Agatha Christie novel when Mother arrived and sat on the opposite end, making it appear as if they weren't together.

"Good morning, Tru," Mother said. "You know there have been mystery novels written in this century."

"I prefer the classics," she replied tartly. "And I prefer not to be summoned. So, tell me what was so urgent. Have you made progress in the search to identify Horus?"

"I'm afraid I'm here on a more pressing matter," Mother replied.

"What could possibly be more pressing than a massive cyberattack on our country?" she asked, peeved, still looking down at her book as if she were reading.

"I need you to look at me," he said. "It's important."

Tru didn't like being bossed around, but she closed her book, placed it on her lap, and turned to face him. "I'm all eyes."

"Is Clemmie your mole inside Umbra?"

"What makes you ask that?" she responded flatly.

"Amazing," Mother said, shaking his head. "I called you out on something huge. Something that I know to be true. That you've hidden from me for nearly six years.

And you didn't even flinch. No quiver. No blink. No expression at all."

"First of all, if you know the answer, you shouldn't bother asking the question," she said. "And second, never forget that in this business, we don't flinch. Flinches get people killed. Do you know who Mansfield Smith-Cumming was?"

"The first director of the Intelligence Service," Mother said. "The original C."

"That's right," Tru answered. "Did you know he had an artificial leg?"

"Where's this going, Tru?" Mother asked, annoyed.

"During the screening process, when he was interviewing potential spies, he would suddenly and without warning pull out a knife and stab himself in that wooden leg to see if they flinched. If they did, he knew they didn't have what it took to do the job."

"Interesting," Mother said. "What part of you is artificial? Your wooden heart?"

"Don't be melodramatic," Tru said.

"I'll be however I want," Mother said. "How could you do it? All those years, I have been searching for Clemmie and the kids, and all along you knew where they were."

"No, I didn't," Tru said. "You can choose to believe

me or not, but the kids were never part of the plan. She was supposed to go undercover for a few months. We didn't tell you because she was worried that you'd try to talk her out of it."

"*She* was worried, or *you* were?"

Tru ignored the question and kept on. "Then things went pear-shaped, and there was the fire. Everyone thought you were dead, and Clemmie disappeared with the kids before I knew what happened. I had no idea where she hid them. I still don't."

"Well, one of them is about to move to the FARM."

"What?" Tru replied, surprised.

"Now, that made you flinch," Mother said. "Clemmie hid a second message in the one you showed us."

"Cleopatra?" Tru shook her head. "I was worried about that."

"She led me to Berlin, where I found Robert," Mother said. "And that's why I need to know her status. I need to know if she can be trusted or if she is working with Umbra and using him to get to me and the others."

Tru didn't respond for a long moment as she considered this. "You know Philby is the reason I come here to think," she said, referring to Kim Philby, the most notorious double agent in MI6 history.

Mother rolled his eyes. "Must you always bring up old spies when you're trying to avoid a subject?"

"It *is* the subject we're discussing," she responded. "The Soviets first met up with him right over there, next to the lake. He sat down on the grass with an agent named Otto, like they were on some sort of picnic, and that's where a man who would become one of the highest-ranking members of the Secret Intelligence Service decided to betray his country. The damage he did was incalculable."

"And this relates to my question how?"

"I come here to remind myself that I can't trust my eyes." She gave him a pointed look and added, "Or my wooden heart. Nobody suspected what Philby was up to. He was a star in the Service, destined for greatness, and he fooled everybody."

"So, Clemmie?"

"I know that she provides us with intel about Umbra," she replied. "I know that her mission was to get inside the organization, but that mission is more than five years beyond its expiration date."

She looked at him with true sadness in her eyes.

"As to whether or not she can be *trusted*?" she continued. "I have no bloody idea."

14.

KV66

DR. IMOGEN GAISMAN LIVED IN A NICE
two-bedroom flat that was kept immaculately clean. It
had a modern kitchen, designer furniture, and stylish
decorations. It also had a lousy security system. Rio had
broken in and disarmed it in less than forty-five seconds.
Now, he and Kat were looking around for anything that
might connect Gaisman to Horus and the cyberattack.

"What are your first impressions of Robert?" Kat
asked. "Think he can be trusted?"

"How would I know?"

"You spent the day with him," Kat responded.

Rio laughed. "We were racing across Europe. All I know is he moves quickly and snores when he falls asleep on a plane." Then he stopped. "Of course, I also know that he'll instantly move ahead of me."

"What do you mean by that?"

"Everyone does," Rio answered. "I'm always last on the list, so now I guess I'll be sixth."

They'd reached the kitchen, and when Kat opened the refrigerator, something caught her eye. "Check this out."

"As much as I like to eat, I draw the line at stealing food from a suspect's refrigerator."

"Not to steal," Kat said. "For clues."

Rio gave her a raised eyebrow and walked over to the refrigerator to peer inside. "What clues do you see here?"

"Strawberries, blueberries, and milk," Kat replied.

"You're right, that is suspicious," Rio said sarcastically. "Let's call Scotland Yard and tell them she's making smoothies."

"The milk's unopened and the fruit's fresh," Kat said. "Would you buy fresh fruit and milk *before* you went on a trip to Egypt? It'll all be spoiled by the time she gets back."

"Okay," Rio admitted. "Maybe you were right about her trip being sudden and unplanned."

"So, what made her leave abruptly?" Kat asked. "Was it connected to the cyberattack? Or was it something else?"

Rio walked into one of the bedrooms and said, "Check this out. It looks like a TV studio in here."

One half of the room was set up as a home office, while the other had been converted into a little studio with two chairs arranged interview-style, a microphone on a boom, three camera lights, and a tripod. The bookcase behind the chair was filled with books by Dr. Gaisman and replicas of Egyptian artifacts. A sign on the wall read EVERYTHING BUT THE KITCHEN SPHINX.

"It's for her video podcast," Kat explained. "She has guests on, and they talk about all things ancient Egypt. I watched part of one about how the pyramids were built. It was good."

"What's the pattern?" Rio asked as he took pictures of it all so that they would have them for reference later on.

"What do you mean?"

"You say there's always a pattern," Rio said. "So, what's the pattern here?"

"For one, she's meticulous. Everything's ordered and put away in its proper place, with three exceptions. Two were in her bedroom: the bed was unmade, and there were shoes scattered in front of the closet."

"The trip's not planned, so she's in a hurry," Rio theorized. "She doesn't bother to make her bed, and she digs around in her closet looking for the right shoes."

"That's good, but what about this?" Kat pointed at Gaisman's desk. "All the papers are organized in neat stacks and piles, but the mail is just scattered across the desk."

"You think she got something in the mail that made her change plans and leave for Egypt?"

"Maybe," Kat said. "But none of it's been opened."

"Because she took whatever it was with her," Rio said.

"That would make sense," Kat reasoned. "If there was something, we have no way of knowing."

They looked at each other, smiled at the same time, and both said, "The envelope."

They searched the apartment, and Rio found it in the kitchen trash. Rather than an envelope, it turned out to be a small package, half the size of a shoebox. The contents were gone, but as was the case for all international packages sent to the United Kingdom, there was a customs declaration form attached to it that listed the address of the sender and a description of the contents.

"There's no name, but according to this, someone in Cairo sent her a handcrafted wooden jar weighing point four kilograms," Rio said, reading from it.

"Why would that make her fly off to Cairo?" Kat wondered aloud.

LOVELACE & HOPPER CYBER SOLUTIONS

Although she was supposed to be playing the role of difficult teenager, Brooklyn had to fight the urge to break out in a grin as they walked through the headquarters of the all-female tech company. It seemed more like a shrine to awesome computer hardware than a workplace, and it filled her hacker's heart with joy. It killed her that she had to downplay her abilities.

"My name's Oriana," said the woman.

"Christina," Brooklyn replied. She recognized the "NY" on the baseball jersey Oriana was wearing and asked, "You like the Yankees?"

"Love them," Oriana said. "I grew up in New York."

"Me too," Brooklyn said accidentally, but she quickly

covered for herself and added, "I mean, I love the Yankees too. I watch their games sometimes with my brothers."

"The knuckleheads who think girls can't code?"

"That's them," Brooklyn said with a grin.

"Tell me what happened with the laptop."

"I don't really know," Brooklyn answered. "I wanted to clear up some space on my hard drive, and I found a tutorial online, but I must have done something wrong because I accidentally deleted some system files."

"It's an easy mistake," Oriana said. "And it has nothing to do with being a girl. I hope that you backed up your files."

"Of course," Brooklyn replied. "But I can't get the laptop to turn back on so I can reinstall them."

"That's because first you have to reinstall the OS," Oriana said. "The operating system."

"Do you have to send it back to the manufacturer to do that?" Brooklyn asked.

"No," Oriana replied. "I've got some custom software that should take care of it in no time. All I have to do is hook it up to our network and let her rip. You can restore your files when you get home."

Once again, Brooklyn had to fight the urge to break out in a giant grin. As soon as Oriana rebooted the laptop, the worm she'd loaded onto it would slip right into the company's network and start doing its work.

KNIGHTSBRIDGE

Considering her job title, it wasn't surprising that Valerie Garfield's home had top-of-the-line security features. Just walking from the front door to the kitchen, Sydney noticed cameras, motion detectors, a biometric control pad, and window sensors. The furnishings were also high-end, but everything still had a warm feeling. Sydney got the sense that it was a home and not just a house.

"Let's sit at the table while I put on a kettle," Garfield said. "Do you have a name, or is that classified?"

"Ellie," Sydney said, offering the cover name she used at school.

"Well, Ellie," Garfield said as she filled a kettle with water. "What makes you ask about KV66?"

Sydney wasn't sure how much she could share of what they knew. She wasn't supposed to talk about any of it, but she was looking for help and information, so she needed to give a little in exchange.

"According to the log-in history on the museum's computer server, someone using that ID accessed your system several times in the days leading up to the hack."

"How could you possibly know who—" Garfield started to say. "Never mind. I'm sure you can't tell me."

"No, ma'am, I can't."

"KV66 isn't a person; it's a company," Garfield said. "Although, that company only has one employee, so I guess it really is a person in a way. His name is Jason Harper—a bit of an odd duck, if you ask me. He's American, although his company is based in Egypt."

"And he did work for the museum?"

"He was supposed to," said Garfield. "He had this idea to use computer mapping, 3D modeling, and video projectors to turn one of our exhibit rooms into a fully immersive experience."

"What do you mean by that?"

"He shot footage of every inch of King Tut's tomb in a way that he could project it on the walls of a specially designed room to make it seem as though you were entering the tomb just like Howard Carter did a century ago."

"'Wonderful things,'" Sydney said, quoting Carter from that moment.

"Exactly," said Garfield. "He did a partial demonstration, and it was breathtaking. I thought it was going to be a huge hit."

"Then why wasn't it part of the exhibit?" Sydney asked.

"Some of the curators weren't big fans," Garfield answered. "They said it was entertainment more fitting for a theme park than the museum. They can get a bit stuffy that way. Then one of them knocked on my door and said she needed to show me something."

"What was it?" Sydney asked, excited by the story.

"Documents that someone had secretly passed on to her that showed Harper was being investigated by Egypt's Ministry of Antiquities for trafficking looted and stolen artifacts."

"Wow," Sydney said.

"He denied it, but my team investigated, and while we couldn't fully confirm it, the mere hint of impropriety made him radioactive. The museum cut all ties with him."

"And it was one of the curators who gave you the information?" Sydney asked.

"A consultant, actually," Garfield said. "An Egyptologist named Imogen Gaisman."

15.

"You'll Never Walk Alone"

THE HEAVY WOODEN CHAIRS WERE uncomfortable, which seemed fitting considering the awkwardness of the conversation. Paris and Robert were failing miserably at making small talk in a room Sister Christine called the library.

With no television, computer, or electronic devices, the only entertainment at the convent was the occasional nun communicating by coded handbells. Paris was desperate to find something to break the ice.

"Want to have a kick around?" he offered hopefully. "We've got proper kits and everything."

"I don't know that I want to wear a tracksuit that's been worn by a nun," Robert replied.

Paris laughed. "No, the sisters don't have the gear. We do. For our cover story, we were traveling as players with the Aberdeen FC Youth Academy. Our bags have sweats, trainers, jerseys, you name it. Who knows, you might even get lucky with a pair of boots if you and Rio wear the same size."

Robert flashed a genuine smile and said, "I could go for some footy."

Twenty minutes later they were kicking a ball across Hyde Park as they jogged toward an area known as the Old Football Pitches. Sister Christine had told them about it when Paris asked her if there were any good places to play nearby.

"How are those boots?" Paris asked, looking down at Robert's cleats.

"A little tight, but they'll do."

The situation was still awkward, but at least out here it felt like they were doing *something*.

"So, let me get this straight," Robert said. "You don't actually play for Aberdeen's youth team?"

"No," Paris said. "It's just a cover identity that was

developed for a mission that got canceled."

"And what is it that you do?" Robert asked, trying to make sense of it. "I can't quite get my head wrapped around it."

Paris hesitated. "I don't know how much of that I'm allowed to tell you."

"Right," Robert said. "Can't trust the new kid. I'm used to that in every school I go to." He paused. "And, believe me, I've gone to a lot of them."

"I didn't mean it that way," Paris said. "It's not about trust. It's literally about what I *am* and *am not* allowed to say. It's a legal thing. We signed the Secrets Act."

"Of course, it would help if my father was here," Robert said. "But he didn't even bother to stay around on my first morning. I guess that's not new. He was gone a lot when I was little. I don't know what I was thinking when I decided to come here."

"It was your decision?"

Robert nodded. "About three months ago, our mum came and told us we could move back if we wanted."

"Where were you all living?"

"I'm not sure how much I'm allowed to tell you," he replied with a smirk.

"That's fair," Paris said. "So, you decided to come back, and Annie decided to stay?"

"She was really torn. She wanted to come back, but she knew that if she did, Mum wouldn't have either one of us, and she couldn't leave her like that. Now I'm wondering if I made the right decision. Like I said, he didn't even stick around today."

"I'm sure he wanted to let you sleep in," Paris said. "Besides, he had to take care of paperwork."

"What type of paperwork?" Robert asked.

"All the stuff he needs to create a new identity for you," Paris said. "Birth certificate, passports, that sort of thing."

"*Passports,*" Robert said. "I've got the only parents in the world who regularly give fake passports as presents."

Paris wasn't sure if this was meant to be a joke or a complaint and decided it was probably a combination of both.

"About your father," Paris started to say.

"Don't you mean *our* father, *brother*?"

"Yes."

"That's strange too," Robert continued. "I mean, my

sister and I were out of the picture, so he just replaced us. Is that how it went?"

"You've got him all wrong if you think that. Your dad—I mean—our dad has literally searched the planet for you two. And while he was doing that, he came across kids he couldn't turn his back on. If he hadn't, who knows what would've happened to us."

Robert let out a deep sigh. "I'm sorry. I shouldn't lay that all out on you."

"You absolutely should," Paris said. "After all, that's kind of what big brothers are for. You can come to me to complain about anything: school, the others, *our* father. Plus there's one thing that you and I agree on that he doesn't. And we can always talk about that."

"What is it?"

Rather than answer, Paris started singing, *"Walk on, walk on, with hope in your heart."*

Robert grinned and responded by singing the next line in the song, *"And you'll never walk alone."*

"You'll Never Walk Alone" was the anthem of Liverpool FC, and by tradition it was sung by the club's supporters at the start of every game. Paris loved the team, and he knew Robert did too because Mother had joked that both picked it because he loved Everton, their bitter rivals.

As they continued toward the Old Football Pitches, they humorously sang the last line of the song together, drawing it out just like fans did at the games. *"And you'll neeeeever walk aloooooone!"*

Royal London Hospital

THE ROYAL LONDON HOSPITAL WAS A patchwork of old and new. Although it was founded in 1740, it was also a modern medical facility with state-of-the-art equipment like the Pentero 900 surgical microscope. That's what Dr. Shakthi Sivasubramaniam was using to remove a small tumor from the brain of a young patient in operating theatre eleven. There were seven members of the surgical team, and they were halfway through the six-hour procedure when the anesthetist had an alarmed reaction.

"My screen's gone," he said.

"What do you mean?" asked the neurosurgeon.

"Just that," he replied. "Everything was fine, and now it's blank."

It was the anesthetist's job to monitor the patient's vital signs, including heart rate, blood pressure, oxygen level, and body temperature. He tracked them on a computer that recorded the results in an ongoing scroll of data.

"We're too far along to stop," said Sivasubramaniam. "Is it just the monitor? What about the anesthesia machine and the ventilator?"

The anesthetist checked his equipment, and everything else seemed fine. "Just the monitor."

"Thank goodness for small miracles," the doctor said. "You're going to need to write all the information down on paper, just like we did back in the dark ages before we had computers. And, somebody else, find out what's going on."

While the anesthetist scrambled to find pencil and paper, similar scenes were playing out in other parts of the hospital. The scheduling nurse could no longer see what patients and medicines were needed in which rooms, a doctor about to perform an operation couldn't access his patient's electronic medical records, and no one in the building could open or send any email.

Horus had shut down the entire communication network for five East London hospitals. Fortunately, most medical equipment like the surgical microscope wasn't affected. It worked independently and wasn't part of the network. This meant the doctors were able to conclude any procedures that were underway. However, within hours, the hospitals were virtually closed for business, and patients had to be directed to other hospitals throughout the city.

Family Business

"CLAY HOBSON?" ROBERT SAID, LOOKING down at the passport Mother had just handed him. "What was wrong with Ben Dobrow?"

"Nothing. I love Ben; he's a great kid," Mother said. "But as soon as you used that passport to go from Berlin to London, a trail was created. Now MI6 is going to reroute it by giving Ben a Twitter account, scheduling him for a doctor's appointment, and enrolling him at a school in Newcastle. If anyone tries to track you with that name, they'll just hit a dead end."

"And by 'anyone,' you mean Mum," Robert said.

"No, I mean *anyone*. This has been such a whirlwind that we haven't had a chance to catch our breath, much less catch up. I don't know who might be interested in finding you, but I'm going to make sure they can't. This is home, and it's safe, and it's absolutely amazing to have you here."

They'd just arrived at the FARM, and after Mother gave him a quick tour, they were sitting in Robert's new bedroom. It had pale blue walls, a bed, a wooden desk, two chairs, and a lovely view of the Scottish Highlands.

"What do you think?" Mother continued.

"It's really nice," Robert said. "I have to admit, I wasn't expecting to live in a castle or—what'd you call it again?"

"A manor house."

"Right," Robert said. "I certainly didn't expect to live in a manor house."

"It's a little grand and a bit drafty, but we try to make it comfortable," Mother said. "And there's an excellent school nearby, Kinloch Abbey. We'll get you enrolled right away."

"I'm used to changing schools. Mum kept us on the move, but a big house and a big family . . . that's all new."

Mother gave his hand a squeeze. "I know it seems overwhelming, but you'll get used to the house, and you'll love the others."

"Not so sure they're going to love me," Robert said, Sydney's comments still fresh in his mind.

"I am," Mother said confidently. "I know them well."

"Yeah," Robert said softly. "Better than you know me."

"We're going to change that right away," Mother said, trying to lighten the mood. "Tell me, have you finally seen the light and dumped that awful football team of yours?"

"Never," Robert said with a grin. "And Paris is with me."

"See, you're already getting along. Albeit at my expense."

There was a knock on the door, and Paris poked his head into the room.

"He's on me about Liverpool," Robert said. "Trying to convert me."

"Don't let him," Paris said, tapping a fist against his chest. "Stay strong." He turned to Mother. "Sorry to interrupt. But we just got an alert from Tru, and we need you in the priest hole. It sounds pretty urgent."

This was exactly what Mother didn't want to happen

while he was trying to help Robert settle in.

"Go ahead," Robert said, forcing a smile. "I can explore the castle." He caught himself. "I mean, manor house."

"No," Mother said, making a snap decision. "You come too."

"But I'm not part of whatever *this* is," Robert said.

"You are now," Mother answered. "Like it or not, this is who we are. Your mother, me, your newly discovered brothers and sisters: we're all spies. It's our family business. Just like a hardware store that's passed down from generation to generation."

"Except, instead of selling hammers and nails, we steal secrets and blow stuff up," Paris said with a grin. "Much more fun if you ask me."

"Now, if you don't like it, you don't have to participate," Mother said. "I'm not going to force you."

"Except you're going to love it," Paris said. "Every bit of it."

Robert tried to contain a smile but failed. "It does sound exciting."

A few minutes later, he was wide-eyed when they entered the priest hole and he got his first look at all the high-tech gear. Except for Brooklyn, who was working at a nearby computer station, everyone was sitting around the sleek black conference table in the middle of the room.

The moment they saw Robert, they knew what it meant. If he was in the priest hole for a briefing, then he was now part of the team. It was a major development, but there was no announcement, explanation, or formal introduction. Just six words from Monty as she kicked off the meeting.

"Hello, Robert. Welcome to the FARM."

Sydney looked like she might jump in and say something, but Mother spoke first.

"What's the latest from Tru?" he asked.

"Up until now, Horus hasn't done anything malicious other than hack the computer systems," Monty said. "They've been letting everyone operate while they negotiate the ransom with the government. But now they've upped their assault on the National Health Service by attacking the computer systems at five hospitals in East London."

"It's an amazing contradiction," Brooklyn said, turning from her workstation. "Hospitals have some of the most amazing tech you'll see. We're talking robotics, surgical microscopes, you name it. But they also have computers older than we are that run on software that is generations out of date. This makes them incredibly vulnerable, which is why they're so frequently targeted by hackers."

"What do the hackers want?" Robert asked, trying to catch up.

"Anarchy, money, the normal Umbra objectives," Sydney said. "Of course, you know all about them, right?"

Robert ignored the dig, and Mother gave Sydney a pointed look.

"It's all part of turning up the heat on the government so they'll make a deal," Monty said. "Horus sent a ransom note demanding twenty million in cryptocurrency to free up the hospitals."

"Even if they pay it, the hackers are still going to keep attacking the NHS and the other targets," Paris said. "I mean, what's going to stop them?"

"We are," Brooklyn said confidently.

"You're exactly right," Mother said. "We're going to stop them cold."

"Or maybe her," Kat said. "Imogen Gaisman's definitely a candidate."

"She's the Egyptologist, right?" Mother asked, still catching up with what they'd been investigating.

"Yes," Rio said. "She's highly regarded and has written numerous books about ancient Egypt, but she's also controversial."

"How do you mean?" Paris asked.

"She's very outspoken about returning antiquities to Egypt," Kat said. "In her flat there's a poster of the great pyramids that says, 'Why are the pyramids in Egypt? Because they were too heavy for the British Museum to steal.'"

"Sounds like my kind of girl," said Sydney.

"But that doesn't make any sense," Paris said.

"Sure it does," said Sydney. "It's implying that if the pyramids weren't so big, the British Museum would've taken them and moved them to London."

"The joke makes sense," Paris said. "Just not the person making it. Wasn't she in charge of the *Wonderful Things* exhibit *at the British Museum*? Doesn't she work for them?"

"Technically, she's a consultant who works for herself," Kat explained. "She coordinated the exhibit with another curator at the Egyptian Museum in Cairo. Her viewpoint is that the artifacts can be shown around the world, but that they should belong to and be controlled by institutions in Egypt."

"If she's the curator in charge of *Wonderful Things*," said Monty, "that might explain why Clemmie mentioned it in her message. Maybe she was pointing a finger at Gaisman."

"Mum?" Robert whispered to Mother.

"Yes," he said. "This all traces back to a message she sent."

Robert nodded while trying to keep up with the flow of the conversation.

"What motive would Gaisman have?" Brooklyn asked.

"I can think of two," Kat answered. "She'd love to embarrass the government. She and a few members of Parliament got into a Twitter feud recently when she said the Rosetta Stone should be returned to Egypt. She's also talked about organizing a boycott of people and businesses that support the museum, hoping they'll put pressure on it to return the artifacts."

"And if she hacked into the museum's system," Brooklyn said, "she has access to all of their financial records, so she would be able to identify who those people are."

"Where is she now?" Mother asked.

"Somewhere in Egypt," Rio said. "She went there suddenly after receiving a package from an address in Cairo. We took a photo of the customs declaration that came with it."

Monty pressed a button, and the picture appeared on the large wall monitor.

"Nice work," Paris said.

"I keep telling you all that I've got skills," Rio said.

"Don't you mean *we've* got skills?" Kat said. "I'm pretty sure I was there too."

Mother read directly from the customs form. "'A handcrafted wooden jar valued at two hundred pounds.' Did you see the jar?"

"No," said Kat. "We think she may have taken it with her."

"What could be so interesting about a jar that it would make her fly straight to Cairo?" Paris wondered aloud.

"Imogen Gaisman's also connected to KV66," Sydney said. "And not in a good way."

She stood up, walked over to the wall monitor, and used a clicker to add a new photograph.

"This is Jason Harper," she said. "He was about to

close an important deal with the British Museum when she accused him of trafficking in stolen antiquities."

"Was it true?" asked Kat.

"We don't know for sure," Sydney answered. "The authorities in Egypt are looking into it but haven't given a definite answer. But, when the museum investigated, they found enough to make them back off the deal."

"Is he an Egyptologist too?" Monty asked.

"No, and that's the problem," Sydney answered. "After Valerie Garfield told me about him, I did a deep dive to find out as much as I could. He had no experience in archaeology but was brought in from America as part of an extensive photogrammetry project."

"What's photogrammetry?" asked Robert.

"Yeah," asked Paris.

"It's advanced computer science that uses photography to create hyperaccurate digital models," Brooklyn answered. "Computer mapping times a hundred."

"He's a total tech genius with a PhD from MIT," Sydney said. "The project was started to create three-dimensional computer models of all the tombs that had been discovered in the Valley of the Kings. You can find them online, and they're really fascinating. But he got it in his head that the same technology could be used to locate missing tombs."

"There are still missing tombs?" Rio asked.

"Probably a bunch of them," Sydney answered.

"How can you be sure?" Monty asked.

"Because all the important pharaohs and queens got them, and there are a lot of those who we know about historically but whose final resting places have never been located. This includes Rameses VIII, Thutmose II, and the biggest prize of all, Nefertiti. The expectation is that those are somewhere in the Valley of the Kings, but the tombs were hidden so that raiders couldn't steal all their treasures."

"And what is KV66?" Paris asked.

"That's the name of his company," Sydney answered. "Each time a new tomb is discovered in the valley, they give it a number. It started at KV1 and goes all the way to KV65."

"So, the tomb he's determined to find would be KV66?" Paris said.

"Exactly."

"Why's it a problem that he's not an Egyptologist?" Mother said.

"No one will sponsor an excavation to test his theory," Sydney explained. "Typically, the digs are overseen by universities or Egypt's Supreme Council of Antiquities, but they won't fund him because he doesn't have a background in archaeology."

"Then what was he going to do for the museum?" Paris asked.

"He figured out a way to use the mapping of the tomb to create an immersive exhibit so that it looked like you were actually entering King Tut's tomb just like it was for Howard Carter a hundred years ago."

"That sounds cool," Rio said. "I would've liked to have seen that."

"And you would've been able to if Imogen Gaisman hadn't accused him of being a criminal," Sydney responded.

"This is cool," Brooklyn said, looking at her computer.

"What is?" Rio asked.

"The 3D maps of the tombs," Brooklyn answered. "I just pulled one up off Harper's website."

"I thought you were busy hacking into Cyber Solutions?" Monty said.

"I can multi-hack," Brooklyn joked. "I mean, multi-task."

"Then maybe you and Monty can also tell us what you found when you went there?" Mother responded.

"Lovelace and Hopper Cyber Solutions is an all-female tech company that seems to be very good at what they do," Monty said. "It's a small operation, but they have big accounts, including the British Museum. They take care of all the computer hardware, which gives them plenty of access."

"Not only that," Brooklyn said. "I've just started digging around, but their clients have also included Parliament, the NHS, and the London Underground."

"That means they have access to each of the targets," Mother said. "Not to mention the technological know-how to orchestrate the attack."

"Absolutely."

"But why would a successful company risk all of their business to commit a hack like this?" Paris asked. "They'd lose everything if they're found out."

"But they could walk away with more than one hundred million pounds if they're not," Mother said. "People have done far worse for far less."

"Here's what I don't get," Rio said. "How is Umbra involved?"

"I've looked into that," Monty said. "Apparently, they've been developing gangs of cybercriminals to work for them on jobs just like this. Typically, someone, like one of these three suspects, comes to them with a vulnerability for them to target."

"Such as the ability to get past an institution's firewall," Sydney suggested.

"Exactly," Monty said. "Then one of Umbra's cybergangs comes in and provides all the dirty work, like negotiating ransom demands or transferring money."

"And what's in it for them?" Paris asked.

"Umbra keeps between fifty and seventy-five percent of the cash, which in this case is quite a lot. They're suspected of having been involved in the similar attacks of several oil companies and half a dozen banks. We don't really know how many because most companies aren't willing to admit they've been compromised. Sometimes they just pay the ransom quietly and the public never learns of it."

"This is going to get worse very quickly," Mother said. "We've got C's order to do what we can to help, so let's do it as fast as possible. Brooklyn, continue looking into Cyber Solutions and find out everything you can about them. Sydney, Paris, I want you two to become experts about all things Jason Harper and KV66. Kat and Rio, you do the same with Imogen Gaisman. We're going to get back together in exactly two hours to see where we are."

"What about me?" Robert asked meekly.

"I figured you wanted to get adjusted, look around the FARM a little bit," Mother said.

"I want to help," Robert replied. "After all, it is the family business."

"What can you do?" Sydney asked tartly. "You don't know anything about the case, and you don't have any training."

Mother went to say something, but Robert beat him to it. "Egypt seems to be a key here," he said. "That's where Imogen Gaisman is hiding and maybe where she hid the jar she got in the post."

"Your point?" Sydney replied.

"I think I'm the only one here who's lived in Egypt," he said.

"You did?" Sydney asked, surprised.

"I spent seven months in Cairo," he answered. "And training or not, I know a great deal about hiding."

18.

Hapi and Pluto

ROBERT AND KAT SAT TOGETHER AT THE conference table, scrolling through Imogen Gaisman's social media accounts as they looked for any times during the past few years when she'd posted pictures from Egypt. They were trying to create a map of locations she'd visited with the hope of finding a pattern. It was an effective pairing because Robert knew Egypt and Kat knew patterns.

"Here's one at a restaurant in Cairo," Kat said, showing him her phone.

"Great," replied Robert as he tagged the location on a map on his phone. "I've actually been to that restaurant. I like it."

Kat thought about this for a moment. She struggled in social situations, especially with new people, but saw this as a chance to connect with Robert.

"I like primes," she said.

Robert gave her a look. "Primes?"

"Prime numbers," Kat said. "I especially like truncatable primes."

Robert wasn't sure if she was joking with him or not. "What's a truncatable prime?"

"A number that remains prime even if you take off the first or last digit," Kat said. "My favorite is 73,939,133, which is the longest of the right truncatable numbers."

Robert looked at her, unsure what to say.

"What's your favorite number?" Kat asked.

He thought for a moment. "Eleven."

"Also a prime," she said happily. "Is that why you chose it?"

"It's Mo Salah's jersey number," Robert answered. "He's my favorite footballer."

"Good choice for both of us, then." Kat smiled and went back to scrolling.

Robert was still trying to wrap his head around the conversation a few minutes later when Mother returned to the priest hole to meet with everyone.

"It hasn't even been ninety minutes," Paris complained. "You said we had two hours."

"The timeline's been accelerated," Mother said. "I need to know where we are on each lead so we can plan next steps."

Everyone regrouped around the conference table except for Brooklyn, who was engrossed in her computer. "I just need a minute," she said, holding up a hand while still focusing on the screen. "I may be onto something."

"Fine, but listen to this while you do that," Mother said. "I just talked to Tru, and there's been a bit of a break."

"What is it?" Rio asked.

"The National Cyber Security Centre set some kind of trap with a root kit or a root canal or something computer-based," Mother said.

"Don't talk tech; you'll embarrass yourself," Brooklyn told him. "Just say they set a trap."

"Fine," Mother said with a chuckle. "They set a trap and were able to get a potential IP address for the hacker." He shot a look at Brooklyn. "And I won't embarrass myself and try to explain exactly what it is either, but I do know that it tells us the location of the hacker's computer."

"That's amazing," Paris said. "Did they catch them?"

"No," Mother said. "The address was for an internet café in Cairo, so they had to coordinate with Egyptian authorities, and by the time the commando team arrived, the person was gone."

"If they were ever there in the first place," Brooklyn said. "Any decent hacker knows how to bounce around IP addresses to confuse someone trying to do a trace. If anyone found it, the hacker probably intended them to, so the searcher would go looking in the wrong direction."

"That's what the Cyber Security Centre decided too," Mother said. "They think it's a dead lead."

"But you don't?" said Monty.

"No. Neither does Tru. Two of our three leads have connections to Egypt," he said. "That could be a coincidence, or it could be a pattern. Where do we stand on them?"

"Jason Harper has gone completely off the grid," Paris said. "Up until four months ago, he was active on social media and trying to drum up business and financing for his immersive museum concept. And then *poof.*"

"As soon as the British Museum canceled its contract, he disappeared," Sydney added.

"So, we don't know where he is?" Mother asked.

"No, but the odds are he's still in Egypt," Sydney said.

"What makes you say that?" asked Monty.

"If he's under investigation, I don't think they'd let him leave the country," Sydney explained.

"What about Gaisman?" Mother asked.

"She hasn't posted anything on social media since she left London, but Kat and I have been going through all the posts from previous visits, and it looks like she's probably in Zamalek," Robert said. "It's an affluent area of Cairo that she often visits. It's popular with internationals, so it's good place for her to go and blend in."

"But why is she hiding?" Paris asked.

Rio said, "It probably has something to do with whatever she got in the mail. The wooden jar spooked her."

"I have an idea about that," Robert said.

"What is it?" Mother asked.

"She left town in a hurry, right? Annie and I have done that more times than I can remember. Mum would just show up and tell us we had to move. We didn't have time to pack and prepare. Sometimes we'd just have to leave things out in the open and hope that no one noticed."

"It's called hiding in plain sight," Sydney said tersely. "We all know it."

Paris gave her a look.

"Sorry," she said to Robert.

Robert let it go and kept talking. "Maybe that's what Imogen did. Instead of taking the jar with her, maybe she just hid it in plain sight."

"We looked all around the flat and didn't see out anything of the ordinary," Rio said, a bit defensive.

"But an Egyptian jar might not look out of place at her flat," Robert said. "Did you take pictures?"

"Of course we did," Rio said, more defensive. "We know what we're doing."

"Great," Robert said. "Then let's look at any picture that shows the backdrop for the podcast. It's filled with Egyptian objects. If she put it there, no one would notice."

"We can compare it to the backdrop from her latest podcast," Kat said, getting Robert's thinking. "See if anything has just been added."

"That's brilliant," Paris said.

Robert smiled, happy to have made a contribution.

They projected the two images on the big screen, and

it didn't take long for Kat to notice what was new in the photograph.

"Right there," she said, pointing at the second shelf from the bottom. "This podcast was made a week ago, and there was nothing on the end of the shelf. But yesterday there was."

Monty expanded the image on the monitor and zeroed in on a jar. It was small, about four inches tall, and the top of it looked like the head of a baboon.

"Where are my mythology books?" Paris said, excited. "I left them on the table just the other day."

"I think they're over there." Sydney pointed at a messy desk in the corner.

Paris ran over, found the book he was looking for, and rejoined the others.

"Look at this," he said. "The head of the baboon means that it's Hapi."

"Who's Hapi?" Rio asked.

"He's one of the four sons of Horus," Paris said. "That's a canopic jar."

The mention of Horus gave everyone a jolt of energy.

"That's not a coincidence," Mother said. "This has to be connected."

Before anyone else could react, they were interrupted

by a shriek from Brooklyn, who was still working on her computer.

"Oh my goodness!" she exclaimed. "I don't believe it!"

"What is it?" Sydney asked urgently.

"I think I just discovered Pluto," she said, a stunned look on her face.

"I'm pretty sure Pluto was discovered about a hundred years ago," Paris said. "First it was a planet. Then it wasn't. Now some people think it should be, and others think it shouldn't."

"Not the celestial body Pluto. And no, Rio," she said, giving him a look as he was about to make a joke, "not Mickey Mouse's dog either. I mean the legendary hacker named Pluto." She was so excited that she momentarily got tongue-tied as she tried to explain. "Pluto hacked everything from Scotland Yard to British Petroleum to Buckingham Palace. And then, five years ago, completely disappeared. There were rumors about an arrest and detainment in a secret prison—all sorts of wild speculation—but none of it was ever verified. The only thing that anyone knew was that there was no sign of Pluto. That is until I just found something while I was looking through these files."

"Pluto hacked the company?" Monty asked.

Brooklyn shook her head and grinned. "Pluto *is* the company. Or rather she's Oriana, the woman we met who fixed the laptop."

"What makes you say that?" Robert asked.

"The company offers custom software to its clients, and it's all written by its founder, Oriana Gutierrez."

"Who you think is actually Pluto?" Mother asked.

"I'm certain of it," Brooklyn said. "Coders have distinct styles, signature patterns, and distinct phrasing. I pulled up some of Pluto's hacks, and they sync up. Not only that, but there's also this."

She pointed to a symbol on her screen: ♇.

"What is that?" Rio asked.

"It's the astrological symbol for Pluto," Paris said.

"It was the consistent signature in all of Pluto's hacks," Brooklyn said. "Like a tag in graffiti."

"If Pluto's gone into hiding, why would they leave a clue like this?" Sydney asked.

"First of all, I'm sure they thought no one would ever see it," Brooklyn explained. "I hacked into the company's internal network. This isn't what their customers see; it's what runs their systems. Second, the one thing that brings hackers down most often is ego. They're artists, and artists like to sign their masterpieces."

"That means a computer security company that has had contracts with all the targets is actually run by a notorious hacker," Rio said. "Unbelievable."

"Former hacker," Brooklyn said. "Pluto hasn't hacked anything in five years."

"Once a hacker, always a hacker," Rio said. "And this would be the ultimate return engagement."

"But the company's here in the UK, and the IP address is in Egypt," Paris said. "Do they have any connection there?"

Brooklyn smiled broadly and said, "Three months ago they signed a contract to develop a cataloging system for the Grand Egyptian Museum."

Now Mother was the one who was smiling.

"Do you know what that means?" he asked.

"No, what?" said Robert.

"We're going to Egypt," replied the others.

"And you're going to need this," Mother said as he walked over to a workstation, opened a drawer, and pulled out a flat rubbery disk the size of a small coin.

"What is it?" Robert asked.

"It's called a nautilus," Mother said. "It's a tracker, and you'll need it if you're going to be in the field, so that we can find you if you get lost."

"Or kidnapped," Sydney said with a wry smile.

"Must you?" Monty said.

"Just keeping it real and laying out the possibilities," Sydney replied.

Robert seemed more worried about the device than the threat of kidnapping. "Do I swallow it, or do I have to have it surgically implanted?" he asked with a gulp.

The others laughed, and Paris said, "We could pull out a knife and give it a try if you'd like, but it would probably be a lot less painful if you just put it in your shoe or pocket like the rest of us."

Robert turned red and laughed at himself. "I guess I've seen too many spy movies."

"Whatever you do, it's essential that you have it with you at all times," Mother said. "It's made of a super-strong polymer, so it's impossible to break and it doesn't set off metal detectors."

"That's really cool," Robert said. "Did you get this in some James Bond lab at MI6?"

"We tried to do that, but requisitions take forever," Monty said. "So I ordered them online from an electronics store in Blackpool instead."

Everybody laughed at this, and the mood in the room was charged with the promise of action and adventure.

19.
Scriptex

IT LOOKED LIKE A NORMAL PEN, SO Monty hadn't paid it much attention when she'd searched Robert's backpack at the convent. She took it apart, tested it, and noticed nothing out of the ordinary before putting it back exactly as she found it. For Monty, whose sharp eyes and thoroughness were trademarks of her spycraft, this was a rare mistake.

Like the tracker, Robert had received the device from a parent, but it wasn't something that could be purchased from a discount electronics store. It was specially made, a gift from his mother, and proof that Umbra's technology development program was far more advanced than MI6 or any other intelligence agency imagined. Known as a "scriptex," the instrument looked and worked exactly like a normal pen but was also capable of stealth writing.

Unlike invisible ink, with which a message was hidden until it was revealed by some method such as exposure to heat or ultraviolet light, stealth writing needed no ink or paper. The user simply had to make the writing motions with the scriptex, and an internal gyroscope converted the movements into digital letters that were transmitted with a simple click.

Like most twelve-year-olds, Robert's handwriting wasn't particularly neat, and it had taken him time to learn how to properly use the scriptex. But now it was second nature, and he was able to successfully send messages with ease.

While the others were packing for Egypt, he composed a quick note to Clementine that described the FARM as well as the members of the City Spies team and their upcoming trip. He'd just finished writing it when Mother came to the door to his room.

"Ready?"

"I hardly have anything to pack, so yeah."

"Come on, then," Mother said. "As soon as we get back, I'll take you into Edinburgh, and we'll get you some more clothes. Build a wardrobe."

"Sounds great," Robert said, picking up his backpack. Just before he slipped the scriptex back into the front pocket, he clicked the button at the top and transmitted his message. "I think this is going to be a fun trip," he said to Mother. "No doubt full of surprises."

The City of a Thousand Minarets

AS THE PLANE APPROACHED CAIRO International Airport, Kat looked out the window at a seemingly endless desert and tightened her grip on the armrest.

"What's wrong?" asked Monty, who was sitting next to her. "Turbulence getting to you?"

"The turbulence inside my head," Kat said softly.

"What do you mean?" Monty asked.

"I'm worried about freezing in Cairo," Kat admitted.

Monty smiled as she looked out the window. "I

know it's November, but the desert still looks pretty warm to me."

"That's not what I meant," Kat said, cracking a smile. "I froze twice at the British Museum. I had a plan that I thought was perfect, and when things went wrong, I didn't know what to do." Kat shook her head slightly as she remembered. "I was saved, once by Sydney and once by Paris, but I still froze."

"That's one of the many reasons why it's great to be part of a team," Monty said. "You're there to pick each other up."

"True, but that doesn't help the anxiety I'm feeling about letting the others down."

"First of all, you should know that you could never let them down, but what is it about Cairo that worries you?"

"Disorder. Everything I've read or seen indicates that it's loud, crowded, total pandemonium. I'm worried it'll overwhelm me."

"Sensory overload," Monty replied. "I used to struggle with that a lot. I still do sometimes."

"Really?" Kat asked, surprised.

Monty nodded. "That's a big problem for you and me. Our greatest strength is also our biggest vulnerability."

"Which strength is that?"

"The ability to see patterns where others see confusion. That's how we break codes and solve puzzles. But that ability comes from a *need* to see order in our environment. It comforts and calms us in a way most people can't understand. And when we can't find it . . ."

"We freeze," Kat said. "That's exactly it." She thought about this for a moment; it was such a relief for her to know she wasn't alone in this. "How do you deal with it?"

Monty smiled, reached into her pocket, and pulled out her tracker. "This helps."

"Your nautilus?" Kat asked, perplexed. "How?"

"If you press on it, you can feel the coil of the antenna," Monty said, running her thumb across the surface. "When I start to feel anxious, I reach into my pocket and trace the pattern with my thumb, and it helps me focus."

"And that does the trick?"

"Usually."

"What'd you use before you had cool spy gadgets?"

"Paper clips," Monty said with a chuckle. "But I like the nautilus because it doesn't snag on my clothes."

Kat took off her right shoe and pulled up the insole

to reveal her nautilus. She took it out and rubbed it between her thumb and her forefinger. It seemed to have an instant calming effect. "That's brilliant. Thank you."

"It's quite soothing, isn't it? I'm just sorry I didn't think to tell you about it sooner."

"Don't be," Kat said.

Neither spoke for a moment, and then Monty leaned in and whispered, "How do you think it's going with Robert and the rest of the team?"

Kat thought for a moment. "It's too soon to tell. Especially because we've been so busy."

"And what about you?" Monty asked. "What do you think about him joining us?"

As a rule, Kat didn't like change at all, which is why things had started off poorly between her and Brooklyn when Brooklyn joined the team. Since that had worked out well, Kat was trying to be more open-minded with Robert, but it wasn't easy for her.

"Too soon to tell for me as well," she answered. "Although we had a nice conversation about prime numbers."

"Oh, that sounds perfect," Monty said, smiling.

It didn't take Kat long to test out the nautilus. The scene inside the airport was anarchy, with lines of people everywhere and little indication of what they were for. First, they had to stand in one to get a visa, then they had to wait in another to get their passports stamped, and finally they had to wade through a sea of noise and people in the massive luggage hall.

"Who are we meeting?" Paris asked Mother as they worked their way through the crowds only to be greeted at the exit by an army of aggressive cab drivers swarming around them.

"Where you need to go?" one asked the team. "I take you there, no problem."

"My taxi is best in Cairo," offered another.

Mother ignored the cabbies and responded to Paris. "This was all sudden, so Tru arranged for transportation with someone at the embassy. They're not typically subtle, so with eight of us, I'm guessing we should be on the lookout for a pair of Range Rovers."

"Or that," Sydney said with a gulp as she pointed toward a beat-up microbus that looked like it had more than one hundred fifty thousand miles of wear and tear. It was a bit longer than a minivan and sported a red-and-blue paint job that had faded in the relentless Egyptian sun. On the side, it read CAIRO INTERNATIONAL STUDENT TOURS, and standing next to it was a bearded man in his late twenties holding a handwritten sign that read WELCOME, FARM.

"So, maybe not quite a Range Rover," Paris said.

"Can we all fit in that?" Rio asked. "Or are some of us supposed to run alongside it?"

"Hello, hello," the man said eagerly. He had a mop of curly black hair and an ever-present smile. "Welcome to Cairo. Is one of you Monty Alexander?"

"Actually, it's Alexandra Montgomery, but yes, I am," Monty replied. "And you are?"

"Marwen," said the man. "The British embassy hired me to give tours to your students." He looked at the team. "Hello, students!"

"Hello," they responded, not sure what to make of his enthusiasm.

"We are going to have so much fun learning about my country, but first, let us take care of the luggage." Marwen deftly climbed a metal ladder built onto the back of the microbus and was instantly in position on the roof. "Hand them to me, and I will tie them down."

"Will our bags be safe up there?" asked Sydney.

"Very safe," Marwen replied. "I am excellent with knots. I used to work at a marina and had to tie up many different boats."

There was a pause of uncertainty, but Mother realized there was no better option, so he handed up his bag and the others followed suit. Marwen skillfully tied the suitcases to a roof rack as everyone else squeezed into the microbus. There were three benches, and the kids piled into the rear two, while Monty and Mother took the one behind the driver's seat.

"The phrase 'packed like sardines' comes to mind," Paris whispered to Mother.

"That makes sense," Marwen said, overhearing as he climbed into the driver's seat. "Sardines are fish. Fish travel in schools. You are students. Students are also in schools."

Mother laughed and said, "I think this is going to be quite all right."

"Do you know where we're staying?" Monty asked.

"Oh yes, very nice," Marwen said. "I make all the arrangements."

In the back row, Sydney and Brooklyn shared a concerned look.

The bus belched to life, Marwen ground the engine into gear, and they wriggled their way into the bedlam that was Cairo traffic. With the push of a button, Egyptian music started to play, and he began his tour spiel. "Welcome to the city of a thousand minarets."

Kat slipped her hand into her pocket and began tracing the nautilus with her thumb as she looked out the window. There were no lanes marked on the road, which was clogged by an endless stream of cars, trucks, scooters, and microbuses inching along to a constant chorus of beeping horns. Sensory overload indeed.

Twenty minutes later, they arrived at the Grand Nile Hatshepsut, a two-star hotel that despite its name was not grand, nor did it overlook the Nile. Still, it was a definite upgrade from the bus that carried them there, and they checked into two pairs of connecting rooms that were comfortable and clean.

"What's our plan of action?" Paris asked as they all met up in the room shared by Mother and Robert.

"It's getting late, and most places will close soon, but I think we have time to check out the two addresses," Mother said.

"Which two addresses?" Robert asked, still not quite up to speed on things.

"The return address from the package that was sent to Imogen Gaisman," Rio said. "It could lead us to her or to whoever sent her the canopic jar."

"And the internet café where they tracked the IP

address with the ransom demands from the hacker," Brooklyn said. "Even though the raid was a bust, I'd like to see what's there."

"Do we let Marwen take us in the sardine can?" Sydney asked. She was standing on the balcony of the third-floor room, looking down below. "He's waiting on the street."

"I don't know if we can trust him," Paris said.

"He seems pretty harmless," Rio said, "and Tru's the one who hired him."

"Actually, someone at the embassy hired him," Kat said. "And I'm sure we seem pretty harmless to people too."

"Okay, let's split the difference," Mother suggested. "Monty, Paris, Sydney, and Brooklyn can go in the van. Tell him you want to visit a few places and throw the location of the café in there. Tell him you want to check on some email."

"And what will you do?" Sydney asked.

"Once you leave, Kat, Rio, Robert, and I will go on foot and find the address from the package. That's a juicy piece of information that only we know about, and I'd like to keep it that way for now."

"So we do all the walking, and they get to ride?" Rio complained.

"We've got Robert, and he knows his way around town," Mother said. He turned to Robert. "Isn't that right?"

"Absolutely," Robert answered.

"Rio, if you want to switch, I don't mind walking," Sydney offered, motivated more by her desire to keep an eye on Robert than her inclination to stroll through the city.

"No," he said. "Kat and I found the clue, and I want to see where it leads."

"Sounds like a plan," Monty said. "Afterward, we'll meet up back here and have some dinner while we figure out what we're going to do tomorrow."

As soon as the first group left on the microbus, Mother, Robert, Rio, and Kat began the twenty-minute walk to Zamalek, a well-to-do section of central Cairo located on a large island in the middle of the Nile. This area was popular with Europeans and home to dozens of embassies, not to mention one of the top football teams in Egypt's Premier League.

"This is the part of town where you think Imogen Gaisman is hiding?" Mother asked Robert as they walked along a busy street.

"Kat and I found it in a lot of the photographs on her

social media accounts," Robert said. "That makes sense because this area is popular with Westerners, and if she's hiding, she could go unnoticed here."

"We have to take into consideration that she may be hiding out in the very place where we're going," Mother pointed out.

"Here's a reminder of what she looks like," Kat said, showing the others a photograph on her phone of a woman in her forties with shoulder-length brown hair and light blue eyes. She had a confident look, like a newscaster.

"If you see her, don't react," Mother said. "Our goal is to let her lead us to the hackers. We don't want her to suspect that anyone is onto her."

"It should be the next left," Robert said, looking up from the map on his phone.

They turned the corner onto a quiet side street lined with small cafés and shops. They found the address over the door of a small grocery at the end of the block. The store occupied the ground level of a five-story building, and a doorway next to it led to the apartments in the top four levels.

"It came from one of those," Mother said, nodding at the balconies above the store. "Was there an apartment number on the address?"

"No name, no apartment," Kat said, "just the street address."

To blend in better while they staked out the building, they ordered sweet potatoes from a street vendor, who baked them in a portable wood-fired oven and served them with honey.

"This is so delicious," Rio said as he savored his first bite. "Who knew they sold these on the streets?"

"They're called batatas," Robert said. "You can get them all over town. When I lived here, this was what I had for dinner many times."

Rio shot him a look. "They're good, but I'm going to need a whole meal."

"Realize that in Egypt, the biggest meal is traditionally lunch," Robert explained, "with a lighter supper at night."

"Realize for me, all three meals are essential," Rio countered. "I don't play favorites."

"Just as a heads-up, Rio doesn't eat—he devours," Kat told Robert. "The most dangerous place to be is between him and his next meal."

Once they'd finished the sweet potatoes, Mother said, "I think we're going to need to go inside and look around. We can't really tell much from here."

"Just a second," Rio said. "Let me update my log." As he entered something into his phone, he explained to Robert, "I track and rate all the food I eat. All around the world. It's for an app I'm developing."

"Rio. He puts the app in appetite," Kat said, like it was an advertising slogan.

"That's good," Mother commented. "Have you been saving that one?"

"For about a week now," Kat admitted. "I didn't quite nail it like I wanted."

"Don't overthink it," Mother said. "It was good."

"What spices do you think he used on the batata?" Rio asked as he typed up his review. "There was salt and cumin, but also something else I can't quite put my finger on."

"Coriander," Robert offered.

"I think you're right," Rio said, impressed. "How'd you know that?"

"I've got taste buds, don't I?" Robert said. "And I've lived all over the world. I know my way around a kitchen."

For Rio, it was as if Robert had become an entirely different person. "Good to know."

They waited next to the entrance, and when someone

came out, Mother caught the door, and everyone stepped into the lobby. The interior was nice but showed its age with faded yellow paint on the wall and a patterned tile floor that looked like it had gone years without a good scrubbing. Two sets of mailboxes stuck out from the walls and had angled tops with slots for envelopes.

"There are names on most of these," Mother said. "Take pictures so we can check them out later."

Kat took out her phone and shot photos of the labels above the mailboxes, one of which caught her eye.

"Elbeheri," Kat said. "I wonder if that is Lina Elbeheri."

"You know someone who lives in Cairo?" Rio asked.

"No. But I know all about the *Wonderful Things* exhibit at the British Museum," Kat replied. "I studied it for the break-in. Imogen Gaisman coordinated with the Egyptian Museum here in Cairo, and the local curator was a woman named Lina Elbeheri."

"Interesting," Mother said.

"Yes, but we only have a last name to go on," Rio responded. "For all we know it's as common as Smith or Jones."

"I never met anyone with that name when I lived here," Robert said. He did a quick search on his phone.

"According to this site, there are only one hundred ninety-seven people named Elbeheri living in Egypt." He looked up at Kat. "That's one of those truncatable prime numbers, right?"

Kat beamed. "It is!" she said. "Left and right."

"Oh great," Rio joked. "We've got another one."

"If this is the Elbeheri who's a curator, she would have access to all sorts of artifacts," Mother said. "But why would she send one to Gaisman?"

"Maybe they're smuggling them," Robert offered.

"It could be as simple as that," Mother said. "But smuggling doesn't have anything to do with the cyber-attack. At least not that we know of. What's her apartment number?"

"Four B," Kat said.

"Let's check it out."

There was no elevator, so they took the stairs to the fourth floor and stepped out into a hallway with two apartments on each side and windows at both ends.

"We can't really blend in here, so let's make it quick," Mother said. "Rio, listen to see if there's anyone inside."

Rio pressed his ear against the door. "I don't hear anything," he said. "Do you want me to pick the lock?"

"Absolutely not," he said. "This is just a hunch on a

hunch; there's no need for us to get arrested on our first day in Egypt."

"Okay, you're the boss," Rio said. "But the lock looks pretty easy. We could be in and out in no time. Just ask Kat; I've got skills."

"And I've got sense," Mother said emphatically. "There's nothing else for us to find here; we should leave."

"Wait a second," Kat said. "What's he doing here?"

She was at the end of the hall, looking out the window toward the street on the other side of the building.

"Who?" asked Rio.

"Marwen and his bus," Kat answered.

They all crowded around the window and saw Marwen standing next to his battered microbus. It was parked down the block, close to the next corner.

"None of you told him the address, did you?" Mother asked.

"Absolutely not," Rio said.

"Then how did he find us?" asked Kat.

"More importantly," Mother said, "why?"

Zamalek

"SHOULDN'T HE STILL BE WITH THE others?" Rio asked as they looked down toward the street where Marwen was waiting with his bus.

"He must have finished with them and tracked us here," Kat said.

"How?" Robert asked. "Do you think he hacked our devices? The nautilus in my shoe?"

"If so, then I doubt he's *just* a tour guide," said Mother.

"Do you think the embassy's spying on us?" asked Rio.

"Could be," Mother said. "But I'm more worried that it could be the Mukhabarat, Egyptian intelligence."

"Well, he's out there, so he figured out something," Robert said.

"Let's give him a closer look," Mother said. "See if that tells us what he's up to."

He was on the next street, so they slipped out of the building and went to the corner to study him.

"He's not really trying to hide, is he?" Kat said. "He's just standing next to that bus, which is impossible to miss."

They were so focused on Marwen that they didn't notice the woman approaching them.

"Mother?"

They turned to see that it was Monty, who was with Brooklyn, Sydney, and Paris.

"What are you doing here?" everyone said in unison.

They were all so surprised and confused that it took them a few moments to figure out what had happened. The apartment building and the internet café were just down the street from each other.

"What are the odds?" Robert asked.

"There are no odds for this," Kat replied. "The package with the canopic jar was sent from the same block as the IP address of the ransom demand. They have to be connected."

"You're absolutely right," Mother said. "And that ties Imogen Gaisman to the cyberattack and moves her to the top of our suspect list."

"Are you sure about that?" Paris asked. "Does she have a good motive?"

"There are several possibilities," Kat said. "It could be money, but my guess is that it ties into her belief that the treasures in the British Museum should be returned to Egypt. She's extremely passionate about this."

"And what? She's going to use the money to buy back the artifacts?" Robert asked, not seeing how these went together.

"More likely as a negotiating technique," Mother said. "She raises the ransom demand high enough and then offers that, instead of money, the government can return the artifacts."

"That could definitely change some minds in Parliament," Monty offered.

"Speaking of Parliament, don't forget that Horus has hacked them, too," Brooklyn added. "With access to emails between members, they might be looking for dirt to use as blackmail."

"Rebellious, clever, and fearless. Sounds like her to me," Sydney said. "I can totally relate."

"But she doesn't have the tech background necessary for this, so there must be a partner," Mother said. "Maybe it's Elbeheri, although as a fellow Egyptologist, I don't know that she would have the expertise either."

"You're forgetting Umbra," Sydney said pointedly. "Never forget Umbra; they're always lurking nearby." She shot a side-eye at Robert.

"I'm happy to stake out the apartment," Paris said. "Gaisman may be hiding in there."

"I'll help," Robert offered. "Paris can show me the ropes, and I know the way back to the hotel from here."

"Count me in," Sydney said. "I love a good stakeout."

"Me too," Brooklyn said.

"Four people?" Rio said. "That's not a stakeout. It's a cookout. It doesn't take that many people to watch a building."

"Actually, I want to stay so I can do some work in the internet café," Brooklyn explained. "I can access Beny and cover my tracks from here much better than at the hotel."

Mother considered this for a moment. "Okay, new plan. Why don't we all spend the evening in Zamalek?

The weather's great, it's a lovely place to stroll, and there are plenty of places to eat. We can brainstorm during dinner, take turns staking out the apartment, and give Brooklyn all the time she needs on the computer."

"I'll tell Marwen to go, and we can just walk back to the hotel after we eat," Monty said.

"Speaking of Marwen, do we trust him?" Rio asked.

"I don't," Sydney said.

"Because . . . why?" Robert asked.

"Because I don't trust anybody until they prove to me that they deserve it," she said.

"I don't trust him either," Rio said. "Something about him seems suspicious."

"Let's see how he reacts," Monty said. "If he doesn't want to leave, that might be a sign that he's watching us."

"Or that he's conscientious about his job," Robert said.

Sydney gave him a look. "You sure are quick to defend him."

"It's all part of our secret Umbra plan," Robert said sarcastically. "Speak up, because he's listening on the microphone I have hidden on me."

Sydney's cheeks burned as the others chuckled.

Marwen left when asked, and the team found a

restaurant that specialized in Egyptian street food and had outdoor seating that let them keep an eye on the entrances to both the apartment and the café. The food was delicious, and they stuffed themselves with local favorites like *hawawshi*, *taameya*, and *molokheya*.

They didn't see any sign of Imogen Gaisman, but Brooklyn was able to make some progress with Beny. She was always careful when she activated the super-computer away from the FARM. She and Monty built a firewall with several layers of protection that required her to access a VPN and then perform a complex series of multi-factor identifications. This let her use his comput-ing power to look into Lina Elbeheri and to learn some information that she was excited to share at the table.

"Before we left, I initiated a search for anything and everything about Oriana Gutierrez," she said as she dipped a piece of pita into a bowl of hummus.

"And did Beny tell you that she was actually a hacker named Pluto?" Sydney asked jokingly.

"Not in so many words, but yes," Brooklyn said. "There's a ton of stuff about her launching her company, even some interviews she did with different tech web-sites."

"What's so suspicious about that?" Paris asked.

"They're all in the last five years, after Pluto dis-appeared," Brooklyn said. "If you go back any ear-lier, there's no indication that anyone named Oriana Gutierrez even existed. She just appeared out of nowhere. Not only that, but I couldn't find a single photo of her."

"Is there anything that connects her to Imogen Gaisman?" Monty asked.

"Nothing I can find," Brooklyn said. "Although we know that the company did work for the British Museum, so they might have met there."

"And we know that they're doing work now for the Grand Egyptian Museum," Kat said. "Which might connect her to Lina Elbeheri."

"Beny's looking into Elbeheri right now," Brooklyn said. "We should have a full rundown first thing in the morning."

"What about Jason Harper?" Sydney said. "Are we dropping him? Because I thought he was a strong sus-pect."

"I agree," Paris said. "He has motive and the techno-logical know-how. But I doubt we'll find anything about him in Cairo. From what we saw, it looked like his work was all based down around the Valley of the Kings."

"*Up* around the Valley of the Kings," said Robert.

Paris gave him a confused look. "Isn't it south of here?"

"Yes, but unlike most rivers, the Nile flows north," Robert explained. "So, even though it is south, that area is known as Upper Egypt, because it is up the river."

Rio laughed. "Just when I thought this couldn't get any more confusing."

As the others discussed the case, Mother slipped away to make a phone call to Tru. He was still angry at her, but he needed to update her on what had happened.

"Good evening, Mother, how are you?" Tru said when she answered.

He skipped the pleasantries and went straight to the information. "We've followed multiple leads and have some information to report."

"That's good to hear. I'm doing well too, thanks for asking."

He ignored this and kept going. "The package that was sent to Imogen Gaisman had a return address from the same neighborhood as the IP address that made the ransom demands."

"That is interesting," she said.

"We believe it may have been sent by a curator from

the Egyptian Museum named Lina Elbeheri. We're looking into her, but you should too."

"I'll put someone right on it," Tru replied. "I have news as well. I set up alerts for the names you gave me, and two have already gotten hits. You're not the only ones who headed to Cairo today. Oriana Gutierrez landed about an hour after you."

"She might be headed to the museum," Mother said. "She has a contract with them."

"And this afternoon, MI5 got a request from the Egyptian government. They want local authorities to execute a search on Imogen Gaisman's flat."

"Why?"

"According to the Ministry of Antiquities, she's suspected of trafficking in stolen artifacts," Tru said.

"That goes against everything I know about her," Mother said. "She has been vocal in her attempts to fight trafficking and repatriate antiquities to Egypt. She even got into a Twitter feud with some MPs about it."

"The Egyptians must think that it's all a cover," Tru answered.

"Did MI5 search the place?"

"No," she answered. "They asked for more information to justify it."

"Does MI5 suspect her in the cyberattack?"

"Not at all," Tru said. "I've kept that information in-house for the moment. I'll set up a meeting for you tomorrow morning. You can pay a visit to the ministry and meet with the investigator to follow up on the request. Maybe he knows something relevant without realizing it. Find out why he suspects her, and see if it somehow ties into the hack."

"Send me the details, and I'll be there."

There was an awkward pause until Tru asked, "How's Robert?"

"Fine," Mother said curtly.

"That's good," she replied. "Let me know if there's anything I can do."

Mother resisted the urge to say something snarky and just replied, "I'll report to you after the meeting."

The *Guardian*

IT WAS LATE AT NIGHT, AND THE AROMA of half-eaten fish and chips filled the air around Alice Natali's desk. She was still hard at work on her computer in the massive newsroom of the *Guardian*. As a journalist, it was her job to figure out if there was any connection between two recent incidents. First, the London Underground shut down for eleven minutes in what was thought to be a Bonfire Night prank. Then, a few days later, the NHS reported that the computer network for five local hospitals had crashed due to a software glitch.

As a science and technology reporter, Alice had written about both for the paper but couldn't shake the feeling that they were in some way related. There'd been no mention of a connection, but their press releases used similar language, and both events were being handled by the same incident response team from the National Cyber Security Centre.

Shouldn't each have its own team? she wondered. *Or is it just one case?*

Stumped, she'd posted a question on her social media accounts that afternoon, hoping some of the paper's readers might know something that could help.

> Does anyone think the stoppage on
> the Tube was more than just a Guy
> Fawkes prank?

She'd been deluged with responses, most of them tired conspiracy theories, but some showed promise, and it had taken her hours to sort through them all. One she found particularly interesting had come from someone named Horus.

> The subway stopped on Guy Fawkes,
> but the worm that shut it down was
> put there the day before. That's the
> anniversary that helps answer your
> question.

Her first thought was that the message was from an American. Brits didn't use the word "subway"; they called it the Tube or the Underground. "Subway" was an American word.

She was also intrigued by the mention of another anniversary, although she couldn't think of one for that date. She ran a search for "this day in history November fourth."

2008—Barack Obama was elected president of the United States

2001—The first *Harry Potter* movie premiered in London

1979—Militants seized the US embassy in Iran, taking fifty-two Americans hostage

1922—British Egyptologist Howard Carter discovered the entrance to King Tut's tomb

None of these seemed remotely related to her story, but she knew Horus was a name from Egyptian mythology and Howard Carter was from London, so she thought the Tut anniversary might be the one. She started digging around to see if she could find a connection between Carter and the hospital or the Underground.

Ding.

The sound signaled the arrival of an email. Natali was intrigued when she saw the subject line: "Horus strikes again."

The message inside was direct:

> First the Underground. Next the NHS.
> Now Parliament. There's a present
> waiting for you at the front desk.
>
> —Horus

Her pulse began to race. She hadn't mentioned any connection between the Underground and the NHS in her post, but now Horus had. Maybe she was onto something. She dialed the extension for the security desk in the main lobby.

"Hi, this is Alice Natali up in the newsroom," she said. "By any chance, has there been a package of some sort left for me?"

"Let me check," said the guard, who took about thirty seconds to sort through a stack of deliveries before getting back on the line. "I have an envelope that looks like it was dropped off a couple hours ago. Want me to have someone bring it up to you?"

"No, thanks, I'll get it," she said, not wanting to wait. "I need to stretch my legs anyway."

Although brightly lit during the day, the newsroom

was spooky at night, all darkness and shadows until each row of lights flickered to life as she walked through the room and set off the motion sensors.

"You must be Alice," the guard said as she approached the desk.

"Here's my badge so you don't have to take my word for it," she said, holding up her work ID. "You said you've got something for me?"

The legal-size envelope was thicker than she expected, which only fueled her sense of anticipation. She was so excited, she didn't even wait until she got back to the newsroom to open it. Instead, she pulled out the contents as she rode the elevator upstairs.

Inside was a stack of papers with a note on top that read:

> In honor of the thirty dynasties of ancient Egypt, here's the correspondence of thirty members of Parliament who don't believe artifacts should be returned to their homeland.

She noticed that the sender used the US spelling of "artifacts," rather than the British "artefacts." "Definitely American," she said.

Natali's pace quickened as she walked across the newsroom while flipping through the papers. Someone had apparently hacked the email server for Parliament and sent her a trove of correspondence. By the time she reached her desk, she thought there was a good chance that Horus was the real deal and had just dropped a major story into her lap.

She dug her mobile phone out of her pocket and placed a call.

"You do know what time it is?" her editor answered groggily.

"I think you're going to want to wake up for this."

Follow-the-Leader

AS THE SUN ROSE OVER CAIRO, PARIS and Sydney were walking back to Zamalek so they could stake out Lina Elbeheri's apartment again. Nothing had turned up the previous night, and with everyone's internal clocks still on Scotland time, they'd volunteered to go early and let the others sleep in, promising to call if there was anything worth reporting.

"It's beautiful," Paris said as the orange glow of light washed across the building facades.

"It would be even prettier if I wasn't half asleep," Sydney joked.

"Nothing like a brisk walk to get the blood flowing," he said, picking up the pace slightly.

The air was invigorating, and they were wide-awake by the time they reached Elbeheri's neighborhood and were greeted by the call to morning prayer playing over loudspeakers throughout the city. As many of Cairo's Muslims knelt and bowed toward Mecca, they tried not to draw any attention to themselves and found an out-of-the-way location at the corner where they could wait and watch the door to the apartment.

Over the next twenty minutes, the city came to life with activity, but there was still no sign of Elbeheri. Paris decided to bring up a subject that had been bothering him.

"Are you going to give him a break?"

"Who?" Sydney asked.

"You know who."

She realized what he was getting at and rolled her eyes. "Don't even go there. All I'm doing is looking out for this team."

"Except we're not just a team," Paris said. "We're a family, and Robert is part of it."

"He may be Mother's son, but that doesn't make him my brother."

"Actually, that's exactly what it makes him," Paris said. "You remember, there was a whole adoption ceremony and everything."

"Being related and being a family are not the same," she replied annoyed. "I specifically remember my relatives abandoning me back in Australia, so don't tell me that blood automatically makes you something it doesn't."

"And don't talk about your past like I don't know what it means to be forgotten and alone."

"Sorry," Sydney said, conceding the point.

"I know you're not big on trusting new people, but it doesn't seem like you're giving him any chance," Paris said. "You take every dig you can, but he seems good to me."

"Of course he does," she replied. "Spies are trained to make you like them. That's what human intelligence is all about."

"Except he hasn't had any spy training."

"You don't think so? He figured out how to find the canopic jar by comparing the picture to the podcast. That's not something you just know. That's something you're taught."

"Paranoid much?" Paris said. "Have you considered that maybe he's just smart? It's not that much of a stretch considering how bright his parents are."

"Tell me you're not the least bit suspicious. After years of hiding him in the far corners of the world, Clemmie just lets Robert come home out of the blue? And now we have this huge mission that happens to take place in Egypt. And it just happens that he used to live in Cairo, so he's instantly essential."

"And you think, what?" Paris asked. "Clemmie's using him to infiltrate us? That she's setting us up for some huge trap? Is that it?"

"Maybe. I don't know. But for the first time in my life, I actually have a family that I can count on, a family that I love, and I don't want anything to hurt it."

"Well, it would be great if you could open yourself up to the possibility that Robert might have a place in that family, because he's here to stay."

"If that's the case, then it doesn't matter what I think," Sydney said. "My problems are my own. It's not your job to worry about me."

"No, it's my job to worry about everyone. And I'll be honest, it can be exhausting."

"What are you talking about?"

Paris gave her a look like he couldn't believe he was having to explain himself. "Among us, I'm the one who has to keep things together. To make sure Kat doesn't disappear into herself or that Rio doesn't feel over-looked. To help Brooklyn find her place, and to keep you from . . ." He stopped for a moment and let out a sigh.

"Keep me from what?"

"From sabotaging something that you love and are trying to protect because you're the most pigheaded per-son I've ever met."

"That's all on you," Sydney said. "No one ever asked you to take care of us."

"I don't do it because I was asked; I do it because it needs to be done," he said. "I was there when each one of you arrived at the FARM. I saw the scared looks on your faces and promised myself that I would always be there for you. That I would help soften the blows and tend the bruises. And now I need to do it for Robert. He has that same scared look, and I'm his big brother. I'm going to help him and trust him until he gives me a reason not to do so. That's going to be hard enough as it is, so it would be great if you didn't go out of your way to make it more difficult."

Sydney stewed for a moment, unsure if she should

push back against what he'd said or acknowledge that some of it might have been true. She was still trying to decide when Lina Elbeheri exited the apartment building and started walking in the opposite direction.

"There she is," Paris said. "Time to play follow-the-leader."

"Okay, but we're not done with this discussion."

"I didn't think we were."

Even though they'd been in the middle of a charged conversation, they each flipped a mental switch and put their focus back on the task at hand. Surveillance was as much an art as a skill, and if they weren't perfectly in sync, they could easily mess it up. Their disagreement could wait.

"She's got a strong sense of fashion," Sydney observed as they took their place about ten meters behind Elbeheri on the busy sidewalk. It was important to stay close enough so that they could see her, but far enough away that she wouldn't notice them if she looked back or caught a reflection in a window.

"You can tell that from this far back?" Paris asked.

"I could tell that the moment I saw her hijab," Sydney responded. "The plum color is bold."

Sydney was passionate about fashion, and ever since

they'd landed, she'd made a point of studying the head coverings worn by many Egyptian women. Hijabs were part of Islamic culture and were greatly misunderstood by most people outside the faith. She liked the way that many women used theirs to show their personal style.

"Look how she drapes it, simple and elegant," Sydney continued. "And the color is striking against that mint green sweater."

"Maybe she knew she was going to be followed and wanted to look her best," Paris joked.

They'd done surveillance training together and had used it so many times in the field that tailing someone had become second nature. They instinctively knew what the other would do without having to say a word.

When Elbeheri turned a corner, they kept going straight and crossed the street in case she was suspicious and looked back to see who might be behind her. Paris pulled a baseball cap from his backpack and slipped it on to alter his appearance. Sydney made a point of looking down at her phone so she appeared to be a typical teenager.

At the next corner, they separated, with Sydney stopping to browse at a flower shop while Paris crossed the street and moved in closer behind Elbeheri. From that point, they rotated every two blocks, alternating who was closer and who was farther away. This lasted twenty minutes until Elbeheri stopped in front of a café.

Before entering, the woman nervously looked both ways to see if anyone was following her. This was a mistake because there was no way she could tell if anyone was, but her actions made it obvious she was hiding something.

"Now *that* was paranoid," Sydney quipped once she caught up with Paris across the street from the café.

"She's suspicious about something," Paris said. "Let's see what it is."

He started to cross the street, but she reached up and put a hand on his shoulder to stop him.

"First, I want to finish the discussion we were having about you looking out for everyone."

"Can't it wait?" he said, a bit peeved. "We're kind of busy."

"I've been thinking about it the whole time we were tailing her, and I don't want to leave it hanging."

"Okay. Let me have it."

He braced himself for her to unleash a stinging rebuke, but instead she just looked at him with appreciative eyes and said, "Thank you."

He was caught off guard and waited to make sure there was no follow-up. When there wasn't, he smiled sweetly and answered, "My pleasure."

And just like that, they went back to work.

It was an open-air café with a dozen tables, each only big enough for two or three people at the most. Even though she had her back to them, they recognized Lina Elbeheri's hijab and sweater. She sat at a table along the back wall and was placing an order. When the waiter moved away, they could see that another woman sat across from her. She wore a hoodie and oversize sunglasses and was keenly watching the door to see anyone who entered.

It was Imogen Gaisman.

Ministry of Antiquities

WHILE PARIS AND SYDNEY WERE ON stakeout at the coffee shop, Mother was at the Ministry of Antiquities meeting with an investigator named Ahmed Farouk. Tru had pulled some late-night strings at MI5 to arrange the get-together, and it was obvious the man wasn't expecting to have a visitor to start off his day. His office was cramped and messy, and he had to pull in a chair from the next room just so Mother had a place to sit.

"I apologize for the surroundings," Farouk said. "I

would have reserved a proper meeting room, but I only found out you were coming twenty minutes ago, and the rooms were already booked. Can I get you some tea?"

"No, thank you," Mother replied. "I had plenty this morning, right after my boss called to wake me up and tell me to be here first thing. It seems like both of us are catching up."

Mother did a quick scan of the room to get a read on Farouk. His desk was covered with stacks of over-stuffed files that seemed to have no real sense of order. There were several framed pictures atop a crowded bookcase, but none showed him with any family mem-bers. They were all photos of him on the job at impor-tant heritage sites.

"How long have you been at the embassy?" Farouk asked.

"Six months," answered Mother, whose cover story was that he worked in the embassy's legal affairs office. "I'm still learning my way around town."

"I hope you are here to tell me that your police are going to search Ms. Gaisman's flat."

"If you convince me there's significant cause, they'll do it today," Mother replied. "But we can't just break into someone's house on a hunch. Why do you suspect her?"

The investigator smiled. "This work is complicated. In this office we are overwhelmed trying to secure the return of thousands upon thousands of artifacts that have been stolen from our land. There are networks of traffickers throughout the world, and we have to protect the secret nature of information so that we don't alert any of them."

"I understand," Mother replied. "But if you want me to recommend that Scotland Yard executes this search, you'll have to give me something. What can you tell me without compromising the confidentiality of your sources?"

Farouk went to a file cabinet and pulled out another thick folder, which he plopped onto the middle of his desk. Mother wondered if that had been the one thing he'd done to prepare for the meeting: put the file back into the cabinet so that he could drop it dramatically. The investigator flipped through some pages and then looked up.

"Have you been to the GEM?"

"You mean to exercise?" Mother asked, confused.

"Not the *gymnasium*," the man said, laughing. "The GEM, the Grand Egyptian Museum."

Mother chuckled. "That makes more sense. I've been

meaning to go but haven't gotten the chance."

"You must. Let me know, and I will arrange a VIP tour for you. Our bureau runs it."

"I hear it's beautiful."

"Magnificent," Farouk said proudly. "As you might expect, it took years to complete, and there were some delays and difficulties. During that time, the staff had to undertake the complicated process of moving artifacts to the new facility from our older museum here in Cairo. As a result, some items are now unaccounted for and missing. We believe they have been smuggled out of the country."

"And you think they were smuggled by Ms. Gaisman?"

"With the help of a partner at the museum. There is someone on the staff who is sending them to her."

"Who's this person?" Mother asked, although he was confident the answer was Lina Elbeheri.

"I'm afraid I cannot share that piece of information."

"It sounds like she's the one you should be after," Mother said. "After all, she's the one stealing the artifacts."

"They are both criminals," Farouk said. "But we believe that Gaisman is the one who has established the network of people necessary to distribute the looted artifacts. She is the mastermind."

"I hope you understand my reluctance to simply believe this," Mother said. "She's a highly respected Egyptologist, and it's my understanding that she's outspoken in her efforts to protect antiquities. She's even clashed with members of our government about returning archaeological treasures from the British Museum."

"Her actions are a clever ploy for exactly this reason," Farouk said. "Her protests make you doubt her guilt, but I believe if you search her home, it will change your opinion."

"In order to get a warrant, you would need to provide us with a specific list of items that you believe may be in her possession."

"Which I have for you right here," the Egyptian man said happily as he handed Mother two pages from the file. Each had photos and descriptions of four missing artifacts. The canopic jar was listed on the top of the second page.

"And do you have any evidence that connects Ms. Gaisman to the disappearance of these objects?" Mother asked.

Farouk gave him a conspiratorial look and said, "I'm not supposed to show these, but I will do so."

From an envelope in the file, he pulled out some

photographs, which he handed to Mother.

"The first are pictures of her with the museum employee," he said as Mother looked at several photos of Gaisman with a woman Mother recognized as Elbeheri. "They were taken at the grand opening of an exhibit at your British Museum."

"They look rather innocent to me," Mother replied.

"These establish that they know each other," said the investigator. "The other pictures show the staffer with the canopic jar at the museum here in Cairo. This is the item we are most interested in."

In these, Elbeheri was wearing a lab coat and latex gloves as she worked with the jar in a sterilized conservation room.

"This jar is now missing, and we believe it was sent from Cairo to Ms. Gaisman in London."

"What makes you think that?" Mother asked.

Farouk grinned.

"We went through the records of the post office near her home and located this customs receipt," he said, handing over an evidence bag that held the receipt of the same shipping form that Kat and Rio had found in Gaisman's trash.

"What you have is interesting," Mother said. "But it's still circumstantial."

"There's one more picture," Farouk said smugly.

He placed the final photograph on the table as though he was playing the winning card in a poker game. The picture was taken from a distance, no doubt by a surveillance team, and showed Gaisman in an alley, meeting with a stocky man in a black coat.

"The man she is speaking to is Sallah el-Kahir, who has been known to help international clients smuggle antiquities out of Egypt."

Mother was impressed with what they had, even more so because he knew that the man was right and that the jar was in her flat. What he didn't know was how any of this connected to the cyberattack.

"Do you have copies of these for me?" Mother asked.

"No," said the man. "I'm not even supposed to show them to you. I just wanted to make sure you knew that we had solid evidence. Once we have proof that one of the items is in her apartment, we can go through with the arrest."

"As convincing as this may be, even if they find what you suspect, there's no guarantee my government will arrest Ms. Gaisman and send her to Egypt."

"That is where we are lucky," Farouk said. "She arrived at Cairo International Airport several days ago and is still in the country. The photograph with el-Kahir was taken yesterday. If you find the artifacts in her home, we will arrest her immediately."

This worried Mother because once she was arrested, there'd be no chance for British authorities to question her about the cyberattack. She'd be tied up in the Egyptian justice system.

"If your plan is to arrest her, then I would insist on being there when it happens. She is a British citizen, and for us to help you, I need to ensure that she is treated properly and make sure she is apprised of all her rights."

Farouk thought hard about this. "I will ask but can make no guarantees."

"Well, if your answer is no, then so is ours," Mother said. "It's a dealbreaker."

"Okay, then," said the investigator. "I will insist on your behalf. Is there anything else?"

"There is," Mother said. "We're interested in someone who I believe you've also been investigating."

"Who's that?" Farouk asked, surprised.

"He's a computer specialist named Jason Harper,"

Mother said. "He runs a company called KV66."

"I don't recognize his name or the company's," Farouk said. "Perhaps another investigator has looked into him, but I don't think it is anything."

"If you don't know who he is, how can you know whether there's anything to it?" Mother pressed.

"You're right," Farouk said. "I would look it up on the computer, but our system is almost as antiquated as the artifacts we protect. If you will excuse me for a moment, I will ask my colleague across the hall." He got up and walked to the door, but before leaving, he turned and asked, "Why would the British government be interested in an American computer specialist working in Egypt?"

Mother smiled and said, "That's funny. I didn't mention that he was American."

"Maybe I've heard the name in passing," Farouk admitted guiltily. "I'll be right back."

While the investigator was gone, Mother quickly rifled through Gaisman's file, taking pictures of the photographs he'd shown him and of as many pages as he could before Farouk returned. He was almost all the way through when he heard the office doorknob turning.

"I have found what you are looking for," Farouk said upon entering. He held up a slender file with a few pages in it. "You were right, Jason Harper was investigated, but he was cleared of any wrongdoing, and the case was closed."

25

Park the Bus

"NO MAMA TODAY?" MARWEN ASKED AS he expertly weaved through the morning traffic crossing the Qasr El Nil Bridge.

"Mama?" asked a confused Monty, who was riding in the passenger seat.

"Isn't that the man?"

"You mean Mother." Monty laughed. "He had to go to a meeting, but he'll join us later."

"A man named Mother," Marwen said, still trying to

make sense of it. "I am beginning to think that you are not like any group I have ever seen."

"Yeah," she replied. "We get that a lot."

Just then, Marwen sped up and zipped in between two cars in the next lane, then did a sudden turn, which had the tires screeching. He noticed Monty nervously clutching her armrest and said, "You told me it was essential to go fast."

"Yes," Monty said. "You're doing an excellent job. Where'd you learn to drive like this?"

"I used to work as a messenger," he said with a grin. "Fastest delivery service in all of Cairo."

They were rushing because Paris had sounded the alarm once he and Sydney spotted Imogen Gaisman. The fact that she might lead them to whoever was orchestrating the cyberattack meant the whole team needed to be on hand in order to run full-fledged surveillance.

"Up ahead, on the right," Brooklyn called out from the back. "There's Paris."

Paris was on the sidewalk, a block before the coffee shop, trying to discreetly attract the bus's attention with what could best be described as modified jazz hands. To keep from driving past him, Marwen had to veer in front of several lanes of traffic, eliciting a cascade of horns in the process. He defiantly made a parking spot where there wasn't one and shouted something in Arabic as he waved for cars to drive around him.

"What's the situation?" Monty asked as Paris stepped up to her window.

"Imogen Gaisman is still in the coffee shop with Lina Elbeheri, but I think they're wrapping up, so she should be on the go at any moment," Paris said. "Sydney's got a good vantage point and is ready to tail Gaisman, but we don't know how she got here. If she has a car or gets into a taxi, we'll lose her. That's why we called you."

"Good thinking," Monty said. "This may be our only chance at her, so we need to cover all scenarios. If she leaves on foot, we can run a leapfrog with you and Sydney starting behind her while the bus pulls ahead so we can get in position."

"That's good," Paris said. "We can use the comms to give you a heads-up if she turns or changes routes."

"Syd's sending a message," Brooklyn said.

Sydney had her right hand in a Y-shape with her middle fingers closed and her pinky and thumb extended. It was British Sign Language for "airplane," and she lifted it from the palm of her left hand into the air.

"Taking off," Monty said, interpreting. "Gaisman's on the move."

"That's her in the hoodie and glasses," Paris said as Imogen exited the coffee shop and started walking away from them down the sidewalk. "I better go and tell Sydney about the leapfrog."

"Paris, wait!"

They were all surprised to realize that Marwen was the one talking.

"I can't—" Paris started to say.

"You must," Marwen said. "Trust me. There are two types of police in Cairo. There are tourist police who have a special patch on their shoulders and are there to help you. Sometimes they will only do so if you give them money, but they are mostly harmless. But the regular police, you do not want to deal with them. They are not harmless, and those police are also interested in your woman in the hoodie."

"What do you mean?" Monty asked.

"You do not notice them, but I do," Marwen said. "Those two men are also following her." He pointed out a pair of men who had close-cropped hair and muscular builds. "And they are working together with the men in that car." He pointed to a black-and-white police car across the street.

"How can you tell?" Paris asked. "They're not in uniform."

"I have lived in Cairo my entire life," Marwen said. "I can tell."

Monty watched them for a moment and saw that the two men had begun to follow Gaisman. As they did, one turned toward the car and subtly signaled the driver.

"You're right," Monty said. "This is not good news."

"What about Sydney?" Paris asked.

"Call it off," Monty said. "We can't let them catch us."

"But—"

"Now."

Paris made an X with his index fingers and held them against his chest for Sydney to see. It was the signal for "cancel." She gave him a confused look, and he flashed the symbol again, this time more emphatically.

She nodded and looked down at her phone as Gaisman walked by because she wanted to make sure they didn't make eye contact. Once she'd passed, Sydney headed for the microbus.

"So, that's it?" Brooklyn said, disbelieving. "Paris

and Sydney actually find her in Cairo, and now we let her get away."

"If I may give a suggestion," Marwen said. "These men are very good at their job. They will follow her."

Paris smiled when he realized what Marwen was getting at. "So, we can follow them."

"Exactly," Marwen replied. "Their ego is such that they would never think someone could do that. Especially someone in a bus like mine."

"And you think you can?" Monty asked.

"Not to be immodest, but, as you said earlier, I am a very good driver."

Monty gave him a curious look and said, "I'm beginning to think you're not like any tour guide we've ever seen."

Marwen smiled and said, "I also get that a lot."

They watched as Gaisman hailed a taxi. When she did, the men in black scurried over to their police car and got in the backseat. Both vehicles pulled away and headed down the street.

"Hurry up," Monty called out to Sydney, who was nearing the bus. "She's leaving."

"I thought the tail was canceled," Sydney said, confused.

"It is, but it isn't," Paris replied, holding the door open for her. "Get in, and we'll explain."

For the next forty minutes, the three vehicles snaked their way in and out of the endless slog of Cairo traffic. Monty noticed that Marwen avoided many of the mistakes novices usually made when tailing a car. He checked his mirrors frequently to make sure no one was onto him, resisted the temptation to hurry through any intersections or run a red light in order to keep up, and maintained a safe distance behind the police car. She wondered if he'd learned all that as a messenger or if he had any specialized training and was maybe something more than he appeared.

"You really are good at this," Monty said.

"I am lucky that the traffic is slow," he said, downplaying it. "It makes it easier to follow without being seen."

"Tell that to the police car," Paris said. "They're right on the taxi's tail. It's like they want her to know they're following."

"They probably do," Marwen said. "They like to intimidate."

The pursuit slowed even more when they reached a web of narrow roads in the heart of old Cairo. Here cobblestone streets ran alongside ancient mosques and were lined with open-air shops and markets. They'd reached a point where it was faster to walk than drive.

"I think this woman you are following is very smart," Marwen said, watching the scene unfold before them. "Definitely smarter than the police realize."

"Why do you say that?" Paris asked.

"Because she is getting out at Khan el-Khalili."

"What's Khan el-Khalili?" Sydney asked.

"It's the souk," Robert said. "A gigantic marketplace and bazaar with endless rows of merchants calling out to you, trying to sell you everything from souvenirs to spice. It's total pandemonium."

"And the perfect place to lose a tail." Monty realized as she saw Gaisman get out of the taxi and head to the bazaar.

"It's like a maze in there," Robert said. "If she turns enough corners, she might be able to lose them."

"Which means she'll lose us, too," Kat said, defeated as the police officers got out of their car and followed on foot.

"What do we do?" Rio asked.

"I may have an idea," Robert said, excited. "We can park the bus."

"Park it where?" Marwen asked.

"No, not park *this* bus," Robert said, trying to explain. "It's a football term."

"Right, right," Paris said, getting it. "When you pull everyone back to guard the goal."

"*Catenaccio,*" Rio said with a sneer, using another term for the style of play. "It's how the Italians play. It's ugly football."

"It may be, but it's an effective defense," Robert countered.

"How does it relate to the fact that everyone we're following just disappeared into the market?" Sydney asked, unimpressed.

"Because if they go in, they have to come out," Robert said. "And we have enough defenders to block all the exits."

Political Affairs

IN ORDER TO MAINTAIN HIS COVER, Mother went directly to the British embassy when he left his meeting at the Ministry of Antiquities. This was essential in case anyone within the Egyptian government was keeping an eye on him. He didn't want to give them any reason to doubt that he actually did work in the legal affairs department. Especially because he wanted to make sure that he was included if they decided to arrest Imogen Gaisman. Soon after arriving in the reception area, he was greeted by a man in a blue suit.

"You must be the one they call Mother," said the man.

"I'm afraid so," Mother replied.

"I'm Devlin," replied the man. "I need you to come with me. There have been some developments."

Mother expected to meet with a lawyer so that he could brief them on his get-together with Farouk, but instead he was taken into the office of political affairs.

"What are we doing here?" Mother asked, a bit confused. "I thought this case was being handled by the legal department."

"The theft and trafficking of a canopic jar is a legal issue," Devlin explained, "but the return of Egyptian archaeological treasures from the UK is very much a political one."

Now Mother was even more confused.

"I'm sorry, have I missed something?"

The man explained that the *Guardian* had published an online story that included the hacked emails of thirty members of Parliament, all of whom had voted against sending artifacts back to Egypt.

"This is an incredibly sensitive issue to the Egyptian people," Devlin said. "This story is about to get very big here."

"I understand that," Mother said. "But what does

this have to do with me? My case only involves the theft of a single item."

"That all changed when they searched Imogen Gaisman's apartment."

"How could they do the search when I haven't even given them a report on what Farouk showed me?" Mother asked.

"They approved it soon after the story broke," explained the officer. "They knew there would be negative publicity, and the government didn't want to be seen dragging their feet on anything involving looted antiquities."

"And they found the canopic jar?" Mother asked.

"They found much more than that," replied Devlin.

This surprised Mother because Kat and Rio hadn't found anything other than the jar.

"What?"

"There was a thumb drive on her desk that contained all the emails and more," replied the man. "They think she's the one who fed the story to the *Guardian*."

27.

Khan el-Khalili

WHEN HE CAME TO GERMANY TO BE reunited with his father, Robert was only able to bring what fit into his backpack. The first thing he stuck into it was his Mo Salah jersey. Salah was his favorite player, and the shirt had been worn and washed so many times, the vibrant red of Liverpool FC had dulled and the numbers were peeling around the edges. He hadn't given it any thought when he slipped it on that morning, but now, in a way, it seemed appropriate because they were employing a football-inspired strategy. But the jersey had an unintended consequence that wasn't a good fit for spycraft. It attracted attention.

"Mo Salah, Mo Salah," cried a souvenir vendor. "Special price for you."

"Come here, Liverpool," shouted another. "I have everything you want."

Merchants had been hawking items in this market since medieval times, and their aggressive tactics were legendary as tourists and Egyptians alike flocked to the Khan to haggle over prices for everything from antique jewelry and replica King Tut masks to papyrus paintings and brass place settings.

Imogen Gaisman was somewhere inside the maze of open-air shops, trying to lose the policemen who were following her. Meanwhile, the City Spies had "parked the bus" and split into pairs positioned on each side of the market, hoping to catch her on the way out.

"Mo Salah," called another, raising his voice to be heard over the clamor. "Try to say yes."

"Why are they so obsessed with you?" asked Sydney, who was with Robert on a cobblestone alleyway called Al-Muski Street.

"Liverpool is extremely popular in Cairo," Robert

answered. "On Saturdays, cafés around town are jam-packed with people watching the games."

"Why do Egyptians care about an English team?" she asked, perplexed.

"Because of Mo Salah," he explained. "He's the greatest player in the history of this country. They call him 'the Egyptian King' and even have murals of him around the city."

"Salah, Salah," bellowed a jewelry merchant. "Lovely necklace for pretty girl."

"I bet you wore that on purpose," Sydney said, frustrated.

Robert had finally had enough.

"You're right," he said sarcastically. "That's how smart I am. I wore this because when I woke up this morning, I thought, 'I bet we're going to chase someone and wind up in the souk, so I should wear this jersey and get shouted at even more than usual.' It had absolutely nothing to do with the fact that I only own four shirts and didn't really have a lot of options."

For the second time that day, Sydney found herself on the wrong side of an argument, and it wasn't even lunchtime yet. She'd conceded the point earlier with Paris and offered a sort of apology, but she wasn't about to do the same for Robert. She may have overstepped, but she still didn't trust him.

"Forget it," she said. "Just keep an eye out for Gaisman."

She walked to the next alleyway so that she could get a better view, but in reality, she just wanted to clear her head.

Why do you do this? she asked herself. *Why do you* always *do this?*

On the opposite side of the bazaar, Paris was having a much better time. He and Rio were at an intersection of alleys, and to blend in, they were interacting with merchants. They'd already eaten delicious deep-fried pastries called *balah el sham*, and while Rio entered his reactions into his food log, Paris became distracted by a craftsman selling hand-carved chess sets. He was drawn to one in particular with Tut and Nefertiti as king and queen and obelisks for the rooks.

"You like?" asked the man.

"It's beautiful," Paris answered, catching himself and regretting it the moment the words came out of his mouth. The vendor pounced on the slightest show of interest.

"I make you good price." The man picked up the board and demonstrated how it folded. "The board closes like this and holds the pieces. Very easy for travel."

"Sorry, I don't want to buy anything; I just want to look."

"Why do you break my heart?" asked the man. "I can't feed my family with looking. I can only feed them with cooking." He flashed a toothy smile, and it was obvious this was a favorite line of his.

"I'm really sorry," Paris said, trying to walk away. "It was my mistake."

The merchant was relentless and followed Paris, taking him by the arm to keep him from getting away.

"Face it, mate, you're done for," Rio said with a snicker. "You better go ahead and buy it, or he'll never let you go."

"Okay, okay," Paris said, stopping. "How much?"

"That depends," said the man. "How much do you want to make me happy?"

Paris slumped, defeated, and Rio cackled in delight.

Brooklyn also made a purchase, but hers was done quickly with minimal haggling. She bought a snow globe that featured the sphinx and pyramids. She got it to add to her collection but also because she figured that once she bought something, the sales pitches would die down a little.

She smiled at Kat, who was about thirty meters away, at the end of a neighboring alley. Kat smiled back, hoping to hide the anxiety she was feeling. She did not like the Khan. At all.

She felt overwhelmed on every level, and no matter how hard she looked for order, she saw only chaos. She felt surrounded by souvenirs crowding every inch of shelf space and hanging from the ceiling above. When she took a deep breath to calm herself, she was overwhelmed by the competing aromas of a spice market and a café brewing Turkish coffee. All of it was accompanied by the noise of relentless selling and the jumble of incomprehensible snippets of conversation in foreign tongues.

Her heart raced, her breath shortened, and she felt nauseous. It was more than she could take. She reached into her pocket and tried tracing her thumb along the nautilus like Monty had told her. She looked up at a ceiling fan, hoping to find some peace in the steady rhythm of the blades. But then, out of the corner of her eye, she saw a face that she recognized and could not ignore.

Imogen Gaisman was five stalls ahead of her, trying to get lost in the crowd.

"I see her," Kat said into the comms, but her voice was too soft to be heard over the surrounding din.

"I see her," she tried again, a bit louder, but still no one responded.

This was the fear that had been gnawing at her since the break-in at the British Museum. Once again, she was frozen, but this time, she couldn't get the attention of the others, to cover for her.

"I see Imogen Gaisman."

There was still no response. She turned and saw that Brooklyn was looking in the opposite direction. Kat closed her eyes and forced herself to take a deep breath. She tried to remember a Motherism that could help.

Courage doesn't end or start; it's always there within your heart.

You can do this, she said to herself. *You can follow her.*

Her plan was to follow Imogen until she got her voice back or hopefully found a quieter location, where she could call the others. But to do that, she needed to go *into* the market, where things were even louder and more frenzied.

The nautilus was no longer in her pocket as she walked. She was now clutching it against her chest, squeezing it between her thumb and forefinger. She fought her instincts and forced herself to walk into the crowd. The steps were labored but got slightly easier as she went. Each one gave her confidence. She focused on the parallel rows of souvenirs lined on a shop table and the straight lines of the shelves in a jewelry market. These flashes of order helped calm her.

"I've got her," she said again into the comms.

"Is that you, Kat?" came the response from Monty.

Finally, somebody heard.

"Where are you?"

"Inside the bazaar," she replied. Then she realized she had no way to describe her precise location in the bazaar. "I don't know exactly where, but I'll follow her and tell you when I see a landmark."

She was just beginning to feel herself again, and then she noticed the policeman scanning faces in the crowd. It was obvious he hadn't spotted Gaisman yet, but he was getting close.

"One of the cops is closing in on her."

"Back away," Monty instructed. "We don't want them to see you."

Even though Monty was the one who had called it off, for Kat it still felt like a defeat.

"I have an idea."

"What?" Sydney asked over the comms.

"I can't talk," Kat said. "You're just going to have to trust me."

It felt good being the one to say that for a change, although she wasn't completely sure she could pull off her plan.

Gaisman was in front of a shop selling brightly colored fabrics and scarves. Kat moved in close and, while reaching for a scarf, "accidentally" bumped the Egyptologist.

She then held up a scarf, as if she were thinking of buying it, and stretched it out in a way that blocked the policeman's view of Gaisman until the woman reached the end of the alley and exited the souk.

She had no idea that Kat had come to her rescue, and she was completely unaware that Kat had slipped something into her hoodie.

"We're done here," Kat said into the comms, her voice proud and confident. "We can meet up at the microbus."

"What'd you do?" Sydney exclaimed, dying of curiosity.

"I put my nautilus into the pocket of her hoodie," Kat replied. "Now we can track her."

There were hoots and hollers over the comms, and despite all the commotion around her, Kat didn't mind the added noise one bit.

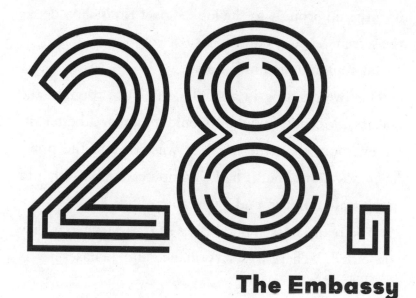

The Embassy

KAT WAS STILL BEAMING WITH PRIDE AS she followed Imogen Gaisman's movements on a computer screen. The red dot slowly made its way through the ancient part of the city, and judging by the speed, the woman was still on foot. People often have a sense of when they're being followed, and the team had decided to give her space in the hope that she might relax and lead them to whoever launched the cyberattack.

"If Horus is in Egypt, I bet she takes us right to him,"

Monty said proudly as she looked over Kat's shoulder at the screen. "And it's all because of you."

Kat couldn't contain her grin.

They were sitting in a small conference room at the embassy. Mother thought it would make for a better situation room than the hotel. It wasn't quite the priest hole back home, but it had a computer for Brooklyn to use, a wall monitor, and a whiteboard.

"You really missed out," Paris said to Mother as they got settled. "There was surveillance and a chase. It was nonstop action."

"Yet somehow, Paris managed to find time to buy a chess set," Rio said, setting off a wave of laughter.

"I haggled with him pretty good," Paris said in his defense.

"I saw the same set go for half the price a few minutes later," Rio said, deflating him.

"I did some haggling too," Mother said. "Trying to get information out of the Ministry of Antiquities."

"How'd it go?" Sydney asked.

"About as well for me as it did Paris, by the sound of things," he said dryly. "But I am so impressed with all of you. What you did was essential because it appears Gaisman is definitely working with Horus."

"How do you know that?" Sydney asked.

"They searched her flat this morning, and in addition to finding the missing canopic jar—"

"Which we'd already found," Rio boasted.

"They also found a thumb drive filled with documents from the Parliament hack."

"Which you did not find," Paris teased.

Kat turned her attention away from tracking Gaisman and asked, "Where did they find it in her flat?"

"On a desk in her home office," Mother answered.

Kat and Rio shared a look, and both shook their head.

"Impossible," Kat said.

"I was just kidding," Paris said. "Don't get defensive."

"There was nothing on that desk except for some papers and unopened mail," she answered.

"She's right," Rio said. "There's no way we missed it."

"Paris is right; you shouldn't take it personally," Mother said. "A thumb drive is easy to overlook."

"Yes, but we're trained MI6 agents," Kat said. "We don't overlook thumb drives."

"I can show you the pictures if you want," Rio said defiantly.

Rio quickly pulled up the pictures he'd taken at Gaisman's flat and AirDropped them to Mother so that he could put them on the monitor. They scanned through the photos and stopped when they reached one of her desk.

Rio nodded confidently as he said, "No thumb drive."

"You're right," Mother said.

"And she's been in Egypt since the time this picture was taken," Kat said. "So, who put it there?"

"That's an excellent question," Monty said.

"It is," Mother concurred. "Although it could simply be a case of miscommunication as to where the drive was found. I'll reach out to Tru and try to verify the information." He chewed on this for a moment before adding, "Either way, we know that the canopic jar was there when you searched and today when the police did. And that is why the Cairo police are planning to arrest Ms. Gaisman."

"I bet it's not the tourist police either," Rio said.

"It's essential that we figure out her connection to Horus before she's arrested," Mother said. "It will be impossible to interview her once she is."

"Let's say for a moment that there's an explanation for the thumb drive and it actually belongs to her," Brooklyn said. "There's nothing in her history to indicate that she has the technical skill to pull off a hack like this. That means she has to be working with someone."

"Yes, but who?" asked Kat.

"Umbra," said Sydney. "One of their cybergangs."

"Could be," said Monty. "But from what I've read, they don't bother with the grunt work. They come in with groups who've already laid the foundation and are about to strike. My guess is that there's a person between her and Umbra."

"Maybe she's working with one of the other suspects, like Pluto or Jason Harper," Paris said.

"Or both," offered Brooklyn, who was at the computer. "I've been focusing on access between the suspects and the server at the British Museum, but yesterday I had an idea and had Beny search through Pluto's files to see if she'd had any separate contact with Gaisman, Elbeheri, or Harper."

"And?" Sydney said hopefully.

"She and Harper emailed back and forth a few times."

"By any chance did the emails mention a nefarious plot to attack the British government?" Rio said.

"I wish. They met through their work with the museum and were discussing hardware that Harper was looking to buy for his company," Brooklyn said. "But it shows that they know each other. So, they could be in it together."

"Maybe they could work together, but I don't buy Imogen working with Jason Harper," Sydney said. "She's the one who got him fired by the British Museum."

"But Pluto makes sense," Rio said. "She's the only suspect with a criminal background, and Tru told Mother she just arrived in Cairo."

"You know, just because she has a criminal past doesn't mean she's still a criminal," Brooklyn protested. "People change."

Rio smirked, "Yeah, but imagine how much change she'll have if she gets a hundred mil in crypto."

"So, we have five people of interest," Mother said as he started writing names on a dry-erase board. "If Imogen's working with someone, it's probably one of these."

He wrote five names on the board: "Gaisman," "Pluto," "Harper," "Elbeheri," and "el-Kahir."

Robert asked, "Who's el-Kahir?"

"Sallah el-Kahir," Mother answered. "A local criminal who's trafficked stolen antiquities and, according to the conversation I just had with the legal affairs team, has been suspected in cases of identity theft and cybercrime."

"That fits," Paris said, "but what connection does he have with Gaisman?"

Mother clicked an image onto the monitor. It was the one he took of the photo on Farouk's desk.

"This was Gaisman and el-Kahir yesterday," Mother said.

"Telephoto lens," Paris said as he got up for a closer look. "I bet it was taken by those cops who were following her."

"So, what comes next?" Sydney asked. "How do we investigate them?"

"Great question," said Mother. He turned to Monty and asked, "What do you think of our bus driver, Marwen?"

Monty smiled. "He's not like any tour guide I've ever met."

"Do you think he's spying on us?" Mother asked.

"I don't think so," Monty answered. "I got the sense that he hated the police officers who were trailing Gaisman, not that they worked together."

"Do you think he can be trusted to drive you along the route that Gaisman's taken since Kat started tracking her?" Mother asked.

"I think it's a risk, but one worth taking," Monty said. "He knows the city inside out and seems to be on our side."

"Then we'll trust your gut," Mother said. "I want Brooklyn with me, and everybody else on the bus tracing Imogen's footsteps to see if you can find any hint of our other suspects."

"What are we doing?" Brooklyn asked.

"I've arranged for a father-daughter behind-the-scenes tour of the Grand Egyptian Museum," Mother said. "We'll visit the treasures of King Tut's tomb, see astonishing works of art, and, while we're at it, hack into their computer system to look for traces of Jason Harper and Pluto." He paused for a moment and made a comical face. "Actually, you'll be doing that last one on your own. I'll just be a lookout."

"I like it!"

As everyone got up to leave, Robert noticed something about the photograph on the monitor and went over to take a closer look. His interest had nothing to do with the photo of Gaisman and el-Kahir. Instead, he was focused on the portion of Farouk's messy desk visible in the picture.

That's where he saw a pen that was unmistakable.

It was a scriptex just like his.

Farouk was working with Umbra.

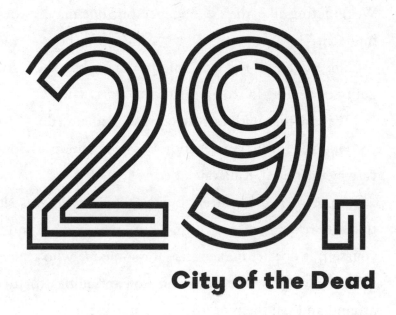

City of the Dead

ROBERT SAT IN THE BACK OF THE microbus and ran through the situation in his head. He was certain Ahmed Farouk was working with Umbra, but he didn't know how it related to this case. This mission. He just knew that if he told everyone *how* he knew, it could ruin his chance to truly become part of this family, and that wasn't a risk he was willing to take.

"What if Kat and Rio are right?" he asked Paris, who was sitting next to him. "What if someone planted that drive in Gaisman's flat to make her look guilty?

We're acting like she's a bad person, but maybe she's innocent."

"She might be innocent of the hack, but she's still guilty of dealing in stolen artifacts," Paris said.

"We saw that with our own eyes," Rio added.

"Plus, the Ministry of Antiquities has built up a strong case against her," Kat concluded.

Robert turned his attention to Sydney, who was sitting one row in front of him. "But, Sydney, you said it yourself. It doesn't make sense for someone who's spent years fighting for the protection of antiquities to turn around and sell them on the black market."

"It may not make sense," Sydney said. "But neither does the idea that she is being framed for two separate crimes—a cyberattack and trafficking. Don't forget, she deposited a lot of money in her bank account last week and rushed down here in a hurry. She's up to something."

"And if she believes in protecting antiquities," Rio said, "why would she meet with a criminal like el-Kahir, who's known to have trafficked them?"

Robert couldn't believe it. "I thought you agreed with me that she was framed."

"I can't explain how the thumb drive got into her apartment, but that doesn't change the evidence against her from the Ministry of Antiquities," Rio answered. "Or do you think they're the ones trying to frame her?"

He said it like a joke, but Robert wanted to scream that that was exactly what he thought. If Umbra had infiltrated the ministry, they were more than capable of framing her.

"I think we should park here, close to the Khan," Marwen said as he pulled over. "We cannot drive on most of the roads she took. She was on foot, and we will have to be as well." He turned to Monty. "I will come to help you find the way and to translate. In this part of the city, most of the people do not speak English."

"Thank you," said Monty. As they got out of the bus, she added, "Kat, let's start where you saw her last."

Kat checked the tracker on her phone and then looked up toward the Khan to orient herself. "Follow me, everybody."

GRAND EGYPTIAN MUSEUM

While the others walked the ancient streets of Old Cairo, Mother and Brooklyn arrived at the country's newest landmark, the gleaming Grand Egyptian Museum. Known as the GEM, the mammoth structure was one of the world's largest museums and an architectural wonder designed to complement the Pyramids of Giza, which it overlooked.

"Look at those," Mother said, gazing at the pyramids. "They really take your breath away, don't they?"

"I've never seen anything like them," Brooklyn marveled.

"And then there's this magnificent building," he said, turning to the museum. "Over four thousand years in architectural history right next door to each other."

After passing through security, they were greeted by Salma, a charming tour guide who dropped facts and figures with ease.

"This is Rameses II," she said as they approached a towering statue that was the centerpiece of the entrance. "He is thirty-two hundred years old, is made of red granite, stands eleven meters tall, and weighs eighty-three tons."

"He's a big boy," Brooklyn joked.

"A very big boy," Salma said to Brooklyn. "Now, here's my question for you. How do you think they got him into the museum?"

Brooklyn scanned the room for clues. The statue was much too big to fit through any of the doors or windows, and there was no way it could be taken apart. She looked up at the glass-and-steel ceiling and considered it, but didn't think a helicopter could lift and lower eighty-three tons. She gave Mother a look to see if he knew, but he just shrugged.

"I'm stumped," Brooklyn said. "How'd they do it?"

"They didn't," Salma answered.

"What do you mean?" Brooklyn asked, confused.

"They brought it here first and built the museum around it."

Brooklyn and Mother laughed.

"Okay," Brooklyn said. "That's brilliant."

Salma smiled. "You think that is brilliant, wait until you see what else we have."

AL-AZHAR PARK

The team had retraced Imogen Gaisman's trail starting at the Khan el-Khalili and then winding through the narrow pathways of the old city. She'd made three stops along the way, spending eight minutes at a women's clothing store, twenty-three at a small restaurant, and another three in Al-Azhar Park, which sat next to the Citadel of Cairo.

The sprawling park was an oasis for this densely

crowded city. With a modern design inspired by traditional Islamic gardens, it featured lush greenery, picturesque fountains, and palm-lined walkways. According to the tracking app on Kat's phone, Gaisman stopped at a café with a patio on the edge of the park.

"Here," Kat said, looking around for anything noteworthy. "She spent three minutes right around here."

"Why a café?" Sydney asked. "The other stops make sense. She buys a new outfit so the police won't recognize her, and she gets something to eat. But why here? Did she get hungry again?"

"It happens," said Rio.

"To meet somebody?" Kat suggested.

"I like that idea," Monty said.

"The loo," said Paris, pointing at a public restroom next to café. "When you have to go, you have to go."

"Okay, she stops here, and where to next?" Sydney asked. "Is she on the move?"

"No. She's been in the same spot for a while now."

"Maybe she's meeting someone," Rio suggested.

Monty nodded and said, "I think it's time we stop tracing where she's been and put our eyes on where she is."

"Across that street," Kat said, leading the way. As the others followed, Monty noticed that Robert was lagging behind and had a troubled look. She walked alongside him and asked, "Everything okay?"

"Fine," he said unconvincingly.

Monty waited in case he wanted to add something, but when he didn't, she commented, "You don't look like you're fine. You look like something's bothering you."

"Just the case," he said. "It's all still kind of new to me, and I'm trying to figure it out."

"It's a lot to get used to," Monty said kindly. "I know we just met, but if you ever need someone to talk to, I'm a good listener."

"Thanks. I appreciate that."

They followed Kat to a setting that was a jarring contrast to the manicured lawns and sparkling fountains of Al-Azhar Park. Stretching out in front them for miles was a series of cemeteries filled with crumbling tombs and crypts. The dirt roads that connected them were littered with trash, and there were people walking along them as if they lived among the tombs.

"She's in there?" Rio asked, surprise in his voice.

"Yes," answered Kat.

"What is this place?" Sydney asked.

Marwen looked out at the grim landscape and said, "The essence of sadness. This is the City of the Dead."

Brooklyn and Mother's tour had brought them to the GEM's King Tut exhibit, the first time since they'd been unearthed a century earlier that all of Tutankhamen's treasures had been brought together.

As they waited in a line to look at the boy king's famous death mask, Brooklyn asked, "Do you think it's true that people don't change?"

"In what way?" Mother asked.

"Once a criminal, always a criminal," she said. "Whenever we discuss Pluto, someone always mentions that since she was a hacker, she can't be trusted. It's like the fact that she hasn't done anything illegal for years just means she's waiting for the opportunity to strike."

Mother saw where this was headed. "You're not a criminal, Brooklyn. You never were."

"Have you forgotten where we first met?" she said. "I'd been arrested and was about to be sentenced to juvenile detention."

"Which would've been a tremendous miscarriage of justice," Mother said. "We both know that. As to your question, I believe people can change."

"I hope so," Brooklyn said. "I know the mission is the mission and we follow it wherever it leads, but I don't want Pluto to be guilty. I met her, and she seemed cool. She started up a company for women, and that's awesome. If she's really a criminal, it will break my heart."

Mother put his arm around her shoulder and gave her a loving squeeze. They were quiet for a moment until they reached the mask, twenty-four pounds of radiant gold that was mesmerizing.

"It's the most beautiful thing I've ever seen," Brooklyn said.

"It is something, isn't it?"

Brooklyn looked over her shoulder to make sure Salma was too far away to hear, and then said to Mother, "I love seeing all this, but aren't we supposed to be working the case?"

"We have to be somewhat sly about such things," Mother said. "But I think it's time."

"What did you think?" Salma asked when they rejoined her.

"Spectacular! Amazing! Words don't do it justice," Mother said.

"It is the jewel of our country."

"And what a fitting museum you've built for it," Mother said. "Speaking of that, Mr. Farouk told me that we would get a peek behind the scenes, as it were."

"Absolutely," she said. "I will take you to our conservation center. It is also spectacular and amazing."

"I can't wait to see it," Mother said.

CITY OF THE DEAD

Kat checked the tracker on her phone as she led the team along a dusty road in the City of the Dead. It was lined with an endless row of small concrete and brick buildings that looked like squat houses.

"These are crypts?" Sydney asked Marwen.

"They are called *hawshes*," he replied, "and they hold the tombs of the family going back for generations."

Paris looked into the doorway of one and could see a tangle of electrical cords powering small appliances inside. "Apparently, not just the tombs."

"Am I the only one creeped out by the idea of living in a house with all my dead ancestors?" Brooklyn asked.

"Not the only one," Rio replied. "I'm having flash-backs of being locked in that sarcophagus."

"I don't know," Kat said. "It's quiet and peaceful."

Rio was walking next to Robert and asked him, "Have you been here before?"

"No," Robert said. "I'd heard about it but stayed away."

"I can see why," Rio replied as they passed a *hawsh* with fractured walls, its corner crumbled into a pile of concrete. "This reminds me of the favelas back in Brazil. I swore I'd never step foot in them again."

"Officially, it's called the Cairo Necropolis," Sydney said, reading from an article she'd pulled up on her phone. "It's four miles long, and there and more than a million people live here."

"More than a million?" Monty asked Marwen. "Is that true?"

"Sadly, it is."

"Kat, how close are we?" Paris asked.

"It's just up ahead," she answered.

They reached a small building, no bigger than a single room, with a makeshift roof of plywood and plastic. A single orange extension cord ran to a neighboring building.

They exchanged uncertain looks and were trying to figure out what to do next when an Egyptian girl came out of the building and looked at them accusingly. She said something in Arabic, and Marwen answered.

They were still talking when Kat noticed something about the girl and sighed.

"The hoodie," she said. "She's wearing Imogen's hoodie."

When the team broke into the British Museum, they snuck in through the basement, and Brooklyn had seen firsthand how the conservation labs were cramped and squeezed in wherever a bit of space could be found in the grand but aging building. That was not the case in the GEM's state-of-the-art conservation center, a separate building next to the museum.

For their behind-the-scenes tour, Salma had taken them into a facility where the hallways were oversize, so that even some of the largest artifacts could be brought in without too much trouble. She took them into a giant lab where scientists and restorers were using the latest technology to study and repair a wooden chariot from Tutankhamen's tomb.

But of all the amazing technology in the building, the one that most excited Brooklyn was a common desktop computer she noticed as they passed an empty office. Somewhere in this building was the server that ran everything in both the conservation center and the museum, and this computer was her way to access it. It was the candy store that would help her rob the bank.

She made a mental note of a nearby restroom, and a few minutes later, when they reached a room where preservationists were repairing a papyrus document, she asked Salma, "Is there a bathroom I can use?"

"Of course," said the tour guide. "There is one just down the hall."

Brooklyn scurried toward the bathroom, and Mother distracted Salma with questions about the papyrus project.

Brooklyn slipped into the office and went straight to work. She opened a connection to Beny and initiated two searches—one for any reference to KV66 or Jason Harper and the other for all things related to Pluto and her company.

Then she noticed something on the desk—a New York Yankees cap. Pluto was a Yankees fan and had been wearing a jersey when Brooklyn met her. Had she come here to work? Was that why she was in Cairo?

KHAN EL-KHALILI

It was a long walk back to the microbus, and the team was deflated after the near miss in the City of the Dead. Marwen talked to the girl who was wearing the hoodie and said she'd found it discarded in the public restroom at Al-Azhar Park. Imogen had gone there to change into her new outfit, discarding the tracker in the process.

They were just about to get back on the bus when

Mother called Monty. She stepped away from the others for some privacy.

"How'd it go?" Mother asked.

"It started off promising but didn't end well," Monty said. "Imogen Gaisman ditched her hoodie, so we can't track her anymore. We have no idea where she is."

"I do," Mother said, to her surprise. "Or at least I know where she'll be in a couple hours."

"Where?"

"The pyramids," he answered. "I just got a call from Ahmed Farouk at the Ministry of Antiquities. They've learned that Gaisman is meeting one of her black-market contacts there, and they plan to arrest her. They're hoping they'll catch her red-handed with some other artifact to go along with the one found in her flat."

"And you're going to be there?" Monty asked.

"The police are going to let me be on hand as an observer," he said.

"Once she's arrested, she won't be able to lead us to the hackers."

"Which is why I need you to get to Giza as quick as you can. Tell Marwen to take you to the parking lot of the Grand Egyptian Museum. I've got a plan."

30

Giza

KAT STOOD AT THE BASE OF THE PYRAMID
of Khufu and looked up at fifty stories of stone. It made
her feel very small and insignificant. Which is exactly
what Khufu would have wanted. The pharaoh's tomb,
which for thousands of years was the tallest structure
on earth, was meant to intimidate and had done exactly
that for countless millions over four millennia.

For some, the Great Pyramid conjured notions of dar-
ing adventures and deadly curses.

Others believed that it could only have been

constructed by so-called ancient astronauts from distant planets.

Kat knew better. That's why she didn't mind feeling small. She reveled in it. To her, the pyramid wasn't a tribute to the second king of the fourth dynasty. It was humankind's greatest monument to math. A flawless geometric masterpiece built with two and a half million limestone blocks, weighing an average of two and a half tons each, arranged with such precision that its corners were within four inches of being perfectly square.

For the first time since she'd landed in Egypt, Kat had found order.

"Scared?" asked Rio.

"About what?" she said nonchalantly, as if she didn't know exactly what he meant.

"You're the key to this whole thing working," he answered. "It's a critical mission. Everybody is going to be in play, including Mother and Monty, and you're the alpha. That's big."

"No," Kat said, looking up at the pyramid. "*That's* big. This is small, and small doesn't scare me."

The oldest of the Seven Wonders of the Ancient World, and the only one still standing, Khufu's was the largest of three pyramids built on the Giza Plateau. Along with the Great Sphinx, they formed one of the most famous panoramas in history. And they were the setting for Mother's plan to have Imogen Gaisman lead them to whoever was responsible for the cyberattack.

"Two teams of three," he'd told them an hour earlier when he laid it out for everyone in the GEM's parking lot. "You're going to be positioned at different locations around the pyramid complex, looking for any of our suspects. The police are focused on Gaisman, because she's dealing in looted antiquities. We're interested in who she's meeting, because it may well be the person behind the hack."

"What are the teams?" Rio asked.

"You're on one with Monty and Brooklyn. The other one's Paris, Sydney, and Robert. I'll be tagging along with the police, and Kat will be watching over it all and calling the shots."

Kat was surprised that she was still in the alpha role. She felt like she'd let everyone down with some mistakes at the British Museum, but she was determined to rise to the occasion. "Where do you want me positioned?"

"There's a spot in front of the sphinx that overlooks

everything," Mother said. "We'll call it the Kat-bird seat, and that's where you're going to set up. For the others, I want you to think football. The pyramids are the goal, and we're going to park the bus and flood the defensive end."

The others shared an incredulous look.

"You did not just say that," Paris said.

"What? Why?"

"That's exactly the strategy Robert came up with at the Khan this morning," Monty explained.

Mother looked at Robert and beamed. "Great minds. Football strategy must be in the genetics."

It was the first time Robert had smiled since seeing the scriptex in the picture of Farouk's desk. It was a hint that he and his dad really were connected.

"To continue with the football metaphor," Kat said, "why am I the manager? Shouldn't it be you? You're the grown-up, and this is your plan."

"I'll be radio silent because I'll be undercover with the police," Mother said. "As for the other grown-up, when I asked her, she recommended you."

Kat looked at Monty, who smiled and said, "It's going to be a zoo with tourists everywhere, and you're the best at finding order in chaos. You'll be brilliant."

"Well, okay, then," Sydney said enthusiastically. "We're all ready except for one thing."

Everyone looked at Kat and waited.

"This operation is hot. We are a go."

Light Show

"I CAN'T BELIEVE MY EYES," RIO SAID. "Every picture I've ever seen of the pyramids must have been taken from this angle. My mind is blown!"

Rio's reaction was common among first-time visitors to Giza. That's because virtually all photographs of the legendary monuments were taken looking west to show only the sphinx and pyramids with nothing around them except for the Sahara stretching beyond the horizon. These made it look as if they stood alone in a vast desert. But a picture taken in the opposite direction would reveal they were actually on the edge of urban sprawl.

"There's a KFC right across the street," Rio said in disbelief. "You know how important I think it is to have food nearby, but even I think that's sacrilegious."

"Maybe here it stands for Khufu Fried Chicken," Brooklyn joked.

There was laughter among the others listening in on the comms, and Paris added, "And your fizzy drink comes in a canopic jar with free refills."

"Okay, gross," Sydney replied. "That image is going to stick."

"Quiet on the comms," Kat said. "If you don't, we're going to be subjected to a Motherism reminding us to focus."

"Mother can't say a word," Sydney said. "He's under-cover with the police. All he can do is listen."

"Then I'll do it for him," Paris interjected. He adopted a humorous impression of Mother and said, *"Don't joke about fizzy drinks; just be silent like the sphinx."*

There was more laughter until Mother surprised them by joining the conversation. "That's actually not bad. A little forced, but a solid effort."

"I thought you couldn't talk," Paris said, laughing.

"Obviously," Mother said, "I was able to step away to

make a fake phone call, and I wanted to check on everyone. I like that you're relaxed. That's good. A tense spy makes mistakes. But don't get too loose. There's a lot at stake, and according to the police, Imogen's meeting is going to take place during the first show."

"That's great intel," Kat said, taking charge. "Open eyes and open minds, everyone. The show starts in thirty minutes. It's game time."

Once the sun set, the area around the pyramids was barricaded off, and visitors could no longer walk up to them. At night, tourists lined up in front of the Great Sphinx to watch the Sound and Light Show, a forty-five-minute production that used music, lights, and lasers that were projected onto the pyramids to tell the story of the monuments and ancient Egypt. It was corny, and more than a little outdated from a technical standpoint, but the pyramids looked magnificent lit up at night, and the darkness at street level gave Imogen Gaisman the perfect cover for her secret meeting.

"Robert, you doing okay?" Monty asked. "Your comms working?"

She'd noticed that he hadn't spoken earlier when the others were joking.

"I'm fine," he said tersely.

Unlike the others, Robert was far from relaxed. He'd been on edge since the moment he realized Ahmed Farouk was with Umbra. He was convinced that meant Imogen Gaisman was being set up, but he hadn't said anything because he hoped that somehow the problem would take care of itself. That they'd figure out she was innocent some other way. But that hadn't happened, and to make matters worse, Farouk was now with his father.

"Dad, can I talk to you?" Robert said into the comms. "Just you and me?"

Mother was sitting in a police car with Farouk and couldn't respond with anything other than a cough.

"He can't answer," Paris answered. "He's probably with Farouk. Can I help?"

"Never mind," said Robert. "It's nothing."

Sydney was the closest to him, so she came over and muted her comms so they could talk one-on-one. "What's wrong?"

Of all people, Sydney was not the one he wanted helping him.

"You can mute your comms and just tell me," Sydney said.

"Like you want to help me."

"I do want to help," she told him. "We're family.

Families can fight, but they're there when you need them."

Robert felt overwhelmed, as if he might cry. "I don't know what to do."

"About what?"

"Ahmed Farouk."

"What about him?"

Robert closed his eyes and blurted, "He's Umbra, which means all of this could be a lie and my dad could be in real danger."

"What makes you think that?"

"I don't think it. I know it."

"How?"

On his phone, Robert pulled up the picture that showed Farouk's desk. He enlarged it to zoom in on the scriptex. "You see that?"

"It's a pen. So what?"

"It's not a pen. It's called a scriptex," said Robert. "It's a device used to transmit secret messages, and the only people who have one are connected to Umbra."

Sydney shook her head, still confused. "How do you know that?"

He looked at her and struggled to say it. "Because I have one too."

He pulled his scriptex out of his pocket and showed it to Sydney, whose eyes opened wide in disbelief. This confirmed her greatest fears about him.

"You're Umbra!" she raged.

"I just use it to contact my mother and my sister."

"Have you done that during this mission?"

He nodded remorsefully. "To let them know I was okay."

"Sydney, Robert, what's going on with you two?" Kat asked. "You're supposed to be spread apart."

From her vantage point, Kat could see the viewing area, but because it was dark and crowded, she was following everyone's locations on a tablet using the trackers they carried. Sydney's green dot and Robert's purple one were clumped together.

"We just need a second," Sydney responded as she tried to wrap her brain around the situation.

"A second's all you've got because the show's starting now."

Everything went dark, and theatrical music began playing over loudspeakers. A deep baritone voice soon joined and began narrating the light show. "You have come tonight to the most fabulous and celebrated place in the world. Here on the plateau of Giza stand together the mightiest of human achievements." A blue light came on dramatically and illuminated the Great Sphinx.

Meanwhile, Sydney was trying process what Robert had told her.

"If Farouk is Umbra, then . . ."

"All of this is a setup," Robert said. "Umbra put the thumb drive on Gaisman's desk, and Umbra sent the canopic jar to her flat. I've been thinking through it all day, and that's the only explanation."

She looked at him, exasperated, and asked, "Are you part of the setup? Are you working for Umbra?"

"No!" Robert said. "I told you; I just use it to talk to my mum and sister. I needed a way to reach them in case this didn't work out. And that's what I told them, that it wasn't working out."

"Why'd you say that?"

"In the convent, I heard you tell Paris that I couldn't be trusted," he said. "So how could I tell you about this?"

"You've used way more than a second," Kat said. "I need you two spread out and looking for our suspects."

"We've got a problem," Sydney said over the comms. "Robert and I have good reason to believe that Ahmed Farouk is working with Umbra."

"What?!" Rio asked, echoing the sentiments of the others.

"How good a reason?" Monty asked.

"Extremely good," Sydney answered. "We can get into details later, but right now we've got to figure out how that changes the situation."

"Completely," Paris said. "If he's Umbra, then this could all be a setup."

"And now we're on the same page," Sydney said.

Just then, there was a crescendo of music, and colored lights washed over the pyramids as the narrator continued telling their story.

"We don't have a lot of time to come up with a new plan," Paris said.

"We don't have any time," Brooklyn said. "I've got eyes on Sallah el-Kahir. That must be who she's meeting. This is all about to go down."

"Where is he?" Kat asked.

"From your vantage point, about fifty meters to the right. He's wearing a black leather jacket and a red ball cap."

"Can you stay close to him so that I can follow his movements with your tracker?" Kat asked.

"On it," said Brooklyn.

"I've got Imogen," Paris said, adrenaline racing through his veins. "She's coming from the opposite direction. I'll get close so you can track her with my nautilus."

Kat watched the dots as they moved across the screen on her tablet and tried to find order in the chaos. She saw Mother's yellow dot.

"Mother, I know you can't talk, but it looks to me like you are very close to el-Kahir," Kat said. "If the police see him and are ready to close in to make the arrest, cough twice."

Two coughs came over the comms.

On the screen, Kat could see that they were about thirty seconds from reaching each other. She looked up at the sphinx as a green laser started to create an outline of its face. They'd come hoping Gaisman would lead them to the mastermind behind the hack, but that plan had completely fallen apart. She was the alpha. It was up to her. And this time, Kat was not about to freeze.

"This is now an extraction," Kat announced confidently. "Mother, I need you to do whatever you can to delay the police. Paris, get Gaisman and head back the other way."

"What about el-Kahir?" Brooklyn asked.

"Keep following him to see where he goes," Kat said.

"We still don't know how he fits into all this. He may be connected to the hack and lead us somewhere."

A gong rang out over the loudspeakers, and a gigantic photograph of a sarcophagus was projected onto the Pyramid of Khafre in a representation of what the structure held within it. "A pharaoh is at rest in his coffin made of gold," intoned the narrator.

"Dr. Gaisman, it's not safe here; you need to come with me," Paris said as he reached Imogen and took her by the arm.

She was confused as she turned and looked at him. "Is this some kind of joke?"

"It is definitely not a joke. You are about to be arrested and charged with stealing the canopic jar that Scotland Yard recovered from the shelf in the spare room of your flat."

Gaisman was completely dumbfounded. This made absolutely no sense to her.

"How do you know about my flat?"

"They're getting mighty close," Kat announced. "Fifteen seconds."

"If you come with me, I'll explain how I know about the jar as well as the poster on your wall about the British Museum stealing the pyramids. But you've got to come right now because I can't explain it to you if you're in jail."

Gaisman nodded, and Paris started to lead her in the opposite direction.

"Okay, everybody, you've parked the bus. Now it's time to play some defense," Kat instructed. "Block the others while Paris and Imogen get away."

Kat used the screen like she was playing a video game, directing everyone where to go and stand. Monty and Rio got in the way of the police. Robert and Sydney intercepted el-Kahir, who was still being followed by Brooklyn. Meanwhile, she guided Paris through the maze of people. Then more police arrived on the scene.

"I see at least five police officers right on top of us," Paris said. "I don't think we're going to make it."

"That is not your decision to make," Kat said. "I'm the alpha, and I say you are."

"How?"

"Keep going in the direction you are, and run as fast as you can."

"To what?" he asked, confused. "The desert?"

"Just run."

Paris turned to Gaisman. "It's time to run."

"Run where?" Imogen asked.

"I guess we'll see."

They sprinted from the crowd and in the process caught the attention of some of the police. Ahmed Farouk got on a walkie-talkie and shouted instructions in Arabic.

"Keep running!" Kat ordered.

By this point, all Paris and Imogen saw was desert in front of them. The police were catching up.

"Where are we going?" she asked between exhausted breaths.

Paris slowed for a moment. Then he saw it, and a giant smile came over his face. "There," he said. "Keep running."

Up ahead, cresting over a desert hillock and coming right at them was Marwen's microbus. He'd broken through a barrier and was off-roading at top speed, throwing up a spray of sand in his wake, with Kat in the passenger seat still using the tablet to direct everyone.

"You're going to have to jump on while it's moving," Kat said.

"What?!" Paris asked in disbelief.

"Marwen says if we stop in the sand, the bus will sink and get stuck."

Kat climbed back and slid open the door as they pulled close.

"You've got to jump," Paris told Imogen, pointing at the door.

The police were too close for her to argue.

Marwen slowed down as much as he dared, and Imogen jumped in through the side door while Paris leaped onto the ladder attached to the rear. Once he had a firm grip, he slapped the roof two times and yelled, "Go!"

The microbus peeled out, and Paris laughed from the thrill of it all as they raced into the cool desert night.

Tomb Raiders

AS THE MUSIC SWELLED TO MARK THE finale of the Giza Sound and Light Show, the dust, or perhaps more accurately *sand*, was still settling in the aftermath of Imogen Gaisman's escape. Ahmed Farouk and the Cairo police were baffled as to what had just occurred. The Egyptologist had arrived as expected, but then, just as they were about to close in for the arrest, she suddenly fled the scene, first on foot and then in a most peculiar getaway vehicle.

It had been too dark during the show for the authorities to get a good look at her accomplices, but they appeared to be young, perhaps even teenagers. Farouk took his anger out on anybody in his vicinity, including Mother.

"Your citizen is a fugitive and will be caught and arrested," he vowed. "And this time, you will not be invited to participate."

There was a hint of threat in the way he said it, as though he somehow wanted to blame Mother for what had transpired but couldn't quite put his finger on how to do that. Knowing now that Farouk was on Umbra's payroll, Mother returned the favor with a veiled threat of his own.

"We want justice too, so we're going to investigate this situation further to make sure we know how the canopic jar came to be in Ms. Gaisman's flat. We were fortunate to get our hands on some security camera footage of the post office and will look to see exactly who put the package in the mail."

This was a lie designed to rattle Farouk, and by the man's expression, it did exactly that. Quite likely, he was the one who sent it, and if such video existed, his career would be over. He went to say something but instead stormed off. Once he'd driven away, Mother headed to the parking lot and joined the others.

"So, how do we get home?" he asked. "It seems our ride has left without us."

"Paris texted us about that," Brooklyn said. "Let me read it to you so that I get it right. 'Marwen has taken us to a safe house and arranged for you to be picked up. Wait in the parking lot.'" She looked up from the screen to Mother. "What kind of tour bus driver has a safe house?"

"The kind whom Tru hires," he replied.

"I don't know who's picking us up, but it's got to be better than the sardine machine," Rio said.

"Don't be so sure," Sydney said. "Look at that."

An old school bus pulled into the parking lot. It was white with blue trim, and its diesel engine belched as it rumbled toward them.

"If I didn't see it with my own eyes," Mother said in disbelief when he read what was painted on the side of the bus. "'The Sacred Sisters of St. Joshua.'"

The bus came to a stop directly in front of them, and the door opened to reveal a smiling nun wearing a habit in the driver's seat.

"Are you Mother and Monty?" she asked.

"We are," Mother answered with a bemused smile.

"I'm Sister Rosemary. Marwen said you needed a lift."

The Cairo convent was not as big as the one the sisters had in London. It was only two stories tall, but they still used handbells to communicate from room to room, which delighted Kat to no end. The City Spies again gathered in the kitchen, where the sisters offered them heaping bowls of *koshari*, an Egyptian staple with pasta, rice, lentils, chickpeas, onions, and spicy tomato sauce.

The conversation around the table was animated as they relived highlights from the night. Paris explained that after hanging on to the back of the bus while it raced through the desert, he had sand everywhere on his body. "Everywhere."

Mother took a seat at the head of the table and, after checking to make sure everyone was okay and there were no injuries, called an impromptu meeting to order. All eyes turned to Dr. Imogen Gaisman.

"I have a question," she said. "First, we were chased by the police. Then I had to jump into a moving bus. And now I'm hiding out in a convent."

"Are any of those questions?" asked Mother.

"Who are you?"

"We're the people who saved you from getting thrown into an Egyptian prison," Sydney said.

"But beyond that," Mother said, "I'm afraid there's nothing more we can tell you."

"We do, however, need some answers from you," Monty said. "Much has happened since you left London, and whether you realize it or not, you've been thrown into the middle of something huge and could face serious charges."

"Charges for what? Receiving an unsolicited canopic jar in the mail?"

"That's the tip of the iceberg," Mother said. "I just spoke with the embassy, and they've sent a vehicle for you. The good news is that they will get you safely back out of Egypt. The bad news is that you will be detained at Heathrow Airport, where you'll be questioned by investigators with MI5 and the National Cyber Security Centre. You're suspected of committing a serious breach of the UK's cyber defense."

"Cybercrime?" Gaisman laughed at the ridiculousness of it. "You're talking to a woman whose password is literally the word 'password' with an exclamation point at the end. My skill set and expertise end about three thousand years ago, during the final days of the New Kingdom. I'm so useless with computers that I had to hire my twelve-year-old nephew to produce my podcast."

"Told you," Brooklyn said.

"We think you were set up," Paris said. "That's why we rescued you."

"But it would help you and us a great deal if you could point us in the direction of who would do that," Monty said.

"Jason Harper," Gaisman said without missing a beat. "And his friend at the Ministry of Antiquities."

"Which friend is that?" Mother asked. He wanted to make sure she gave the names and they didn't lead her at all.

"Ahmed Farouk. You know it's a problem when the person policing the criminals happens to be a criminal. There are so many great and hardworking people at the ministry, but he's not one of them."

"Why would they do that?" Monty asked.

"Jason blames me for ruining his business, and Farouk is worried I'm going to blow the whistle on his illegal side hustle of selling artifacts," Imogen said. "That's why I came down here. I wanted to find Harper, get some proof of what they're up to, and turn it over to one of the good guys at the ministry."

"And the fifty thousand pounds you deposited in your bank account?" Brooklyn asked.

"I don't know where that came from. It was just there. But I've done work for the Grand Egyptian Museum, and when I do, they deposit my paycheck directly into my bank account."

"And the museum is overseen by the Ministry of Antiquities," Mother said. "Farouk could've accessed the information."

"Exactly," replied Gaisman.

"Is Harper here in Cairo?" Monty asked.

"I don't think so. I've been looking for him for days and haven't had any luck. He must be in Luxor, which is where I was planning to go tomorrow."

"What's in Luxor?" Brooklyn asked.

"The Valley of the Kings," said the Egyptologist. "That's where Jason's company was based before it went out of business."

Rio gave her a look. "You mean, before you convinced the British Museum not to work with him."

"It's a good thing I did. It would've been a huge scandal if the museum was connected to any of this. He likes to tell everyone that he's the next Howard Carter and is going to discover KV66, but Howard Carter never got mixed up with tomb raiders."

"Tomb raiders?" Sydney scoffed. "Like Indiana Jones? Is that still a thing?"

"Don't knock Indiana Jones; that's what got me into archaeology in the first place," Gaisman said. "But yes, it is still very much a thing. And these guys aren't finding tombs using the headpiece to the staff of Ra. They're using drones, night-vision goggles, ground-penetrating radar, you name it."

"How'd he get involved with them?" Brooklyn asked.

"He believes the only thing standing between him and finding the next great tomb is financial backing," Imogen said. "But he's gotten so desperate for the money, he's willing to take it from anyone."

She continued telling them about Harper until three officers from the embassy's legal affairs department arrived to take her away.

"One more question before you go," Brooklyn said. "Do you know Oriana Gutierrez?"

"Name sounds familiar," she said, trying to remember.

"Lovelace and Hopper Cyber Solutions," Brooklyn said. "They handle computer work for the museum."

"That's it," Gaisman said. "Yes, we've emailed back and forth."

"About what?" Monty asked, hoping it might be relevant to the case.

"My password. She said I needed to make it more difficult. That's why I added the exclamation point."

Once she was gone, the focus turned to Robert. He took out the scriptex and showed it to everyone. He admitted that he'd used it twice since he'd been with them. "Once at the FARM and last night at the hotel."

"Which means if Umbra can track it, they know where the FARM is, and they know that we're in Cairo," Mother said, concerned.

"Mum told me they couldn't," Robert said. "She made a point of telling me that the only ones who could see it were Annie and her."

"No offense," Sydney said. "But your mum's not exactly high on our to-be-trusted list."

Robert considered this for a moment and conceded, "I can see that."

Everyone was quiet for a moment until Paris said, "So, what do we do?"

"Well . . . ," said Mother, trying to figure it out.

"We put it behind us and move on," Sydney

interrupted. "We all make mistakes, and families forgive each other." She looked at Robert and smiled. "Besides, we're going to need all the help we can get when we go down to the Valley of the Kings looking for Jason Harper."

Clementine

AT A DINGY RESTAURANT ON THE outskirts of Luxor, Clementine sat with her back against the wall and her eyes on the front door. Jason Harper was late, and she wasn't happy about it. When he finally arrived, he was almost comical, wearing dark glasses and nervously peering over his shoulder to make sure no one had followed him.

"You're late," Clemmie said when he sat down across from her.

"I had to be certain no one was tailing me." He studied her face for a moment. "Who are you, anyway?"

"It doesn't matter who I am," she replied. "All that matters is who I work for."

Jason nodded. "Umbra?"

Clementine shook her head disdainfully and put a finger in front of her lips. "Shhh."

"Sorry, right," he said. "I'm a computer programmer, not a terrorist. I'm not used to any of this."

"A little advice," she said. "Don't say the name of the organization aloud, and don't use the T-word."

He nodded.

"Why did you want me to come here?" he asked, fidgety. "I'm extremely busy right now. This is not convenient."

"I think maybe you forget who you're working for," Clementine said. "Your *investors* want to know how their business agreement is progressing."

Harper couldn't believe his situation. Six months earlier, he thought they really were investors, businesspeople looking to finance his dream of locating a missing tomb. But in reality, they wanted him to use the technology to find artifacts they could sell on the black market. And when he couldn't find enough of those, they wanted more. That's when the plan for the cyber-attack was born.

"It would be progressing better if I were at my computer and not wasting time here," he said, trying to sound tough but failing.

"I'm going to ignore your attitude, Jason," she said. "You need to calm down and eat something. You're a wreck, and that's not giving me confidence that you're up to this."

"Okay," he said apologetically.

Although he was nervous, Clementine was the one taking the big risk. Her bosses at Umbra had no idea she was here. She'd come looking for information, and as they talked over two bowls of *koshari*, she pushed him to tell her as much as he could about the cyberattack.

Luxor

THE CITY SPIES WERE THE ONLY
passengers dropped off at Cairo International Airport
by a nun driving a school bus. Not that anyone noticed.
Terminal three was beyond chaotic, and the group
had to go through three separate security checkpoints
before being escorted out onto the tarmac to board
their plane. A friendly face greeted them at the base of
the mobile stairway.

"Tell me you're not the pilot," Mother said to
Marwen, only half joking.

"No," Marwen said. "I have many talents, but flying is not one." Then he shot a look toward Paris and Kat. "Although, I think we were nearly airborne once or twice last night in the desert."

"It certainly felt that way hanging on to that ladder," Paris said with a proud grin.

"Are you here to see us off?" Monty asked.

"Actually, I am also traveling to Luxor. Your embassy has asked me to continue on as your tour guide."

"Well, we certainly appreciate everything that you did last night," Mother said.

Marwen smiled broadly. "We at Cairo International Student Tours do whatever we can to ensure you have a memorable visit to Egypt."

Mother laughed. "You have more than succeeded at that."

The flight was short, and an hour later they touched down and took a shuttle to their hotel. Even on the shuttle bus, Marwen couldn't resist the urge to play the role of tour guide once again. He turned in his seat to face the others.

"Welcome to Luxor, which rose from the ruins of Thebes, capital of the Middle and New Kingdoms. This is where Tutankhamen, Rameses II, and the pharaohs of

Upper Egypt reigned. As in Giza, and all cities of ancient Egypt, Thebes was built along the eastern banks of the Nile."

"Why's that?" asked Robert.

"Because the ancients believed the sun god Ra was born every day in the east and died every evening in the west," he explained. "This side of the river was for the living while the dead were buried on the other. That's where you'll find the Valley of the Kings."

"And hopefully where we'll find Jason Harper too," Mother added.

Luxor was known as the "world's greatest open-air museum" because of its extraordinary array of temples and tombs. In addition to the Valley of the Kings and the neighboring Valley of the Queens, it was home to the temples of Karnak and Luxor.

Nearly half a million people lived in the city, and life revolved around the monuments and the visitors they attracted. Tourism was the main industry, and with so many hotels to choose from, Mother decided to splurge and got two sprawling suites at a five-star resort over-looking the Nile.

"If I'd known there was going to be a pool, I would've brought my bathing suit," Rio said.

"We're on a mission," Sydney said. "We don't have time for swimming."

"Weren't you the one who wanted to postpone the break-in at the British Museum so you could watch fireworks?"

"That's different," Sydney said. "I was being patriotic."

The team gathered in Mother's suite, anxiously waiting as Brooklyn used her laptop to connect with Beny. The supercomputer had been scouring files all night, and now it was time to see if that had yielded any valuable intel that might help them find Harper. Brooklyn smiled.

"What is it?" Kat asked. "Good news?"

"Very," Brooklyn said. "The email chain between Harper and Pluto has given us two addresses."

"Really? Pluto's part of it?" Sydney asked, disappointed.

"No," Brooklyn said. "The messages had nothing to do with the hack. He was just asking her about hardware."

"Then how does that help us?" Rio asked.

"Since it was just a normal email and not a ransom demand," Brooklyn replied, "Harper didn't try to hide his IP address. After all, at the time he was still just a businessman, not a criminal. That IP address led to an office here in Luxor."

"Does that mean we know where his computer is?" Paris asked hopefully.

"Not necessarily," Brooklyn answered. "But we know where it was when he sent the email."

"What's the other address?" Monty asked.

"It's from a receipt," Brooklyn said. "A little over a month ago, Harper spent thirty-six thousand Egyptian pounds at a store here in town."

"How much is that in pounds sterling?" Rio asked.

"One thousand five hundred three," Kat said, instantly doing the calculation in her head. "At least, based on yesterday's conversion rates."

"Really?" Robert said in disbelief. "She just does that?"

"All the time," Paris replied.

"What did Harper buy?" Mother asked.

"The receipt doesn't list the item, just that he bought twenty of whatever it is."

"What kind of store is it?" Monty asked.

"It's in Arabic, but Beny translated it into something like 'Hassan's Shop.'"

"That's great work," Mother said. "We've got two addresses, just like when we landed in Cairo. Let's use the same teams we used there and check out both places."

Neither address was far from the hotel, so both teams set out on foot. Mother, Robert, Rio, and Kat were looking into the receipt. It was a twenty-minute walk to Hassan's Shop, which meant they passed no fewer than eight places where Rio wanted to stop and sample the local cuisine. Mother gave in at a kebab shop that smelled too good to pass up.

"This is delicious," Rio said, happily eating as they resumed walking. "Can you taste the turmeric and curry? Simple and exquisite."

"I love the cardamom," Robert said. "It's in a lot of Egyptian dishes. I really grew to love it when I lived here."

"You know cardamom?" Rio said, pleased. "Finally I'll have someone who I can talk to about food."

Robert was happy for any connection with the team. "I'm looking forward to it."

"Just be warned," Kat said. "When it comes to food, Rio has some strong opinions."

"I have strong opinions about many things in addition to food," Rio said. "It's just that nobody ever asks me."

"Okay, I'll bite, so to speak," said Mother. "Why don't you share one of your non-food-based opinions?"

"I bet no one agrees with me, but I feel bad for Jason Harper."

"The man who launched a giant cyberattack against the United Kingdom and is endangering people's lives just so that he can extort millions?" Kat asked. "Maybe there's a reason people don't ask your opinion more often."

"I think he's a bad person and deserves to be punished," Rio said. "But look what led him there. He had a very good idea, but it was rejected because he didn't have the right background. We should be judged on our ideas and not our heritage or education."

"Does that mean you're willing to be operated on by someone who hasn't been to medical school but has some good ideas about surgery?" Robert asked.

Rio gave him a look. "I think you are twisting my words."

Kat laughed. "That's Rio's way of saying you're right and he doesn't want to admit it."

"The important thing to remember, though, is that we need to own our decisions," Mother said. "Jason Harper has made some very bad ones and has to accept the responsibility for doing so."

They reached the address and were surprised to discover that Hassan's Shop was a tire store.

"He bought twenty tires?" Robert asked, bewildered. "Does he have five cars?"

"This is going to be tricky," Rio said. "It's not really a store for tourists, so I doubt they speak English. And even if they did, they probably don't want to help underage MI6 agents."

"So, how do we figure out what he bought?" Robert asked.

"We'll solve it the way I solve anything," Kat said.

"Uh-oh, here comes math," said Rio.

"Absolutely," Kat said. "He bought twenty of one item, and the total was thirty-six thousand pounds. All we have to do is figure out what one thing cost eighteen hundred pounds."

"Sounds good," said Mother. "Let's go shopping."

The store also sold car parts and automotive necessities, and as the team browsed the shelves, they got some strange looks, but no one bothered them. It didn't take long for Robert to find what they were looking for.

"Check it out," he said. "One thousand eight hundred pounds."

It was a car battery.

"What could he possibly want with twenty car batteries?" Mother asked.

A half mile away, the other address led the rest of the team to a two-story strip mall. On the bottom floor, there was a restaurant, a souvenir shop, and a laundromat. Above, there were four offices, one of which belonged to Harper.

A small plate on the door read KV66 EXCAVATIONS, LLC.

"This is his company," Sydney said.

"Or used to be," Brooklyn replied. "It looks abandoned."

The curtain was open just enough to peek inside. There was nothing left except for a desk and some papers scattered on the floor. Paris picked the lock, and they entered to look around.

"All the computers are gone," Brooklyn said.

"Maybe these papers will give us a clue," Sydney said, and she squatted down to look at some files. She picked up one of the brochures Harper had printed to show clients. She was particularly interested in the company's logo. It looked like a hieroglyph and featured a man with a falcon's head. She held it up for Paris to see.

"Look familiar?" she asked.

Paris smiled and said, "Hello, Horus."

Cartouche

"TWENTY CAR BATTERIES?" PARIS SAID. "What could you possibly do with twenty batteries?"

The teams were comparing notes after running into each other on their way back to the hotel.

"How many batteries does a bus use?" Brooklyn asked. "Or a camper?"

"Are car batteries the same as boat batteries?" Sydney wondered. "Maybe he's using a boat to get up and down the Nile?"

"They could be for the *tuk-tuk* black market," Robert suggested.

"Aren't *tuk-tuks* those three-wheeled covered scooters that are all over the place?" Sydney asked. "Why is there a black market for them?"

"They're a nuisance, and the government is trying to get rid of them," he answered. "Since they're not really cars, anyone can drive them, even kids as young as nine and ten. They're bad for the environment and make traffic even worse than it already is. The government has made it so you can't buy new ones and you can't sell parts to fix old ones, so people have to use the black market instead."

"That's a thought," Monty said. "But I can't imagine it's worth Harper's trouble. Selling artifacts on the black market is profitable, but how much money can *tuk-tuk* drivers pay?"

"Tell us more about what you found in the office," Mother said.

"There wasn't much left," Paris answered. "We found a couple of the packets he'd made for investors. They explained the technology and how he planned to use it."

"We did find a journal that listed some of his research notes," Sydney said.

"Each page was for a different tomb in the Valley of the Kings," Monty added. "But the information was all in his personal shorthand. When we get back to the hotel, I want to look at it with Kat to see if we can make some sense of it."

They were just about to reach the hotel when Kat asked, "What if the batteries aren't for a vehicle?"

"Then what are they for?" said Robert.

"When I was studying heists and robberies, I came across one at a winery in California. The vineyard stored their wine in caves where the cool, damp conditions are perfect for aging. But a gang of robbers managed to steal a ton of it because they found another cave that connected to it. It had a remote entrance, so nobody saw them coming or going. The only way the police figured out what happened was when they found car batteries in the other cave."

"What were they for?" Rio asked.

"The robbers needed electricity to run lights so they could see what they were doing."

"If it works in a cave, then it would work in a tomb," Sydney said. "Maybe he's hiding out in one."

"Yeah, but which one?" Paris asked.

"Hopefully, his notes will give us an idea," Monty said.

When they got to their suite, a large fruit and nut basket was waiting for them in the entryway. "Now we're talking," Rio said at the sight of more food. "I think we should stay in resorts more often."

He started digging into it while the others got comfortable in the sitting room.

"If there're any chocolates in there, bring me some," Sydney said as she plopped onto a couch.

"I want some nuts," Paris said.

"I'm not your waiter," Rio answered.

"Why don't you just bring the whole basket?" Monty suggested.

He brought in the basket and put it on the coffee table.

"Brooklyn, we were so focused on trying to find Harper through his emails that we never talked about what was in them," Mother said. "What type of hardware was he asking Pluto about?"

"Most of it had to do with getting Wi-Fi and internet in remote areas," she answered. "He said he needed to be able to access the web from his excavation site."

"Except he never got an excavation site," Rio said.

"Maybe he did," said Monty. "We might be making the wrong assumption about that."

"What do you mean?" Robert asked. "Wouldn't we have heard about it if he did?"

"Yes, if he had a full excavation for a tomb," Monty answered. "But there aren't only tombs in the valley. Sometimes they find ancient storage spaces or workrooms that still have priceless artifacts. Maybe he found one of those."

"Which would explain where he got the items he sold," Sydney said.

"So, what are you saying?" asked Rio. "He's moved into it, and that's where he launched the cyberattack?"

"Why not?" asked Paris. "It would be a great place for him to hide from authorities. A hidden chamber in an ancient tomb."

"Except the computer wouldn't work," Brooklyn said. "You could power lights, small appliances, even the hardware needed for remote internet access from a car battery. But a computer uses too much electricity. A battery would only be strong enough to run one for about half an hour. The best it could be is backup in case there's a power outage. You couldn't stay on as long as he'd need to for this."

"They give tours of the tombs," Mother said. "That means they must have electricity and lights in some of them. I wonder how many."

Brooklyn went over to her laptop and did a quick search. "Eleven," she said, excited. "Eleven tombs have electricity."

"Maybe he's in one of those," Sydney said. "He uses the electricity to power his computer and the car batteries for everything else."

"Why not use the electricity for everything?" Robert asked.

"If he uses too much, he could throw the circuits," Mother explained. "That could lead to him getting caught."

"So, we have to figure out which of the eleven tombs he's in," Rio said.

"Let's compare the list of tombs that have electricity to the ones he wrote about in his journal," Monty said. "Maybe we can narrow it down."

While they did that, Sydney went over to the fruit basket to look for a snack. "There's a card with it," she said.

"It's probably a welcome note from the front desk," Mother replied. "Happy that we were willing to pay for two overpriced suites."

Sydney opened the card. "It reads more like an Egyptian fortune cookie than a thank-you note," she said. "'Karnak and Thebes resurrect old spirits every time they align.'" She looked up. "That's kind of spooky. Like a curse in some old mummy movie."

"Except it doesn't make sense," Paris said. "Thebes and Luxor are the same thing, right? And Karnak is in Luxor, so how can Karnak and Thebes align?"

Kat was focused on the notes in Harper's journal, but something caught her ear. She turned her attention to Sydney. "Read that again."

Sydney read the note, only this time with an exaggerated dramatic voice. "'Karnak and Thebes resurrect old spirits every time they align.'"

Kat's eyes opened wide as she figured it out. "It's not an Egyptian fortune cookie. It's a message from Clementine."

"What?" Sydney exclaimed.

"It's an acrostic, just like she used before. You take the first letter of each word. 'Karnak and Thebes'— that's 'Kat.' She's writing to me. 'Resurrect old spirits every time they align' is 'Rosetta.'"

"As in the stone?" Rio asked.

"As in the key that was used to break the code of hieroglyphics." She looked to Sydney. "Are there any hieroglyphics on the card?"

"Yes, but they look like they're just decoration for the card," Sydney said.

"Here," Brooklyn said, reaching for the card, "I'll check it out."

"We've been in Egypt a few days, and you can suddenly read hieroglyphics?" Rio asked.

"No, but the internet can," Brooklyn said. "I'll just take a picture and do an image search."

"Her sending a message here is a major problem," Sydney said. "How does Clemmie know where we're staying?" She shot an accusing glare at Robert.

"I didn't tell her," he said defensively. "I swear I didn't."

"You wouldn't have to," Mother said. "If she can track the scriptex, she can find us."

"Does that mean she's here in Luxor?" Sydney asked.

Mother nodded. "Probably."

"This is a cartouche," Brooklyn said.

"What's a cartouche?" asked Rio.

"These hieroglyphics are drawn with an oval around them," Brooklyn answered. "It's called a cartouche, and it was how a royal name was written in hieroglyphics."

"And who does this cartouche belong to?" Mother asked.

"Sety I."

"That's one of the ones that he's written about in his notebook," Monty said.

"Does the tomb have electricity?" Paris asked.

Brooklyn checked the list she'd pulled up on her computer. "Yes."

"So, that's the one we're looking for," Rio said. "That's where Harper is."

"Or it's where Clemmie is," Sydney said. "This could all be a trap, her luring us into some tunnel, away from the world and totally helpless."

36.

Valley of the Kings

ONE HUNDRED YEARS AFTER A TWELVE-year-old boy entered the Valley of the Kings and accidentally discovered the tomb of Tutankhamen, the City Spies arrived looking for Jason Harper. Just like the boy, they were destined to be left out of any official record of what was about to happen. They were anonymous.

But not invisible.

Hidden among the sightseers, Clementine watched carefully as they arrived in a yellow tram with hieroglyphics painted on the sides. Marwen was waiting for them and held up a sign that read CAIRO INTERNATIONAL STUDENT TOURS.

"Welcome to the Valley of the Kings," he said with a broad smile. "I finally get to show you around an actual archaeological site."

"We're particularly interested in the tomb of Sety I," Paris said.

"KV17," Marwen replied. "An excellent choice. Follow me."

The Egyptians called the site *Wadi al-Muluk*. "Wadi" was the Arabic word for a valley or ravine that was dry but vulnerable to flash flooding. Such a threat seemed unimaginable as the City Spies walked along the gravel path through the rocky landscape. Everything was dusty and barren.

"No wonder they buried people here," Paris said. "Nothing could live in these conditions."

"Why didn't they use pyramids like they did in Giza?" Brooklyn asked.

"Excellent question," Marwen said as he began a spiel he'd given countless times. "The pharaohs of the New Kingdom learned from the mistakes of their royal ancestors. Although the pyramids were mighty and awe-inspiring, they were also conspicuous and easy to rob. That's why kings like Rameses the Great and Tutankhamen hid their tombs in this mysterious desert wadi. They built them directly into the cliffsides and covered the entrances with debris in the hope that their treasures would remain undisturbed so they could use them in the afterlife."

"Did it work?" Rio asked.

"No," Marwen said with a chuckle. "Most of them were robbed thousands of years ago. That is why Tutankhamen's tomb was so special. It had been undisturbed until its discovery in 1922."

"And there it is," Kat said as they walked past the entrance to a tomb. The sign next to it read TOMB OF TUT ANKH AMUN NO. 62. "That's where Howard Carter discovered King Tut's tomb."

"Actually," Marwen said, stopping for a moment. "That is where a boy named Hussein discovered King Tut's tomb."

"What are you talking about?" Paris asked. "It wasn't Carter?"

Marwen told them the story of the water boy and his role in Carter's great archaeological find. At the end, he added, "Young people have often changed the course of history, but it is rare for history to acknowledge their role." He looked at them and smiled. "Perhaps you know something of this."

"They do indeed," Mother said. "They do indeed."

"Now, on to Sety."

They walked into the southeast branch of the wadi and up a slope until they reached KV17. An informational sign next to the entrance featured a map diagramming all of the tomb's corridors, stairwells, and chambers.

"With eleven chambers stretching four hundred fifty feet into the mountain, this is the longest and the deepest of all the tombs in the valley," he explained. "I want you to pay special attention to a feature unique to KV17. This stairwell here"—he pointed to the map—"extends beyond the burial chamber, to corridor K."

"What's corridor K?" Brooklyn asked.

"We don't know," Marwen answered. "Some think it was meant to be a pathway for Sety to reach the mythical waters of Nun. Others wonder if it might lead to an as yet undiscovered crypt. All that we know for certain is that it connects to a web of robbers' tunnels that bandits used to loot the tombs."

"That's where we'll find him," Rio said softly.

"Or where we'll find a trap," Sydney replied.

"It's not a trap," Robert said. "I know it."

Sydney looked at him and said, "I hope you're right."

"Show us the way, Marwen," Mother said with a smile.

"Unfortunately, this is as far as I can go," he replied. "Tour guides aren't allowed inside the tomb. But I'll wait here for you."

"I'm not sure how long we'll be," Mother said, "and if we still haven't returned by closing time . . ."

"Don't worry," Marwen said, smiling. "I will be wherever you need me."

Mother grinned. "I have no doubt."

The team descended into the tomb along an ever-deepening series of stairs and corridors, their walls and ceilings decorated with hieroglyphs depicting the journey of the dead into the underworld. When they reached the first landing, Mother stopped to talk to everyone.

"We didn't have a chance to scout this location, so I don't know what we're up against," Mother said. "We need to—"

"Um, if you don't mind," Kat said, interrupting, "I have an idea."

"Okay," Mother said happily. "What is it?"

"We should think of the tomb as a museum, just like

the one we broke into in London," Kat said. "That's fresh in our minds, so you know what to look for: any security measures that could be a problem for us. We'll even break into the same teams. Brooklyn and Paris, you take everything to the left, including walls and connecting rooms. Sydney and Rio, you do the same on the right. Robert and I will be the fail-safe and double-check everything down the middle. We'll meet up at the end, in the burial chamber. By then we should have a good idea of the entire security setup."

Mother and Monty shared a look, delighted at Kat's take-charge attitude.

"And what about the old people?" Mother asked.

"You get to be tourists," Kat said.

"Sounds like a plan," Monty replied with a smile.

It took about twenty minutes to make it all the way through the tomb. Sydney and Rio came across two guards; one stood near a painting of a sacred cow, and the other was picking at his teeth in a chamber with four pillars. Both seemed bored.

"Look, it's Horus," Paris said to Brooklyn as he pointed to a painting of Horus escorting Sety into the underworld.

"And over there is a motion detector," Brooklyn

responded under her breath. "Just like the ones at the British Museum."

Even though they were on a mission, it was impossible to ignore the breathtaking beauty of it all, and they still found time to admire the art. At the end of the tomb, they arrived at the burial chamber, which was divided into two parts. The first half had pillars decorated with images of Sety accompanied by different deities. Stairs led down into the second half, where there was a vaulted ceiling painted with the constellations of the northern sky. This was where Sety's mummy once rested in a sarcophagus. When it was removed, it revealed an unexpected staircase descending down into the mysterious corridor K. These stairs were in a rectangular pit protected by a wooden railing.

"What'd you find out?" Kat asked when they got together around the pit.

"Four guards total," Rio said. "Two at the door, taking tickets, and two roaming around. It's been a long day, and they all seem like they're counting the minutes to closing time."

"What about cameras?" Kat asked.

"Interesting," Paris said. "Because all the artifacts that were once in the tomb have either been looted or put in a museum, the focus of the security is on the walls, protecting the art that is painted on them. The cameras are pointing toward them and not this staircase. I think we should be able to sneak down here as long one of the roaming guards doesn't come through."

Brooklyn popped up the stairs into the first half of the chamber to look.

"I think we're clear," she said. "Let's go."

One by one, they climbed over the railing and went down the stairs, only to reach metal bars and a gate blocking access to the corridor.

"All right, Rio," Paris said. "You keep talking about your lock-picking skills; let's see them in action."

Rio grinned as he moved to the front of the group.

"You want us to time you?" Sydney asked.

"Just watch and enjoy," Rio replied as he quickly went to work and picked the lock in no time.

Mother muffled a laugh as he shook his head in amazement. "Skills indeed."

Rio beamed next to the now-open gate. Sydney started to walk through, but Paris grabbed her and said, "Wait."

"What's wrong?" Sydney asked.

"Look there." Just inside the gate, a series of sensors ran up the wall. He leaned in to examine them and realized that they were laser trip-wire sensors, just like the ones that had been installed at the British Museum. He turned to Sydney and said, "Tell me you brought your hairspray."

"Sorry, no hairspray," Sydney said.

Paris slumped.

Then she smiled and said, "I told you, it's *mist elixir*. And, yes, of course I brought it. I'm not going to let my hair get dried out in this desert."

Mother and Monty exchanged a confused look.

"I feel like we're missing something," Mother asked.

"Just a little trick we learned from the Antwerp diamond heist," Sydney said.

"I feel like we're missing a lot," Monty replied, even more confused with the mention of a diamond heist.

Sydney got the mist elixir from her backpack and carefully sprayed it on each of the sensors.

"Now we can enter," she said, "I think."

They held their breath as she took a few cautious steps forward. Once she made it past the sensors without setting off an alarm, everyone breathed a sigh of relief and followed her into corridor K.

"There's the juice," Mother said, pointing toward a large electrical switch box mounted on the wall. "If

Harper is pulling electricity from this source, we should be able to follow the wiring to him."

"What happens if you pull down that handle?" Rio asked.

"Everything goes dark," Mother said.

"Yeah, so let's not do that," added Brooklyn.

"Come on," Paris said.

"Not so fast," Mother replied. "Sydney's right about the possibility that this is a trap, so we're going to split up. Robert and I are going to go first, and I want the rest of you to follow in two and a half minutes. That should give us enough distance so that if something goes wrong, you'll be away from the danger but close enough to help."

"Why you two first?" Sydney asked.

"Because if Clemmie is up to something, it should be us," Mother answered. He looked at Robert, who nodded his agreement.

"But—" Sydney started to protest.

"It's not a debate," Mother said. "Two and a half minutes."

Unlike the well-lit chambers of the rest of KV17, corridor K only had sporadic lighting. Within thirty seconds of walking down the passageway, Mother and

Robert were already shrouded in darkness. Mother pulled out a flashlight but kept it pointed low so it didn't alert anyone ahead of them.

"Are you okay?" Mother asked in a whisper.

"Yeah," Robert answered. "But it's not a trap. Mum wouldn't do that."

"We're just being extra cautious," Mother replied.

"You hate her, don't you?" Robert said. "Just like they do."

"I don't hate her," Mother said. "How could I? She gave me you and Annie. But my feelings toward her are *complicated*, all things considered."

"She told us about the fire. She said that the plan went wrong and you weren't where she thought you would be. She wanted to rescue you but worried that if she didn't make it, there would be no one to look after Annie and me."

"She was right," Mother said. "She wouldn't have been able to get me in time."

"Then who did?"

"Paris," Mother said. "He was only ten years old at the time. But he saved my life. Imagine that."

"I like him," Robert said. "A lot. He's been the nicest one."

"He's something special, that's for sure," Mother said.

"Mum also told us that you didn't forgive her for what happened."

"That's interesting," Mother said, peeved. "How would she know such a thing?"

"I don't know. But she said that's why she never came back."

They were quiet for a moment before Mother said, "We need to focus on this mission right now. But I promise we can talk more about this later."

Two and a half minutes after Mother and Robert left, the others started down the corridor with Paris in the front and Monty in the rear.

"You remember when I said I was all good if we stopped using creepy tunnels and passageways?" Brooklyn said. "This is what I was talking about."

"Three thousand years of mummies, grave robbers, and ancient curses," Paris said. "What's there to worry about?"

"Unless Sydney's right and Umbra's waiting up there to capture us," Rio said.

"I don't *think* it's a trap," Sydney said. "I just think it's a possibility."

"What about you, Paris?" Brooklyn asked. "Are you scared it's a trap?"

"You know me," Paris said. "I'm not scared of anything."

Rio reached over and ran his fingers like a spider crawling on Paris's shoulder.

"Spider," Paris said, startled as he frantically reached back and tried to swipe it off.

The others laughed, and Rio said, "I thought you weren't scared of anything."

"Okay," Paris said, laughing with them. "I'm not scared of anything with fewer than eight legs."

They heard a crackle over their comms and what may have been Mother talking.

"Did any of you get that?" Monty asked.

"No. Too much static," answered Brooklyn.

"Yeah," said Kat. "Impossible to decipher."

"I'm sorry, Mother, we couldn't hear you," Monty said. "Can you repeat?"

There was another crackle of distorted words, but they couldn't make it out.

"Let's pick up the pace," Monty said. "Quick but careful."

It was hard to move fast in the corridor because the

lighting was poor and the rocky floor made it difficult to get good footing. They also had to be cautious because they could've been walking into a trap. Ninety seconds later, they reached Robert and Mother.

"Is everything okay?" Sydney asked, panicked.

"It's fine," Mother said in a whisper. "We found another tunnel."

He shined his flashlight a few meters up the corridor to where a small crawl space had been cut into the wall. An electrical cord ran through it.

"And it's been wired," Paris noted.

"Yes," Mother answered. "The problem is, not all of us will fit through it."

The crawl space was narrow and went one meter before emptying out in another corridor. Paris squatted down to examine it.

"There's no way I can fit through there," Paris said.

"Neither can I," Sydney admitted.

"I can," offered Rio.

"So can I," said Kat.

Brooklyn eyed it. "I think I'll fit."

"Me too," Robert added.

"Wait a second," Sydney said. "Jason Harper is a full-grown man. There's no way he fit through there."

"He's just using this to tap into the electricity," Mother said. "He probably used a robber tunnel to get inside."

"Then let's find that," Sydney said.

"We don't have time," Kat said. "The four of us are going to go in there and stop Jason Harper."

"Who made you the alpha?" Sydney asked.

"That crawl space," Kat answered.

"Just like that?" Sydney said. "You don't have a plan."

"I'll make it up as we go."

Kat turned to Mother, who nodded reluctantly.

"You have got to be careful," he said. "You're so—"

"What, small?" Kat answered. "Being small doesn't scare me. Zero is small, but it's the most powerful number of all."

37.

The Chamber

ROBERT INSISTED ON BEING THE FIRST to go. "If it is a trap, then I want it set on me," he said.

Once he signaled it was all clear, Rio and Kat followed, with Brooklyn coming last. She was the biggest of the four and couldn't actually *crawl* through. The only way she could make it was by doing a modified soldier crawl on her belly, pushing her way forward with her toes.

"It's not worth it," Sydney said. "You could get stuck."

"I need to go," Brooklyn said. "If Harper's in there,

I'm the only one who can get onto his computer and stop the hack."

Brooklyn had never felt so claustrophobic before. It was as if the rocks were squeezing in on her. At one point, she thought she was permanently stuck, but Robert and Rio were able to reach in and pull from the other side.

After two of the longest minutes in her life, she finally emerged into the robber tunnel.

"Made it," she said back to the others, spitting out the dust and dirt in her mouth. "I don't even want to think about getting back through there later on."

"Shhh," Kat said, pointing. "Look."

Twenty meters ahead they saw a hint of light.

"There's a light," Rio whispered through the crawl space to the others.

"Careful," Mother reminded him, but it was too late. Rio had already gotten up to be with the others.

"What's the plan?" Robert asked Kat.

"First, we've got to see what we're up against," Kat answered. "One of us needs to go first and be a scout."

"I'm on it," Rio said.

He was stealthy as he approached a doorway cut into the rock wall. There were a couple beams of light shining out from the room, and as he peered around the edge, he saw a small chamber that tomb raiders had used as a storeroom. This was where they hid their pillaged treasures for safekeeping, and it was where Jason Harper had launched his cyberattack.

There were some LED lights on stands and a mattress on the floor. The lights were plugged into extension cords, and a few small appliances ran off car batteries. Harper had his back turned to Rio as he sat at a makeshift desk and typed on his computer. Rio carefully took a couple pictures with his phone and moved back to join the others.

"What did you see?" Kat asked when he returned.

Rio smiled and said, "Wonderful things."

38

Horus

THEY WERE LOOKING AT THE PHOTOS RIO took of Harper in his chamber and trying to come up with a plan of attack when Kat had an idea.

"The Hatton Garden heist," she said. "The so-called grandpa gang of six elderly robbers, average age sixty-three, broke into a safe-deposit vault over two days during Easter holiday and stole fourteen million pounds in gold, diamonds, and jewelry."

Robert shook his head in disbelief. "She knows everything about math *and* robberies?"

"When she studies something, she studies it all, and she never forgets," Rio said. "Don't ever play trivia against her. Or Scrabble. Or anything, really."

"How'd the grandpas do it?" Brooklyn asked Kat.

"There was an underground fire in Kingsway that burned for two days and caused a diversion," she said. "The authorities were too occupied with the fire to notice the criminals."

"You want us to start a fire?" Robert asked.

"No, just a diversion," Kat said.

She took Rio's phone and zoomed in on one of the pictures.

"These batteries," she said to Brooklyn. "They're the backup for the computer?"

Brooklyn studied it. "Definitely."

"How long will it run off them?"

"Can't guarantee anything more than ten or fifteen minutes."

"Is that long enough for you to stop the hack?"

"More than."

"Great," Kat said. "I'm about to make Sydney's day."

Kat went back to talk to the others through the crawl space.

"We found Harper," she told them.

"So, it wasn't a trap?" Mother said, relieved.

"No, it wasn't," she said. "Sydney, do you have any explosives like the ones you set off in the British Museum?"

"I may have a banger left," Sydney said slyly. "Why?"

"We need a diversion," Kat explained. "I also need someone to go back to the electrical switch box and be ready to cut the power."

"I can do that," Paris said, eager to help.

"What's your plan?" Monty asked.

"When Sydney sets off the banger, Paris will throw the switch, and everything will go dark. Harper will be in a hurry because he will only have ten or fifteen minutes to figure out what's going on. As soon as he leaves the room to investigate, Brooklyn will sneak in and go to work on his computer."

"That will turn off the power for the guest area too," Mother pointed out.

"True, but we're past closing," Kat said. "Hopefully it will take them a little while to get in and turn it back on."

"Why the explosion?" Paris asked. "Wouldn't it be enough to just throw the power?"

"That would get his attention, but the explosion will

confuse him," Kat replied. "And when you're confused, you make mistakes." She shot a look at Sydney through the crawl space and added, "Besides, sometimes you just need to make some noise."

A few minutes later, everyone was in position, with Kat, Brooklyn, Rio, and Robert hiding in a darkened recess in the robber tunnel, Sydney with the banger at the crawl space, and Paris at the electrical box.

"Can you hear me?" Kat whispered over the comms.

"Loud and clear," Sydney said.

"Our ears are covered; let it rip."

BOOM!

The sound of the explosion echoed through the robber tunnel and the corridor. Rio pulled the switch, and all the lights in KV17 went dark.

"What's going on?!" Harper exclaimed.

He got up from his computer and came out of the chamber to check on things in the corridor. Kat and the others pressed themselves against the wall and tried to hide in the darkness.

Rather than head toward the crawl space, he followed the robber tunnel in another direction. Once he was gone, they rushed into the room, and Brooklyn went to work while the others kept an eye out for Harper.

Brooklyn quickly began her assault on his computer. The first thing she did was connect it remotely to Beny so she could use his firepower against it.

"First thing, find the cipher keys," Brooklyn said, narrating for the others. "Once I get those and send them back to the victims, I'll kill the computer."

"What?!" Harper exclaimed at the doorway. "Who are you?"

They turned and saw that he had returned, spinning as he tried to figure out what was happening.

"Get away from my computer!" he screamed.

Brooklyn kept typing as Kat and Rio moved between Harper and her.

"I said get away from my computer!" he thundered.

He charged at them, but just as he was about to reach Kat, Robert leaped on his back from behind and dragged him down to the ground.

"I need more time," Brooklyn called out as she pushed a USB drive into the computer.

Kat and Rio piled on Harper too, the three of them straining to keep him on the ground. They were only able to do so for about fifteen seconds, but that was all Brooklyn needed.

"Finished," she said as she hopped up from the computer, which now displayed the blue screen of death.

"What have you done?" he cried.

As Harper frantically tried to bring his computer back to life, the others sprinted out of the room and back to the crawl space.

"Quick! Quick!" Kat said as they ran.

"We're going to need some help," Rio called out to everyone on the other side.

"You go first!" Kat said to Brooklyn.

She got into position and did her crawl, but the others all jumped in to help. Kat, Rio, and Robert all pushed her feet while Monty and Mother pulled on the other side.

"Get back here!" Harper yelled as he came out the doorway and raced toward them.

The extra adrenaline was exactly what they needed. Brooklyn made it through first. Then Kat and Rio. Robert was crawling through when Harper reached the crawl space and grabbed on to his foot.

"I said come back," Harper bellowed.

"Dad!" Robert cried.

"Don't worry, son; I've got you!" Mother said as he wrapped his arms around him and pulled.

"Don't let go, Dad."

"Never," Mother said. "Never."

He gave a mighty heave and pulled Robert loose and into the corridor with them.

For a moment, they both laid there on the ground, tears streaming.

"You're okay, sweetheart. You're okay."

"What about the hack?" Monty asked Brooklyn.

"His computer has been neutralized," Brooklyn said, "and now Beny has control of everything. Harper's done."

They looked through the crawl space and saw that Harper was fleeing into the robber tunnel.

"He's going to get away, though," Sydney said, frustrated. "There's no way we're going to be able to find him out in the desert."

"About that," Robert said, calming down a bit. "At one point, he and I were wrestling on the ground, and—" He inhaled deeply, trying to catch his breath. "I stuck my tracker in his pocket."

After a stunned silence, Mother beamed and said, "Just like I told you, it's the family business. You're a born spy."

There were high fives and a couple hugs as the team congratulated Robert on his quick thinking under pressure. The mood was broken, however, when Brooklyn posed a difficult question.

"How do we get out of here?" she asked.

"Back the same way we came?" suggested Rio.

"It's well past closing," Monty said. "If everything's locked up and all the alarms are set, that won't be easy."

"I say we keep going," Sydney said. "These tunnels have to lead somewhere."

Forty-five minutes later, the entire team emerged from the tunnel in a wadi near the ancient town of Deir el-Medina. It was dark, and the temperatures had dipped greatly. Mother was trying to get reception on his phone when a pair of headlights approached them.

"This is not good," Paris said nervously. "Should we try to hide back in the tunnel?"

"No," Mother said, looking at the vehicle. "I think we're just fine."

"Hello, hello," Marwen said as he pulled up in a van. "How did you like KV17? It's fascinating, isn't it?"

"How did you find us, Marwen?" Sydney asked.

Marwen smiled. "A good tour guide always knows where his clients are."

Cairo

FOR THE SECOND TIME IN JUST OVER A week, Tru made the trip from London to Aisling to visit the FARM. The first time, she came to assign them the mission. Now, she was in the priest hole to follow up on what had happened since.

"With the help of Robert's tracker, the Egyptian authorities were able to find Jason Harper," she told the team. "They arrested both him and Ahmed Farouk. There's no extradition treaty between our countries, but negotiations are underway to bring Harper here to stand trial." She winked at Sydney and added, "I've suggested we sweeten the deal with the offer to return a few antiquities from the British Museum."

"The Rosetta Stone?" Sydney asked hopefully.

Tru laughed. "I have some sway, but no one this side of Buckingham Palace has that much sway. Still, baby steps."

"What about Imogen Gaisman?" Kat asked.

"Dr. Gaisman has been cleared of all charges, both here and in Egypt," Tru answered.

"And Oriana Gutierrez?" asked Brooklyn.

"That one's a bit trickier," Tru answered. "Brooklyn was right. Oriana Gutierrez is the hacker formerly known as Pluto."

"Told you!" Brooklyn said.

"It turns out her identity is actually a cover created by MI5. She's been working for them and the Cyber Security Centre."

"She's a spy?!" Sydney exclaimed.

"That's why she was in Egypt. She was searching for Horus just like you were."

"Except she didn't find him like we did," Rio said proudly.

"No, she didn't."

"This is all great news," Mother said. "But you didn't have to come up here from London just to tell us this."

"No, I came here because we have a new team member, and I wanted to welcome him in person." Tru turned to Robert and said, "It's so nice to see you again. Believe it or not, I was at the hospital the day you were born."

"I kind of remember you," he joked. "It's nice to meet you."

"I heard you played a pretty important role on this mission," she said. "Not bad for your first week on the job."

"It was a memorable experience, to say the least," Robert said.

"MI6 owes him a shoe," Paris said. "It got pulled off during the human tug-of-war."

"I will get right on that," Tru joked. "But first, on behalf of C and the few at Vauxhall Cross who know about this operation, I'd like to welcome you to the City Spies, Robert."

The others started to clap, but Sydney held her hands up to stop them.

"I'm sorry, but no," Sydney said. "You and C can

think what you want. But it's not right. Robert can't be part of the City Spies."

The others couldn't believe it, and Paris was about to confront her when she flashed a smile and said, "The name just doesn't work." She turned to him and asked, "How would you like to be called Cairo? That sounds like a City Spy."

"Cairo?" he said, considering it. "I'd like it very much."

The others swarmed around and congratulated him. Tru stayed and listened as they talked about the mission until it was time for dinner. Monty led the pack up to the kitchen, but when she did, Robert lingered behind.

"Aren't you hungry?" Mother asked.

"I'll be right up," Robert said. "I just want to soak it in."

"Don't soak too long, or Rio will eat all your food."

"Good point."

They shared a smile, and Mother left him.

Robert looked around the room at all the high-tech equipment and marveled. The colored lights running along Beny were mesmerizing.

He walked across the room to a desk and opened the

drawer to reveal the scriptex. He held it for a moment and felt the weight against his palm. Then he began to write a letter.

Dear Mum,

You were right. I'm part of the team now. Everything is going according to plan.

UK EYES ONLY

Secret Intelligence Service/MI6

Vauxhall Cross, London, UK

Project City Spies (aka Project Neverland)

Evaluations prepared by teammates

BROOKLYN

DEFINING CHARACTERISTIC: Brooklyn has an amazing quality that blends enthusiasm with fearlessness. Since the day she arrived at the FARM, she's been totally committed to everything she does, whether it's climbing up the outside of a wall to save a mission or pranking Rio by rehemming his pants to make him think he was suddenly taller. If she were an emoji, she would be _100_.

CLASSIC MISSION MOMENT: She once had to hack the computer of a particularly ruthless Russian oligarch, and in addition to stealing the files that MI6 needed, she changed the background on his monitor so that it permanently displayed puppies wearing top hats and bow ties.

SOMETHING ABOUT HER SHE DOESN'T KNOW THAT I KNOW: She uses her incredible hacking skills to keep track of her former foster siblings and make sure they're doing okay in school. If she notices a dip in their grades, she'll email the teacher pretending to be the foster parent—or the foster parent pretending to be the teacher—to make sure they get the help they need.

—Paris

PARIS

DEFINING CHARACTERISTIC: I learned the meaning of loyalty from watching Paris. He never wavers in his support, whether it's for his favorite football team (Liverpool), his favorite candy bar (Cadbury Crunchie), or any one of us. I sing in the school choir, and he's never missed a single performance. Not even when it made him miss a huge Liverpool game. And on every mission, he's always exactly where he said he'd be, exactly when he said he'd be there.

CLASSIC MISSION MOMENT: Paris once rescued Sydney after she fell through the ice into a frozen pond. He didn't hesitate before sliding out there and using a cricket bat to break open a larger hole so that he could pull her to safety. I thought it was the bravest thing I'd ever seen. Then, that night, he admitted to me that he didn't know how to swim! I couldn't believe it. He didn't tell the rest of the team until a few weeks later, after he'd started taking swim lessons.

SOMETHING ABOUT HIM HE DOESN'T KNOW THAT I KNOW: I think he wants to go to college in America, but he's afraid to do it because he's worried that he'll be letting us down.

—*Rio*

SYDNEY

DEFINING CHARACTERISTIC: Her sense of right and wrong has nothing to do with rules and everything to do with fairness. She would have no problem helping overthrow the government but would never think of cutting in front of someone in a checkout line. Unless that person was a member of Parliament. Then she'd totally cut in front of them.

CLASSIC MISSION MOMENT: We were in Latvia and needed to break into a building that was surrounded by a massive stone wall with a wooden gate. Paris and Rio got into a disagreement over how to pick the lock on the gate and were going back and forth when it suddenly opened. We thought we were burned until we saw that it was Sydney. While the boys were trying to figure it out, she'd just climbed over the wall and opened it from the inside.

SOMETHING ABOUT HER SHE DOESN'T KNOW THAT I KNOW: She looks cool on the outside, but inside she's a total nerd. She knows everything there is to know about *Doctor Who*, and when she doesn't think anyone's around, she sings show tunes at the top of her lungs. She's horribly off-key and gets the lyrics all wrong, but she loves it so much that it's adorable.

—Brooklyn

KAT

DEFINING CHARACTERISTIC: Kat is the most honest person in the world, even when you don't want her to be. Like the time I got a pixie cut and asked her what she thought of it. But that honesty can also make you feel incredible—like when I asked her what she wanted for her birthday, and she answered, "To be more like you."

CLASSIC MISSION MOMENT: Kat's not a natural actor, but her fake fainting is Oscar-worthy. She'll be in the middle of talking, and then she'll freeze her face and collapse to the ground. She did it once when we were being detained by the Albanian secret police. Two officers rushed to her aid, and by the time she "came to," she'd managed to steal the keys to our jail cell.

SOMETHING ABOUT HER SHE DOESN'T KNOW THAT I KNOW: About six months ago, Kat started watching makeup tutorials online. I only know this because our rooms are next to each other, and I can hear them through the wall. If she's interested in fashion and beauty, I am here for it, but I don't want her to know I can hear her, so I'm waiting for her to bring it up.

—Sydney

RIO

DEFINING CHARACTERISTIC:
Rio likes to act tough, but
more than anything he's kind.
He used to disappear some
Sundays to go play football
with some friends. One time
I was bored, and I followed
him to watch. It turned
out that instead of playing football, he was
taking the train to Aberdeen so that he could put
on a magic show for the kids in a children's hospital.

CLASSIC MISSION MOMENT: The greatest diversion I've
ever seen was in a Moscow gift shop. I needed the salespeople
to be distracted long enough for me to slip through a door
behind the counter. With no preparation, he stepped up to the
counter and started to do magic tricks with a set of nesting
dolls. He didn't speak Russian, but it didn't matter. He had the
whole room mesmerized. I could've driven a truck behind the
counter, and they wouldn't have noticed.

SOMETHING ABOUT HIM HE DOESN'T KNOW THAT I KNOW:
Rio loves food, but he loves Monty even more. Sometimes
she'll make him a Brazilian coconut custard treat called a
queijadinha. I happen to know that it's one of the very few
sweets that he doesn't like, but he'd never let Monty know
it. He always eats an extra serving and compliments her on
how delicious it is.

—Kat

Acknowledgments

The world of middle-grade fiction is one of the nicest, funniest, and most supportive communities a person can call home. The City Spies team is made up of professionals, colleagues, friends, family members, experts, and others who I hijack with the question "Do you think you could help me with something?" I'd like to give a little shout-out to some of these fantastic people.

Kristin Gilson is an amazing editor and a good friend. (You may recognize her from the dedication at the front of the book.) She's always available, always helpful, and always supportive, even when I wander off track and get lost or text at inappropriate times. She's joined by Valerie Garfield, a wonderful publisher and the type of person who would brave Covid and three trains just so we could have lunch.

This is my tenth book with Aladdin, where I have the pleasure of working with an all-star lineup that includes Anna Jarzab, Alex Kelleher-Nagorski, Tiara Iandiorio, Nicole Russo, Caitlin Sweeny, Michelle Leo, Amy Beaudoin, Christina Pecorale, Emily Hutton, Victor Iannone, Alissa Nigro, Erin Toller, Ginny Kemmerer, Sara Berko,

Nadia Almahdi, Nicole Benevento, Lisa Moraleda, Kilson Roque-Fernández, Nicole Tai, Elizabeth Mims, Chel Morgan, Lauren Forte, and Jeannie Ng. I'd like to give a special thanks to Yaoyao Ma Van As, whose illustrations bring the characters to life, and Lisa Flanagan, who gives them their voices in the audiobooks.

When I decided that the book would involve ancient Egypt, I instantly reached out to Dr. Kara Cooney, a very kind and talented Egyptologist with UCLA. She was extremely helpful, and I highly recommend her books and podcast. Jason Harper channeled his National Geographic experiences in Luxor to help me better understand the Valley of the Kings, and Amber Woodard was kind enough to share her travel photos to help round out the picture. For cultural and linguistic advice, I'm grateful for the assistance of Ahmed El-Ashram and Hena Khan, who is both a talented author and true friend.

For some very specific expertise, I'd like to thank Caroline Danforth for explaining the inner workings of museums, Drs. John Reynolds and Todd Snowden for explaining procedures in the operating room, and Clementine Ahearne and Alice Natali for always being my go-to experts on all things British and London. Huge thanks to my nephew Keith Cavanaugh, who provided invaluable computer knowledge. (Bad news, Keith—I'm going to need your help on more books in the future.)

Pat Devlin has done a tremendous job editing the trailers for all the City Spies books, and I am beyond grateful for his talent and years of friendship. Likewise, I'm so fortunate to have friends such as Christina Diaz Gonzalez, Alyson Gerber, and Rose Brock, who generously provide reading, brainstorming, and counseling services. You are the best! I also want to thank my young reader brigade, which includes Elizabeth, Annie, Lea, Shakthi, and Pluto.

Most of all, I want to thank my incredible family, without whom none of this would be possible.